THE SECOND COMING OF ANGELA

Copyright © [2022] [George Thomas S.]

All rights reserved. No portion of this book may be reproduced in any form without permission from the publisher, except as permitted by U.S. copyright law.

This is a work of fiction. Names, characters, places and incidents either are products of the author's imagination or are used fictitiously. Any resemblance to actual events or locales or persons, living or dead, is entirely coincidental.

THE SECOND COMING OF ANGELA

by
George Thomas S.

Chapters

1. A rude awakening
2. A wonderful new acquaintance
3. A worthwhile adversary
4. The reunion
5. Out of the lions' den
6. Antonio's surprise
7. The mother load
8. I never drink vodka
9. Time to do some banking
10. Care to trade?
11. The Escape
12. It's only just begun
13. Good morning Carlo
14. The Queens connection
15. Paola's story
16. The little bundle of joy
17. Mother and child reunion
18. The river runs deep
19. Carlos is on the hunt
20. Gathering in the flock
21. Rattling Carlos' chain
22. Check your schedule
23. Say hello Pauly
24. Slaughter on Rio Negro
25. Leaving might be wise
26. The City of the belltowers
27. Care for a twist?

The Second Coming of Angela

CHAPTER 1

A RUDE AWAKENING

It was three in the morning in Huntsville, a small tourist-oriented town in middle Ontario about two hours from Toronto and Thomas DeAngelo had been jolted awake by the relentless ringing of the telephone. When he realized that it was not a dream, he made a few erratic flails at the nightstand and managed to grab the receiver, press it to his ear, and grunt out a barely audible "Hello". He knew someone was speaking to him, but his mind was a fog as he mumbled back without a clue what was being said. Suddenly, the voice at the other end became forceful and unrelenting.

"Thomas, will you please wake up and listen to me?"

Suddenly he bolted upright. This voice sounded too familiar, but it was impossible. It couldn't be. It belonged to someone who had been dead for almost five years. The cool morning air wafting through his open window raised goosebumps on his arms as he asked, "Who is this?" almost afraid of the answer.

"It's Angela," the voice at the other end replied. He sat in total silence, his body enveloped in an eerie chill, as the constant breeze through the window grew even stronger and ever chillier.

He had half expected, from the sound of the voice, to hear that name and yet he still couldn't wrap his mind around the reality. He sat motionless, confused, and in total disbelief. It couldn't be true. It wasn't the least bit possible. No! This was beyond cruel. He could feel the build-up of anger within him and, now wide awake, his voice firm and harsh, he finally spoke. "What kind of sick person are you? Angela is dead."

The voice on the other end began to respond but was cut off by his continuing tirade.

"I don't know why you're doing this, but God help you if I find out who you are. You are one sick person."

A distinct click at the other end left no doubt the caller had hung up. With the phone dropped back into its cradle, Thomas lay back on the bed. "Rotten jackass," he muttered as he pulled the covers over him and tried to return to what had been a much-needed slumber.

Despite his best efforts, sleep was now impossible. This malicious caller had dragged forth memories long buried under a deep layer of self-imposed armor. Insulated against all things painful in life, Thomas had proceeded along his path to the ultimate end, certain that he would never again allow anything or anyone to cause him such pain. Sleep was not an alternative at this point.

When he had stashed an unopened pack of smokes in his sock drawer, he wasn't sure it was such a good idea. Quitting had been a serious struggle. Now, he knew that the hidden stash had been a bad decision. Sitting upright on the edge of the bed, he tore the pack open and lit up.

With cigarette in hand and lungs heaving from this now unfamiliar invasion, he headed for the kitchen. Desperate for some coffee, he poured a cup from yesterday morning's pot and stuck it in the microwave. Some milk and sugar should make it palatable, he thought. His mind flashed back to the day her car had been found. They had separated more than six years ago when their daughters were ten, twelve, and fourteen. Her reason for leaving for another man was that there was more to life than being a wife and mother. Thomas was suddenly a single parent raising three daughters by himself. A year after their separation, when Thomas had mostly overcome the pain of it, Angela disappeared without a trace.

Her vehicle was discovered, weeks later, in the St. Lawrence River. Recreational divers had come upon it as they were exploring for old shipwrecks. The door was open, and the windshield smashed. A small fragment of her blouse was caught on the door handle. Her body was never found. The St. Lawrence River runs very deep and very fast, and it was assumed that she had been washed downstream, perhaps entangled on the bottom or even carried to the Atlantic. After two weeks, the search was called off. She was ultimately declared dead and a funeral, complete with an empty casket, was held by the grieving family, including Thomas and his daughters.

The door of the microwave had no sooner closed than when the phone rang again. Standing there, frozen in place, he stared at the kitchen wall. He was in no mood for another intrusion by this weirdo. "Might as well get it over with," he muttered as he picked up the receiver. Before he could speak, he heard that same voice.

"February, nineteen ninety-nine, you and I, one waterbed, a guitar and your song, 'Early Morning Sunshine'. Remember, Thomas? It was our first time."

Thomas' mind went numb, and his legs grew weak beneath him. Very few people knew that story. There was a tremor in his voice as he spoke.

"Angela? Is it really you? It can't be possible."

His mind traveled back and forth between elation and, strangely, disappointment. He was elated for his children's sake that she was alive, yet disappointed that she had now been reinserted into his life. After all, he had spent so much time cleaning up the wounds from their relationship that this was like reopening them and rubbing in some salt for good measure. As difficult as the separation had been, accepting her death had been even worse.

"I know how unbelievable it may seem, but it's true," she replied in a voice that was almost a whimper of helplessness. "It's a long story and no time to explain. I desperately need your help. I beg of you, please believe me. Please help me!"

"What kind of help? Are you in some sort of trouble?"

"Yes! I'm scared and worried and you're the only one I can turn to."

It was difficult for Thomas to erase the suspicion from his mind as he replied. "How could you have disappeared like that and left everyone to believe you were dead? What am I to think?"

"Thomas, I promise, I'll explain everything when I can, but for now I need you to come to Brazil. Quickly!"

"Brazil?" he shouted as the coffee cup fell from his hand and shattered on the floor.

"Sao Paulo, to be exact," she said.

There was complete silence as he pondered the insanity of it all. "Sao Paulo, Brazil?" he muttered as he lit another cigarette. What possible trouble could she be in that would require him to go to Brazil?

"Thomas? Are you still there? Answer me, please." Finally, he managed to speak.

"Sao Paulo?" he said sarcastically, his baritone voice dramatically forceful. "Not Sao Paulo! Couldn't you have picked somewhere more exciting to have a problem? Rio? Curitiba? Damn, woman, Manaus would have been a total pleasure. Sao Paulo? You've got to be kidding. And why me? Why not your sister or brother?

"It has to be you, Thomas. You are the only key to my safe return home. I promise you will understand when you are here."

Thomas had been to Brazil twice, on vacation. Sao Paulo was his least favorite city there. The crime and pollution are horrible, and the traffic is even worse. It was not a fun place to be, and he was certain that this situation would make it even less so.

"Sao Paulo, Thomas. That's where I need you. I beg of you to take this very seriously. I'm sorry for doing this to you, but I have no choice. My life depends upon it."

By now he was pacing the floor endlessly, trying to avoid the scattered pieces of glass that threatened to shred his bare feet. Almost in a daze, he replied, "Sao Paulo then. Let me see what I can arrange. I need to check on flights."

"Toronto Pearson International, Delta Airlines departing on flight nineteen-ten at six-forty-five tonight, connecting in Atlanta and arriving in Sao Paulo just after eight in the morning. I know it's a long wait between flights, but it's the best connection possible on such short notice."

"Angela! Are you crazy? Tonight? That's just a little fast, don't you think? What about my travel visa? I need a visa for Brazil! That takes at least a week or two."

"You were in Brazil two years ago. Remember? You were in Fortaleza."

His eyes widened with surprise and the hair on the back of his neck tingled as he asked,

"How did you know that?"

"I saw you there, outside your hotel!"

Her words were a wound inflicted upon him as he wondered why she would have ignored him in Brazil.

"You saw me and didn't speak to me? You didn't contact me? This is all very confusing, Angela. Almost insanely so."

"I saw you but had no memory of you. It haunted me for months, desperately trying to remember who you were. I had amnesia resulting from a head injury. I was told it was a car accident. Then, one day, I remembered. That was when I realized I was in serious danger."

"Angela, I'm a little overwhelmed here. This is just too strange. Where in Sao Paulo? You have the address?"

"No, Thomas. I am not allowed to give you the address. You will know when you get here."

By now his heart was beating erratically and he felt more nervous than he could ever remember. For a fleeting moment, he considered contacting the U.S. Embassy in Sao Paulo and having them sort it out. The problem with that was that he had no idea where in Sao Paulo she is, and it is a city of twenty-two million people. Add to that the fact that she was calling from a blocked number. If she truly was in danger, by the time the Embassy got around to looking for her it could well be much too late. It seemed he was on his own.

"Just catch that plane, Thomas. Flight nineteen-ten. You're already booked. Check-in two hours before your flight. I need you here quickly. Everything will become clear then."

There seemed no hope of debating the issue further and finally, with a tone of resignation in his voice, he agreed, "OK, fine, but I'll have to look into a hotel."

"Hotel Transamerica! You're already booked there, too. It's on the Av Nacoes Unidas. There is an airport bus that will drop you off at the front door. Don't let me down. Please! And

Thomas, not a soul, not anyone must know about this. Not my family, not anyone. Promise me."

He couldn't help but wonder why she was insisting on such secrecy, but he decided not to argue the point. She said that her life depended on it, and he chose to believe her. A giant leap of faith, considering their history. In truth, he would do this for their daughters if for no other reason.

"Somehow I knew I could depend on you. There is no one I trust more. I'll see you in Sao Paulo."

With those words, she hung up, leaving him worrying about what the hell he was getting into. He leaned, weakly, against the wall as a lump lodged in his throat and with a heart rate that alternately pounded uncontrollably and then subsided.

Thomas was a sales manager for a car dealership and had banked some vacation days. He had an understanding boss who never denied him time off when he needed it. He would call when the dealership opened and let them know he would be gone for a week or so.

"Holy shit! It's four o'clock," the words were almost a yell as they left his lips. Only twelve hours until he had to check-in for his flight. And where the hell was his passport? No problem, he thought. It was bound to be somewhere. He would find it when he packed. He had no idea how long he would be there and wasn't sure how much to take with him. As usual, he would cram about a week's worth of clothes into one carry-on bag. He hated checking luggage.

It made for an easier time when he arrived at his destination and no lost baggage. Carry one bag on, one bag off, and bypass all those people struggling at the baggage carousel.

"Brazil? For Christ's sake, I sure hope I wake up and find out this has all been a bad dream?" he said aloud as he swept up the pieces of glass from the kitchen floor. Then he returned to the bedroom and flopped onto the bed. A few hours of sleep would still give him plenty of time to make his flight, despite the two-hour drive to Toronto. At this moment, what he needed most was sleep, but within minutes, the phone rang again. Angela's voice was almost hysterical.

"My God, what about the girls? How are they? What will you do with them?" she asked. In the confusion of their earlier conversation, they had overlooked any discussion of their three daughters. All three of them lived with Thomas and had done so since the separation.

"Don't worry. They're fine. I'll make arrangements for them," he said.

"What will you tell them? They'll be curious!"

"I'll come up with something. Even if you hadn't asked me to keep this secret, I would never tell them anything until I knew more than just the fact that you're still alive. I'm sure you understand the logic of that."

"Yes. Of course, I do," she said, with the slightest quiver in her voice. "I really do understand. That's the wisest choice. Have a safe flight. I'll be waiting."

Thomas had sensed in her voice that the thought of her daughters had opened a well of emotion and, certainly, pain. It was a rarity when one discovered any degree of vulnerability in Angela. Rare enough that it had an immediate effect and brought about a degree of sympathy not normally associated with feelings towards her. Suddenly, any doubt in his mind was swept away. Yes, this was Angela, no question. That was the only thing about which there was a certainty.

The issue of what to tell the girls would be handled simply. They had been asking about visiting their aunt in Mississauga, Angela's sister, Theresa. This would be a perfect time. It would be easy enough to drop them off there and then a short drive to the airport. As to why he was leaving on such short notice and to where? For what reason? That might require some creative explanation. There would be time enough to think of something while he was in the shower.

Standing beneath the shower massage as it beat upon his neck, he was lost in a total state of confusion over the events of the morning. The dead resurrected and reinserted into his life. What could be more bewildering? Finally, as time marched on, he had finished his shower, shaved, found his passport, and packed as best he could. He had still not awakened the girls or called their aunt. It was seven in the morning, and he had to wake them now so that they had time to pack some things and perform their ritual grooming.

Thomas made the call to Theresa, realizing at that early hour he would probably not wake her. By now, her two young sons, Marc and Julien, would be up and looking for breakfast. He explained only that he had received an urgent call from a friend and had to leave for a few days or perhaps a week. Despite her curiosity, he avoided further details. As always, it was clear that the girls were welcome to stay with her family as long as need be. Of course, there were questions and Thomas' insistence that he didn't know much, only that a friend needed his help. To her credit and despite her desire to know more, she didn't pry.

Until he understood more about the situation concerning her sister, he couldn't possibly bring himself to tell her that Angela was alive. He advised Theresa that he would arrive sometime around noon, and the conversation was finished. Now it was time to wake the girls.

He had decided at that point to say nothing more than the fact they were going to visit their aunt. That explanation would serve to eliminate any questions for the moment and the rest he could deal with later. With everyone now awake and set about the business of getting ready, Thomas sat with a cup of freshly brewed coffee and pondered the situation. The realization that Angela was still alive brought too many memories rushing back to his mind. Not all of them pleasant. Any romantic feelings for her had faded away years ago and there was no resurrecting them. Friendship was all he could offer. He had no idea what to expect in Brazil and had resigned himself to a journey of uncertainty. How long and difficult the journey, and how it would all end, was an open question.

CHAPTER 2

AN INTERESTING NEW ACQUAINTANCE

Thomas was quite thankful that Angela had booked an aisle seat for him. There were few things he hated more than being cramped against the bulkhead of an airplane. Even in the spacious first-class seats, it would have been intolerable. He'd always had a bit of claustrophobia in certain situations, and on an airplane that's not a good thing. He stowed his bag, settled into his seat, and began to watch the other passengers as they boarded. One, in particular, caught his eye.

Dark hair had always been one of his weaknesses and hers was a beautiful brunette color with that natural tight curl that is not uncommon in Brazil. Dark eyes were another of his soft spots and they were even darker than the long and lustrous hair that cascaded so sensually about her shoulders. Her knee-high skirt served to accentuate an incredible pair of legs; typical of the many Brazilian women he had seen, and in three cases, dated on his previous visits there. One thing was certain. His mind was, at least temporarily, not preoccupied with the misgivings and uncertainties of his sudden need to go to Brazil, nor by what unwelcome surprises might lay ahead.

After slowly making her way down the aisle, smiling continually, she arrived next to Thomas' seat and stowed her bag in the overhead. He realized that she must be the occupant of the window seat and rose to give her access. As he stood back, she turned around to slide past his seat to her own. Thomas found the view from behind to be as amazing as it was from the front. This was one more asset he found to be common to many Brasileiras. This was one gorgeous lady. Despite the events of the day, for a few moments, his mind was certainly elsewhere. Perhaps, he thought, this would be an interesting trip after all. If it took his mind off his troubles, all the better.

Settled in his seat for the short flight to New York, Thomas was carefully trying to avoid looking at the vision to his left. The problem was, it was impossible to avoid seeing those beautiful legs unless he looked at the ceiling. No matter how hard he tried, he couldn't avert his eyes. While he fumbled in his mind for words to start a conversation, she beat him to the punch. Suddenly, that stunning face turned and leaned slightly towards him.

"Hi! My name is Sofia," she said very sweetly and not in the formal way one might expect from a stranger. As Thomas wondered why he hadn't thought of that uncomplicated approach he stammered his reply.

"Hi, uh…my name is Thomas."

"Oh, is a very nice name," she replied in an almost flirtatious manner. "I like that name very much. You are going to Sao Paulo?" Her English was almost flawless with just the right degree of wonderful accent. Thomas had always found it interesting that Brazilians, and most South Americans in general, don't shortcut the vocabulary the way English speakers do.

He was sure that he had never heard one use a contraction. It was always "it is" instead of it's, "we are" instead of we're and likewise for every other possible combination. The often-misplaced English verb was also something that Thomas found pleasing to his ear.

"Yes, I'm going to Sao Paulo. And you?"

"I am on my way to Fortaleza."

"Fortaleza? I love Fortaleza. I was there two years ago."

"Really? You were there and I never met you? I am very disappointed." With that comment, her wonderful full lips parted, and she gave him the most beautiful smile. "Well, now we have met," she said with a gentle shrug of her shoulders, "so no need to be disappointed any longer."

"Why are you going to Fortaleza?" he asked, hoping he wasn't being too inquisitive.

"I must negotiate a contract. It is a one-day trip. I must negotiate another contract in Sao Paulo when I return there."

The flight from Toronto to Atlanta was about four hours. During that time, they managed to exchange some personal information. She somehow found it unusually interesting that he was a sales manager for an automobile dealership, although he couldn't imagine why. He, on the other hand, was immensely impressed by the fact that she was an apparent computer whiz specializing in software design and computer security. Fortunately, other than a brief explanation of what she did, there was no desire on her part to bore him with things way beyond his ability to comprehend. He was very grateful for that. He would have hated to sit there looking confused and in full display of his ignorance of the subject.

During the layover in Atlanta, they decided to have dinner together and engage in some casual conversation while waiting for their connecting flight. Thomas thought it best to avoid any conversation regarding his real reason for going to Sao Paulo, particularly since he knew so little about this new acquaintance. He simply said it was a vacation. The connecting flight would be an opportunity for each of them to sleep for a few hours. Unfortunately, Thomas' preoccupation with what may await him in Sao Paulo denied him any possibility of sleep. Sofia, on the other hand, was out cold.

As the plane began its descent to the airport at Sao Paulo, Thomas couldn't help but recall his previous visit. It had been a few years ago and yet it felt like yesterday. Only time would tell how much of it he would see on this visit. Soon, Sofia awoke, stretched, and gazed out the window at the city below.

"Well, Thomas, soon our time together will be finished. It has been a pleasure. If you do not mind, I will give you my business card. Perhaps you will know someone in need of my security services. Or, maybe, when I return to Sao Paulo tomorrow, you can call, and we can go to dinner again."

"That would be very nice, Sofia. I doubt that tomorrow will be possible, but when I know which day I'll be free, I'll call for sure. That's a promise."

Sofia proceeded to her gate for the flight to Fortaleza and Thomas exited the terminal to catch the hotel shuttle bus. It was early enough in the morning as to make for even worse traffic than would be usual. Despite this, the bus made good time and he arrived at the hotel by about ten o'clock. One look at the place and Thomas realized it had to be expensive. He was certainly hoping that it had been prepaid as well. He wasn't disappointed. Whatever Angela's problem was, so far it was giving him a first-class trip in every way. He simply had no idea how she could ever afford the cost of it.

When he arrived at the reception, it was as if they had discovered some celebrity who had come for a stay. He had never, anywhere, been treated so royally. He assumed that it was the normal courtesy displayed to all their guests. Soon, however, he noticed that others were only being given the normal yet polite service you might expect in any hotel. He was beginning to wonder what sort of influence the resurrected Angela had in Sao Paulo.

Despite his insistence that he was more than capable of carrying his only bag to the elevator, and then to his room, he ended up with a bellboy for company. He didn't mind really, just didn't see the need for it. When they exited the elevator and the bellboy opened the door to his accommodation, Thomas discovered that it was quite a bit more than just a room. His eyes opened quite wide when he walked in and saw the size and luxury of his suite.

He offered what he thought was a reasonable tip and, to his amazement, it was refused. He insisted on knowing why, concerned it was too small and therefore insulting. He was told that everyone in the hotel was under orders to accept nothing in the way of money from him and that they would be provided for by his host. He would, it seemed, be spared any expense at all. Now he was damn curious about Angela's apparent wealth. After years of struggling to support his daughters on his own, it was somewhat annoying to realize that she could afford so much luxury on his behalf. He was certain that just the cost of plane tickets and the hotel bill could have supported his kids for a year.

Once settled in his new environment, he phoned the front desk to see if there were any messages. There were none. He had never thought about how Angela and he would get in touch once he was in Sao Paulo. He supposed that now he would just have to wait for her to contact him. With nothing but time to kill, a shower seemed to be a perfect choice, followed by a nap. He had that sticky and uncomfortable feeling that comes with enduring almost an entire day of traveling. It would be very refreshing to wash it away under one of those wonderful Brazilian rainfall showerheads that he loved so much. They gave him the feeling of bathing in the rain. If anything, he tended to spend too much time under one.

With his shower completed, it took about two minutes for him to fall asleep on the bed. Still wrapped in one of the hotel's remarkably soft cotton bath towels, he had found it impossible to even attempt to remain awake. He hadn't slept much at all during the flight, and certainly not the deep sleep that one needs to be well-rested.

CHAPTER 3

A WORTHWHILE ADVERSARY

Thomas' nap was brief as the phone rang soon after he had nodded off. The voice on the other end turned out not to be Angela. It was the front desk telling Thomas that a driver was there to pick him up. Not sure what to think, he simply said he needed time to dress and would be down shortly. Still, no contact at all from Angela herself, and this was becoming more and more strange by the minute.

Upon his arrival in the lobby, he walked directly to the front desk. The desk clerk, a very pretty, young Brazilian girl, with those typical dark eyes, pointed to a man standing at the front door. His mere appearance gave Thomas pause. This guy was huge. He stood at least six foot three inches and was about two hundred and eighty pounds. If Thomas didn't know better, he would have thought he had been chiseled from a block of granite. His black and somewhat greasy hair was combed in a fifties-style ducktail. His physique reminded Thomas of Babe Ruth with that barrel chest and everything else tapering down to legs not much larger than spindles. Thomas couldn't help but smile as he wondered how such thin legs could carry that enormous weight. He was dressed in a suit that looked as if it had been pulled off the rack at the Salvation Army and then left to lie in a pile for a week or so. Thomas wasn't sure a suit of any quality would have looked good on this guy. He was just too damn huge and strangely proportioned. Even more interesting, he didn't look the least bit Brazilian, something Thomas noticed right away. Finally, Thomas walked over to him.

"My name is Thomas, and I understand you're here to drive me somewhere?"

It was somewhat intimidating for him to be dwarfed by this huge man.

"Yeah, how ya doin. Let's get outa here," he answered, turning towards the door.

The minute he spoke, it was clear to Thomas that looks did not deceive. This guy was New York all the way. Could have been the Bronx, Brooklyn, or even Queens. It was hard to say. He supposed that he would learn which soon enough. "Do you mind if I ask where we're going?"

"We're goin to meet Rico. Takes about fifteen or twenty."

"Fifteen or twenty?"

"Yeah, minutes. You know, those little lines on your Mickey Mouse watch?" Apparently, this guy had an insulting sense of humor to go with the almost humorous appearance. Thomas laughed somewhat nervously and said nothing.

At the curb in front of the hotel was a long black Mercedes limousine. This mountain of a man strode to the car, opened the back door, and Thomas climbed in. Settled in the plush leather seat he tried to slow a heartbeat that was now giving proof of his concern about his situation. He was still trying to absorb the gravity of it all when he realized he didn't know the driver's name. Not that it really mattered, but the thought struck him, so why not ask?

"I didn't get your name," he said.

"Yeah, well you didn't ask. It's Antonio, if ya really gotta know."

Thomas tried to be polite, "Ok, nice to meet you, Antonio."

The reply came with an almost sinister laugh, "Yeah? Most people who meet me can't say that." There was no temptation on Thomas' part to even ask what that meant.

They were no more than a few blocks from the hotel when one of those typical Brazilian drivers honked his horn and pulled so closely in front of them that he nearly hit the front bumper. Antonio was, to say the least, pissed.

"Friggin Brazilian drivers. And people back in Queens think they drive nuts there. They don't got a clue."

So, Queens it was. What was this giant of a man from Queens doing in Sao Paulo? It might be better not to ask. It was much wiser to be quiet and discover as things progressed. What he did know was that this entire endeavor had quite possibly just taken an unfortunate turn in a bad direction. He actually felt a cold shiver down his spine, and he had to admit, finally, that a certain amount of fear might be setting in.

About twenty minutes had passed before the car swung into a gated driveway. There was a security booth and Antonio stopped to wait for the guard to open the gate and wave them through. Once in, the limo continued up a long curving driveway lined with trees and foliage typical of a Brazilian rain forest. The house itself was a magnificent mansion that Thomas guessed might date back to the mid-eighteen-hundreds. It had been faithfully restored to its original glory. Antonio parked in front of a stone staircase that was perhaps thirty wide at the bottom and curving on both sides to perhaps twenty feet at the top step. As he exited the limo, Thomas' eyes couldn't stop admiring that magnificent place. He stood there gawking at the splendor of it all while Antonio was already at the top of the stairs. As Thomas continued to take in his surroundings, Antonio looked back at him.

"Hey, put your eyeballs back in your head and try climbin' the stairs. Rico don't like to be kept waitin. And believe me, you don't want me to have to come and get ya."

On that point, Thomas fully agreed. As he made his way up the staircase towards the front door, Antonio was already inside. Inside the doorway stood a maid, perhaps in her late thirties. She smiled shyly, closed the door behind him, and began to lead him acFedir the massive foyer. He had no doubt that his entire house would fit inside of it and there would be room left over. The floor was a mosaic of colored tiles; reds, blues, yellows, greens, and every piece part of a scene that appeared to be a depiction of traditional Brazilian dances. It was quite mesmerizing to look at. The ceiling was at least thirty-five feet above the floor and from it was suspended a huge chandelier embellished with ornate crystal and holding what looked to be forty or fifty candles. It was obvious that it was the original source of light for this huge area and had been preserved for its beauty. The staircase, about thirty feet past the entryway, was a work of art. Not being familiar with typical Brazilian wood, Thomas wasn't sure what it was made of. The banisters and stair treads reminded him of black cherry while the spindles were much lighter in color and more along the shade of ash. The contrast was beautiful to look at. This magnificent staircase led to a balconied hall that surrounded the middle level of the foyer. He had never seen anything to compare. He was able to count twelve doors facing the upper balcony before his attention was drawn to the maid who was trying desperately to have him follow her.

Finally, he was led to a large room that seemed to be both library and office. It was certainly a masculine room and, in many ways, cold. The furniture was all the overstuffed leather variety, and the floor was a hardwood that looked very similar to that in the staircase banisters. A few animal heads were hanging on the wall, a jaguar possibly, a lion, something reminiscent of the deer family, and a few stuffed birds, but not much that Thomas could put a name to. One entire wall consisted of a huge bookcase that was full to overflowing. At a glance, some of the volumes appeared to be quite old.

The maid showed him to one of the leather chairs and asked if he would care for a drink. He settled on just a plain Pepsi for the time being. He tried to engage her in some conversation and managed only to determine that her name was Paola. She seemed almost afraid to speak and as he continued to attempt conversation, she became even shyer. A voice from the open door broke the resulting silence.

"Paola knows better than to become too friendly with my guests."

Thomas turned to see a somewhat average man, nothing more, though immaculately dressed in a blue Armani suit, off-white shirt, and floral print tie. He thought it was kind of late in the day to be wearing a suit, but that was just his own taste. As the man walked towards Thomas he looked rather sternly at Paola and said, "Surely you have work to do! Please see to it."

The little maid, appearing embarrassed, left the room as he turned and walked over to sit opposite Thomas. Once settled into that huge chair he almost appeared lost. He wasn't a large man, maybe five feet six inches at most. His hair was short and a sort of ash brown with just a touch of gray. His eyes, more gray than blue, had a very cold look to them. More than cold, they looked cruel. He was a very different contrast to Antonio. If he was from Queens too, then surely, they had not only attended different schools but also frequented different tailors. He sat there, legs cFedired, hands firmly placed on each arm of the chair, and just stared at Thomas for what would have been only a few moments and yet seemed to Thomas like an hour. It was truly that uncomfortable to have those eyes focused upon him.

"How was your trip, Tommy?"

He hated to be called Tommy, with rare exceptions.

"The name is Thomas, and to be perfectly honest, so far the trip has been a pain in the ass. I'm only here because Angela supposedly needs my help. As for who you are, and why I'm in your house, I have no clue. Maybe you would care to fill me in?"

Thomas was taken aback by his own aggressive tone of voice, but he had been through a long day and was tired of waiting for the details of why he was there. If he had thought this man's eyes were cruel before, he now saw how truly frightening they could be. It was apparent that his host was attempting to control his anger. His hands were squeezing the arms of his chair to the point of his fingers going white while his face was developing that reddish hue that Thomas just knew meant trouble. As the normal color returned to his face, he released his grip on the chair and reached out for the drink that Paola was carrying. Thomas hadn't even noticed her return to the room. Just as quickly, she was gone.

"I provided you with first-class accommodations all the way. And for that, you speak to me in such a manner? But I'm going to forgive your rudeness," he sneered, as he made a point of saying his name properly. "Thomas," he said with a slight smile that was quite obviously insincere.

"As for who I am? I'm Angela's husband." With that, he put the glass to his lips and looked intently for a reaction. He certainly got one.

"Well, that's very interesting. Truth is, since we never divorced, I would still be her legal husband. Quite a dilemma, don't you think?" No matter how hard he tried, Thomas just couldn't remove the sarcasm from his voice. He never did seem to know when to control his mouth. He did notice that this character almost choked on his drink when he heard that Angela and he were still married.

"You were never divorced?"

"Nope. Never. We could never agree to the terms of it."

"Oh, Tommy, that's rich. Never expected that. Not that it matters a bit. But I must admit that it is rather funny."

"It doesn't matter? They must have different laws in Brazil regarding bigamy."

By now Thomas' glass of Pepsi was empty and, out of nowhere, Paola appeared with a fresh one. She was very much like some ghost that appeared without warning or sound.

"You'll understand soon enough, Tommy boy. I think you'll find it a fascinating story."

"I told you, my name is Thomas."

"In my house, you're who I say you are. Soon, I think, it will be time for you and Angela to see each other," and with that, he rose from his chair and walked to a phone that sat, along with a computer, on a very large walnut desk at the opposite end of the room. For once Thomas thought better of letting his mouth run away with him.

"We'll be going down in twenty minutes," were the only words the man spoke into the phone before returning to his chair.

It was about this time that Thomas began noticing various pictures on the walls. There were many with Angela in them and some, for whatever reason, looked very familiar. If they were recent, Thomas thought, she was holding up well for someone who was by now forty-eight years old. She always did look younger than her years.

"You've believed for years that Angela had been killed in a car accident," his host said as he repositioned himself into his chair.

"Yeah! Me and everyone else in her, life."

"Well, she did have an accident, but, obviously, she didn't die. I'm sure you'll find this confusing. But believe me, every word is true. So, I'll explain."

"That would be what I'm here for. One hell of an explanation."

"I'm sure you'll agree that it qualifies. To begin with, I don't travel out of Brazil often. There are serious reasons for that, reasons which don't concern you, but when I do need to conduct business out of the country, I choose little-known places where I'm assured of privacy. On one occasion, I chose Cornwall, Ontario. Anyway, as Antonio and I were returning to our motel we see this woman walking, somewhat dazed, along the road. At first, we drove past, thinking she was just drunk, but for some reason, I told Antonio to turn around and go back. There we find this beautiful woman in a torn blouse, bleeding from the forehead and soaking wet. We stopped the car, thinking we would do the considerate thing and drop her at the hospital where they could provide her with medical care, and we would be done with it. There were only a few problems with that idea."

"Problems?" At this point, Thomas was leaning forward in his chair hanging on to every word.

"Yes, Tommy. Problems. She was almost the spitting image of someone who had stolen my heart long ago. We were together for ten years. The similarity in appearance was amazing. Unfortunately, she had passed away under less than pleasant circumstances many years earlier and I never quite got over it. As for Angela, she didn't know her own name, where she lived or even what had happened to her. She blurted out that fact before I had even asked a single question. She was obviously suffering from amnesia as a result of her head injury. Why I did what came next, I will never know. Well, I do know, but it just defies all logical explanation."

Thomas stared at him in total curiosity as he asked, "What? What did you do?"

"I told her she was my wife."

Thomas lurched forward in his chair gasping for air. "Why the hell would you do that?"

"Oh, Tommy, you know what you saw when you looked into those eyes. It was the same spell that CarEarla had cast on me twelve years ago. You know that you would have done anything to have her. Anything at all! Tell me that it's not true. Tell me that she wasn't like some sorceress casting a spell that you couldn't run from if you tried."

Thomas was incredulous, "Whatever effect she may have had on me, I would never have done anything that stupid. That's totally sick. Are you nuts?"

"Nuts? Am I nuts?" There was that frightening look on his face again. "I can assure you I'm not. Now if you don't mind, I'll finish the story."

"By all means. I can't wait. It's getting better by the minute. What could possibly be next?"

"We backtracked until we found her car partly submerged in a shallow area near the bank of the river. Apparently, she had veered off the road, hit a tree and caromed into the water. Antonio recovered her purse, checked her identification, and then hid it in his shirt. With her personal information safely in hand, Antonio, bull that he is, managed to push the car farther into the river so that the current began to carry it downstream before it sank completely. The man is like a human bulldozer."

"Good lord. This is too bizarre. You can't be serious."

"Oh, I'm very serious, Tommy. By now, I had a complete plan. I've always been a good planner. I create solutions to problems very quickly. This woman was returning with me to Brazil to live as my wife."

Thomas sank back in his chair, "No, ok, I'm sorry, you are nuts. How could you accomplish that? What about documents?"

"Documents are no problem, and if you don't stop calling me nuts, you're going to lose yours. Whether it's Brazil or anywhere else, money buys you what you need. We returned to the motel and being very groggy from her head injury, Angela fell asleep. Medically that's probably not the best idea when you have a concussion, but not much choice. I needed her to sleep so that we could carry out the beginning of the plan. In fact, I gave her a mild sedative to help the process along."

By now Thomas was fidgeting in his chair. This was too far out for him to even comprehend. It was time for something different to drink.

"I think I need something stronger than Pepsi right now."

"What would you like? Scotch? Rum? Beer? Your choice."

"A nice Caipirinha would be great, I think."

"Good choice. Great drink. "Paola? Did you hear?"

There she was again, the ghost maid with not just a glass, but also a pitcher of caipirinha, and then gone once more.

"Shall I continue?"

"Please. I can't wait to see where this ends up."

"Where it all ends up depends on you. Anyway, while Angela was asleep, trusty Antonio drove to her place in Ottawa. There he retrieved just enough clothing to make it look as if she had indeed been traveling and staying in the motel with me. He gathered some pictures that would be needed to create digital copies in Brazilian scenes, as well as in pictures with me. He also searched for any information he could discover about her family."

As the story became even more convoluted, Thomas found himself unable to remain silent. "I have to say that I almost wanted to believe this was some sort of a gag, some sick joke, but this is all for real?"

"Now seriously, I'm not one who has time for games. This is all very real. Now, where was I? Oh yes. I made a phone call to an acquaintance that delivered a new birth certificate for her. We made it American so that she wouldn't recall a Canadian connection. Then there was a passport and, of course, a Brazilian visa. Those documents were backdated to a few years earlier along with the phony marriage license. I had my bank issue credit cards in her new identity and instructed my household staff to prepare the house, complete with a wardrobe based on her clothing and shoe sizes, makeup, and anything else they could think of to give the appearance that she had lived there for some time. The pictures were scanned and emailed to someone in Brazil who created new ones to be displayed around the house. When we arrived there, she would see herself in Brazilian locations and pictures with me. All of this was accomplished throughout the night and the next morning as she slept."

Suddenly Thomas realized why some of those pictures looked so familiar. He had seen them before. He had even taken some of them himself. He was sure now that he was hearing the truth.

"Your household staff actually went along with this?"

"This is Brazil, my friend. Good work is hard to find and, truth be known, they are just a little afraid of the consequences if they ever fail to do what I tell them. I know where their families live."

There was a very unpleasant look on his face as he spoke those words. If Thomas hadn't realized it before, he was suddenly aware that this was a dangerous man. He was beginning to wonder if he would be able to help Angela at all. Everything seemed too impossible, even hopeless.

"Anyway, all things were arranged, Angela accepted my story about us, and we returned to Brazil. My only hope was that she wouldn't recover her memory on the plane. That would have been slightly uncomfortable. Once again, a sedative helped relieve that concern. When we arrived here, a psychologist friend of mine provided her with counseling. Rather than help her find her own memory, his job was to give her a new one. The memory I wanted her to have. Everything was fine. Until that day."

"That day? What day?"

"You just had to be in Fortaleza that day, at the same time we were. How the hell could I ever predict that she would see you in Brazil? Hell, I didn't even know about you. There was no way to anticipate that possibility. In any event, see you she did, outside your hotel. She was never the same after that. She kept bringing you up, saying that she knew you somehow. It was a daily preoccupation with her to remember who you were. I would hear her talking to herself about it. I sent Antonio back to Fortaleza and to the hotel where you stayed. He bribed a clerk and discovered only one guest from Canada at that time. Of course, that was you.

I did nothing with that information, just held on to it for the time being. Despite more intensive counseling by my psychologist friend, almost two years later, she remembered everything. She was totally livid. She actually came at me with a butcher knife. She was furious and wanted to return to Canada. I gave her one hell of a great life here. All the money she could ask for, clothes, furs, jewels, everything. She showed no appreciation at all."

"Appreciation? For being kidnapped? Are you serious? My God! Anyway, I'm sure you see the need for her to go home now. The cat is just slightly out of the bag."

"Oh, she can go, Tommy. But it won't be without a price. Definitely not without a price. Everything has a cost."

"What price? What could I possibly have that you could want? I have nothing and you seem to have everything."

"Quite the contrary, you have just what I need."

Before Thomas had the chance to ask what that might be, Antonio entered the room.

"It's time, boss."

Thomas couldn't hold his words as he rose from his chair, "Rico, what price? Tell me." His host turned and looked at him with a screwed-up face that had question mark written all over it.

"Rico? Why did you call me Rico?"

"Because that's your name, isn't it?" The truth is he never had introduced himself. Thomas just assumed he was Rico. He had never seen someone so slight of build deliver a belly laugh of such magnitude.

"I'm not Rico, you ass. Whatever made you think that?"

"Antonio. He said we were going to see Rico."

"Sometimes I admire his sense of humor. You are indeed going to see Rico. I'm not sure you'll like the experience, but you will see him."

"Then who the hell is Rico?"

"Let's just say that he's a tool I use in certain situations. There are some things I wouldn't even ask Antonio to do. The big dumb ox that he is, he would gladly do them, but Rico is much better at certain tasks."

"What does this Rico have to do with all of this?"

"Actually, at first, when all of this blew up, I considered giving Angela to him. A gift for faithful service perhaps."

"Give her to him? What the hell are you talking about?"

"Rico isn't very good with women. You'll see why. They don't tend to last very long with him. The fact that they have no desire to even be near him tends to hasten the final act. It would have been a good way to dispose of her."

Thomas was now standing up to follow this sick bastard out of the room and his knees almost collapsed underneath him as he heard those words. What the hell had Angela gotten herself into? Not to mention, what the hell had she gotten him into? He was sure, if not for Angela, he would have been looking for a place to run. Somehow his mind stayed focused on her and what might happen if he failed in whatever he was expected to do for her release. One thing kept him going. The knowledge that he would never be able to look his kids in the face again if he failed to at least try and help their mother.

"So, for the record, would you care to tell me what your name is then?" Thomas asked.

"My name is Carlo," he replied without turning around.

Thomas followed Carlo and Antonio into the foyer and to a door behind the main staircase. Antonio opened it and Carlo approached the stairs with Thomas close behind. He had no idea where they were going, but there was no choice in the matter

CHAPTER 4

THE REUNION

At the bottom of the stairs was a long hallway. Its slate-colored stone floor was surrounded by walls of what appeared to be handmade bricks that were somewhat rough and irregular in appearance and with a rusty hue. Thomas could see that there were four doors accessible from the hall. As they proceeded on their way, he could hear the most disturbing sound of muffled screams and uncontrollable sobbing. His first thought was that it was Angela, and his heart leaped into his throat, almost choking off his breath. He was only temporarily relieved when he discovered that it wasn't her at all. His relief was only fleeting because what he saw next was horrific.

As they approached the first door on the left, he could see that it was slightly ajar. Carlo, displaying a look of extreme displeasure, pushed the door open wide. It was then that Thomas saw something he was sure he would never forget no matter how long he lived. There, against the wall, was a young girl that appeared to be about sixteen or seventeen years old. She was, to say the least, filthy. Her clothes were little more than dirty rags that hung loosely from her body. Standing before her, naked from the waist up and groping with his pants as he held her against the wall by her neck, was the most disgusting human Thomas had ever seen. His torso was so covered with dark brown hair that Thomas' immediate thought was that one could skin him and make what would pass for a bearskin rug. Given the look of him, he thought it would be well advised to shoot him forty or fifty times first to make absolutely certain he was dead. This beast of a man heard the sound of the door being swung open and turned to look in their direction. If there was a place on his disgusting face that wasn't scarred or inflicted with some form of horrid blemish, Thomas couldn't see it at a quick glance. His teeth were green, or something close to that, and appeared to be caked with years of built-up tartar. The faces of some people are a dead giveaway that they are very simple of mind. This face belied any trace of intelligence at all. Thomas was still frozen by that image as the remaining clothing was torn from the girl's body. Unable to scream with a hand tightly gripping her throat, all she could do was look at the doorway in the hope that someone had come to save her. She would be disappointed.

It was at that point that Carlo bellowed.

"How many times have I told you not to bring your damn playthings here? Do you realize the risk you put me in? Why? Why? You damn moron. You and these filthy little things from the favelas are a scourge. Damn you!"

There was an instant reaction to Carlo's scolding that totally surprised Thomas. Immediately, this beast was like a dog being scolded by his authoritative master for soiling the carpet.

"I've had enough of this shit, Rico. Now finish this thing. Just get to the end. Now!"

"So, this was Rico?" Thomas thought. Carlo had been right. This was not in any way a welcome experience. Not in the least. There was a certainty that he would have preferred almost anything else in its place.

No sooner had those words left Carlo's mouth than Rico turned to that poor frightened girl and, while still holding her by the throat, his other hand twisted her head until Thomas heard the distinct snap of her neck and she slumped to the floor. The girl was dead, and Thomas was trying everything to avoid vomiting. Despite the unmistakable taste of bile in his throat he managed to maintain, or so he believed, the appearance of someone not totally frightened. He could never have imagined he would see anything so gruesome in all his life.

Carlo's voice was almost an echo as he spoke. "So now you've met Rico. Can you imagine if I had given Angela to him?" he said with a cruel chuckle. "He would have liked that. He's always had a sick sort of passion for her. I swear he would drool at the sight of her. What disgusting ideas were going through his mind when he looked at her, I can only imagine. She, on the other hand, was frightened of even seeing him on the property. Petrified! Not hard to understand why she would be so fearful of him. I'm sure he frightens you, too."

With that remark he looked up at Thomas' face, frozen in disbelief at what he had just witnessed.

"It takes a great deal to frighten me, Carlo," he said with a forced air of confidence that wasn't quite honest.

"Fear shows in a man's eyes, Thomas. I can see it in yours right now. In fact, I do believe I see more than that. I see panic."

There was a tone of self-satisfaction in Carlo's voice that he felt he could read Thomas so well. Or so he believed. He was right about the fear. But panic? No way! Panic was something Thomas had never known. Somehow, he had always seemed to realize that fear can be your friend if you understand it. He knew that fear makes you aware of danger and allows you the opportunity to deal with it. Panic, on the other hand, causes you to lose any opportunity to evaluate the situation and then react appropriately. More than likely, it can get you killed. No, there was none of that.

His mind was already working overtime. He realized that this situation would result in both of their deaths, no matter what price anyone paid for Angela's and his release. There was no way Carlo could afford to let them live. If he thought Thomas believed otherwise, then he was not as smart as he imagined. All that remained was for Thomas to determine what Carlo wanted and use it against him. He could only hope there was an answer to that question. For the moment, let Carlo believe what he wanted to. Let him feel sure there was panic. Allow him to convince himself that Thomas would be much too afraid to do anything other than what he demanded. Let him feel comfortable while Thomas worked out a plan.

Carlo gave one more instruction to Rico, "Get rid of that. Make it fast and get your ass back here."

Carlo began walking down the hallway as he continued to speak, "I can't imagine why that dumb shit takes my abuse. Truth is, he frightens even me just a little. Maybe he tolerates it because I retrieved his sorry ass from the slums and gave him the opportunity to practice his apparent passion, killing people, all the while being well paid. If you go by Brazilian standards, that is. In terms of what you and I think of as money, he's one huge bargain. I'm never quite sure if he'll turn on me one day. I suppose at some point he will have served his purpose long enough, and I'll have to deal with it before I lose my ability to control him. Such a pity, really! He can be so damn useful"

Thomas was in no mood to talk, his mind still attempting to overcome the terror of what he had seen, so he followed quietly behind Carlo. Antonio, ever-present, was close behind as well. When they reached the end of the hallway, Carlo punched the keys of a coded lock and opened the door.

"There she is, Tommy. I'm sure you have a lot of catching up to do." Antonio gave Thomas a firm push into the room and closed the door.

What lay before him was a very simple bedroom. It appeared to have been recently constructed and the materials were not what one would associate with the rest of the house. The walls were a soft yellow and the floor was covered with mint green and off-white Berber carpet. He noticed immediately that there were no windows. Off to one side, there was a sofa, a coffee table, and two matching end tables. There was a television, a stereo, a computer and a small bar fridge against another wall.

At the opposite end was a four-poster bed. In that bed, under a white duvet, laid Angela. She was either asleep or drugged and had not heard his arrival. He walked over and sat down beside her. It was strange looking at her there. He hadn't seen that face in five years and yet he found that his memory of it was flawless. She looked exactly as he remembered her. Tears were running down his cheeks as his hand reached out to touch her face. It wasn't an emotion of finding a lost love, or one with any romantic attachment at all. What he experienced was a feeling for someone who, because she had been such a significant part of his life for so many years, still had at least some right to his compassion. Not the same place in his feelings, but still a place. He imagined the torment she had been through since recovering her memory and worried how it would all turn out. His only hope was that somehow, he would miraculously manage to save them both. He would settle, however, for just being able to save her, and giving his children back their mother.

After a few moments of his hand stroking her cheek, she gradually awoke. At first, she looked at him through sleepy eyes and made a face of disbelief. Then, her eyes suddenly wide with recognition, she threw her arms around him and began to cry. Her tears flowed so heavily that in no time the shoulder of his shirt was more than a little wet. She held him so tightly that he struggled to breathe. It would be many minutes before she would even talk. Thomas just held her in his arms, silently, until she could find her breath to speak.

"Thomas, you came for me. I was so afraid you wouldn't. I'm so happy to see you. Thank you so much," and the tears flowed again as she returned to hugging him.

It was as if she were afraid that he would disappear if she let go. Thomas knew that this was a person filled with fear and desperate for hope. He wasn't sure what to say and had yet to utter a single word. Finally, he moved her back from his shoulder so he could look into her eyes.

"Angela, I'm glad I'm here but I have no idea what they expect from me."

With that, he pulled her close to him so that he could whisper in her ear. He wasn't foolish enough to think they would be left alone without someone eavesdropping. He had no doubt the room was bugged. Ever so softly he said, "I'm sure they're listening. Be careful what you say. I'll come up with a plan when I know what it is they want from me. We can't let them hear anything that might help them."

Angela leaned back and nodded her head.

Over the next four hours, they had quite a talk concerning her experiences in Brazil and about family back home. Early in the conversation, it became apparent that she had not regained her memory completely. It seemed as if once she had recovered her recollection of Thomas, anything after that was still lost. In her mind, they were still a couple, and she had no apparent recall of the fact that they had broken up. He didn't think this was the appropriate time to tell her the truth. Eventually, he assumed, she would recover the rest of her memory, and everything would become clear. Right at this moment, the primary concern was to keep her calm and give her some hope that everything would be fine, even if he had no way of knowing it would.

Angela asked so many questions about their daughters and absorbed every detail he could provide her. She hadn't seen them since before they became teenagers. Thomas had a small picture of them in his wallet that he showed her. She held it in her hand and stared at it for the longest time as she alternately smiled and then cried. After what seemed an hour, she assumed he wanted it returned and handed it to him. He placed it back into her hand and told her to keep it. She smiled and held it to her heart. Thomas had no way to prevent the tears from collecting in his own eyes. He began to realize that Angela had indeed enjoyed a good life in Brazil. There were expensive jewels, clothes, parties, and numerous trips around that beautiful country. She had never lacked for anything she wished for, except to find her past. As for her relationship with Carlo, she admitted that she never could understand how she ended up married to him. There was no attraction, either physical or emotional. She said that she simply accepted the facts as they appeared and assumed that she would eventually remember what she saw in him. She only knew that he was in the import business.

It seemed he mostly worked from home and only rarely left the country for any reason. He could, she said, be alternately kind and yet cruel. Though he had never struck her, more than once she feared that he might. They had arguments, and often things ended up broken. At one point, she told him that she might wish for a divorce. He glared at her and told her to never mention the idea again. She had seen the same cruelty in his eyes that Thomas had seen, so she took that advice and simply went about enjoying the good things in her life.

After many hours of sitting on the bed in conversation, they both simply lay down and held each other. It was now after three in the morning. Thomas was totally exhausted and fell asleep with Angela nestling her head against his shoulder. He awoke hours later feeling Angela breathing warmly on his ear.

"Thomas? Are you awake?"

He was still half asleep but managed to answer, "Uh, yeah. Sort of."

"Make love to me? It's been so long since we've been together."

Now, he was suddenly wide-awake. It seemed the time had come somewhat early when he would have to deal with the truth. He would never take advantage of her lack of memory for the sake of sex.

"I think we need to talk, Angela."

"What is it? You look confused."

"No, I'm not confused. I'm not sure how to tell you all of this, but you need to know.

Angela, we hadn't been together for almost two years before you disappeared."

There was a look of total shock on her face as she spoke, "What? I don't understand. What are you talking about?

"Angela, you left me. You left us all. More than six years ago."

"No! You're lying to me. I would remember that. Why are you saying that? That's cruel, Thomas."

"Because it's true. I have no doubt you'll remember everything, sooner or later."

"But why? Why did I leave?"

"I suppose for the same reason most people leave a relationship. You weren't happy in it anymore. The truth is, neither of us was. It really was for the best."

"I can't believe this. I call you, you come here for me, and yet we have no relationship anymore? Why would you even bother?" she asked as she began to cry.

"We have a relationship, Angela. It's just not the same one we used to have."

"Well, I don't remember, so let's just forget a breakup ever happened. We can just start over."

"I can't do that."

"Why? Tell me why."

"For one thing, it would make me no better than Carlo. I would be just another person who took advantage of your loss of memory. For another thing, sooner or later, I'm sure it would fall apart again. Once is enough for that kind of pain. We were just not meant to be together."

"No! It wouldn't fall apart. We would make sure it didn't. Why would you come all this way if you don't care anymore?"

"I never said I didn't care. I will always care, in some way. I could never have turned my back on you in this kind of trouble."

"I still don't understand why you don't want to try."

"Well, that may be something to discuss later." Thomas then whispered into her ear again to remind her that they were surely being listened to. Angela took the warning.

"OK. Whatever you say. Maybe you'll change your mind. I'm still very happy you came."

"So am I. No matter the past, I could never live with myself if I turned my back on you in a situation like this. All those years count for something. Besides, the girls would kill me if I left you here," he said with a laugh.

"I'm glad you feel that way," she said, as she once again rested her head on his shoulder.

At just that moment, the door swung open, and Carlo made another appearance. Antonio and that disgusting Rico were close behind. When Angela saw Rico, she cowered behind Thomas. Her fear was obvious in the way her body was shaking uncontrollably against his back."

Carlo sneered as he spoke, "You feel her fear, Tommy? She knows that Rico is her fate if you fail to help me with what I want. She knows what her future is after he's had his fun with her."

The response from Thomas was stern.

"How about if we get to the point and skip the drama. Don't you think it's about time you told me what it is you expect from me?"

"Yes, it is," Carlo said as he sat down on the sofa and placed his feet on the coffee table. "When I discovered what it is that you do for a living, the idea struck me."

"What idea was that? What could my line of work possibly offer you?"

"Think, Tommy. Think! Do you know the value of imported vehicles in Brazil? The high cost of them?"

"They're very expensive. That much I know. I even investigated the possibility of exporting used vehicles here, but it wasn't possible. Too many restrictions and the import duties were huge. I gave up the whole idea very quickly."

"At least you understand how lucrative it can be. But you have to think in terms of new vehicles."

"There's still the issue of almost forty percent duty."

"Duty doesn't bother me. It's certainly not important when the vehicles don't cost me anything, to begin with."

"I beg your pardon?"

"That's where you come in. You have the access and the means to acquire what I need at no cost to me."

"Are you trying to tell me you want me to steal vehicles for you? You better be kidding!"

"Steal? Acquire, Tommy. I'm sure there are ways. And no, I'm not kidding at all. Twenty F350, crew cab 4x4 XLT diesel trucks and Angela goes free, back to Canada, back to her daughters. It's a simple arrangement."

Thomas was quick to appreciate the motive. In U.S. dollars these trucks would be worth at least sixty thousand each in the States. In Brazil, more like a hundred thousand each. Likely even more. Even after whatever reduced duty rate Carlo can bribe his way into, plus shipping costs, there would be a tidy profit of over at least a million and a half dollars. Carlo had dollar signs in his mind, and sometimes that blinds a person. Thomas could only hope it would dull

Carlo's senses enough to allow him time to come up with a final plan. He was well on his way to knowing exactly how to fool him completely. Carlo was right, there were certainly ways Thomas could at least make him believe he was getting what he wanted. Once that was accomplished, he could concentrate on what to do next. Buying time was the only option at this point.

"Listen, even if I do what you ask, how can I trust you to keep your end of the bargain?"

"What choice do you have? You can agree, or you can sit and watch as I give Rico what he wants. You can witness the whole sick thing. And trust me, I would make you watch. You'll just have to take my word, Tommy. My word is worth something."

His word wasn't worth shit, but Thomas had to let him think he believed him.

"Fine, I'll do what you want, but believe me, if you break your word, I'll find a way to get my revenge. That you can count on."

"Then we understand each other. Now, I need to know how you will accomplish what I ask. I need some proof that you're capable of it."

At that point, Thomas felt he might as well offer some details so that Carlo would feel comfortable that he had the knowledge, and ability, to pull it off.

"Do you have a way to establish a bogus company in Ontario, Carlo? You seem to be good at forged papers. I need a registered company in Ontario for the phony bills of sale. Then, with the help of some friends, I can arrange shipping and customs details. I'll provide you with copies of the purchase agreements, ownerships, and shipping documents. The problem is it will take at least a little time to accomplish it all. I can't do it from Brazil."

"I'm very aware that you can't do it from here. My biggest concern has been that once allowed to go back to Canada, you might simply leave Angela here to her fate. You may begin to think only of saving yourself."

"You don't know me, or you would never believe that."

"Actually, I was about to say that I see in the way you are together that I don't have to worry about it. I'm positive that you could never leave her to that fate. So now we only need to talk time frame and get you back to Canada so you can begin your work. The sooner those vehicles arrive, the sooner she gets to go home. I'll have some breakfast sent down and we can continue this later."

Having ended the discussion, Carlo stood and walked out the door, followed by Antonio and Rico. They were alone again, and Thomas could see the questions in Angela's eyes.

"You would do that for me? You would risk all of that for me?"

"Did you think for a minute I wouldn't? It's not just for you. I'll do it for the girls, too."

"Yes, I was afraid you might not. You'd be throwing everything away, maybe go to jail, all because of me."

Thomas forced out a small chuckle as he stated firmly,

"I'm not going to jail! Don't worry about that."

"How can you do this? Maybe it's impossible."

"I've been around this business long enough to know every in and out. Just have faith."

"I trust you, but it will be torture being left here and not knowing what's happening. I'll be petrified every day that I'll find out you couldn't do what he wants."

Thomas took her in his arms and whispered, "Don't worry, everything will work out. Let's not talk anymore about it in a negative way. No point in causing him to have doubts. Only speak positively about it. Ok? Act like you know I am very capable of doing what he demands."

She looked at him, and nodded in agreement as she spoke, "I shouldn't doubt you, Thomas. I know if anyone can do this, it would be you. I have faith in that."

"Good. When breakfast comes, let's just relax and not think about this situation for a while."

Almost the second he mentioned breakfast, the door opened. It was Paola, wheeling a food trolley and followed by Antonio. She placed it at the foot of the bed and was gone. Antonio closed the door, and they were alone again. The sWaltl of freshly cooked bacon made Thomas realize how hungry he was. He hadn't eaten since the night before, during the layover in Atlanta, and his stomach was telling him that it was very much prepared for something to satisfy it.

He moved the trolley over to the sofa and Angela and he began a quiet breakfast. When he had finished his bacon and eggs, tomato, rice, and fresh fruit, he reached for his napkin. As he opened it to wipe his face and hands, a small piece of paper fell into his lap. He picked it up and read the awkwardly scribbled words, "I will help you if you need. I hate him. Paola." If this were not some sort of trick, then it would appear that the little ghost-like maid had been through more than enough with Carlo. Thomas had a feeling that she might come in very handy. There was now another piece of the puzzle to build on. He let Angela see the note, and then went into her bathroom and flushed it. He was beginning to feel even more self-assured. The question was whether that confidence was misguided.

CHAPTER 5

OUT OF THE LIONS DEN

Shortly after they had finished their breakfast, which they both ate quite ravenously despite the situation, the door to Angela's room opened. It was Antonio displaying a serious look on his face.

"Let's go, sport. Times up. Carlo wants ya."

"Will I be coming back down here?"

"Kinda doubt it, pal. I think you're gonna be on your way"

"Then be a nice guy and give us a minute, will you?"

"Carlo said now, and that's what he means."

"Come on, Antonio. A few minutes won't hurt."

Antonio looked around the room as if he were searching for something, "Fine! Whatever. Two minutes. No more."

"Thanks. I really appreciate it."

Antonio stepped into the hallway and closed the door behind him. Thomas turned to Angela, placed his hands on her shoulders, and looked straight into her eyes.

"I don't want you to worry. You have to trust in me. Everything will be fine. I'll do what he wants, and you'll go home." With that, he pulled her close to him and whispered, "Don't ever forget to always be careful what you say out loud."

She looked at him knowingly and winked.

"I have faith in you. I know everything will be fine." Just then the door burst open again and Antonio barked out, "Ok. Times up! Let's go. Carlo's gonna be pissed."

Thomas left Angela alone, in what could only be considered her prison, and headed upstairs. Once back in the library, he sat again in the same leather chair. Paola brought him a Pepsi and gave him a slight smile. So, it appeared it was true, he thought, she did want to help. As Paola was making her exit, Carlo came in and sat opposite him.

"So, Tommy boy. We have an understanding! Right?"

Thomas was getting fed up with Carlo not calling him by his proper name but managed to bite his tongue.

"Yes. We do. Not a problem. Let's just get it done."

"Good boy. You realize, of course, that the price Angela will have to pay if you fail me on this will be nothing short of gruesome."

"Believe me, I'm aware of that. You made your point quite well. I have no intention of failing."

Carlo handed Thomas a piece of paper, "This is my email address. All contact will be made that way. You don't discuss this kind of business on the phone. I expect to be kept fully informed. You understand?"

What Thomas understood was that the man was not as smart as he imagined. He immediately thought of his recent new acquaintance, Sofia. With his email address, Thomas was thinking that she would be able to arrange some wonderful things. Assuming, of course, she was willing to get involved in this mess. How lucky to have met someone like her, with so much knowledge about computer security. He couldn't help thinking that this might very well be a potential key to a happy ending to all of this.

"I understand. No problem. But I'm going to want to hear from Angela regularly to know she is still safe, and unharmed."

"Fine. I'll let her email you."

"Yeah, right! You can't believe I would accept that! As if I would ever be able to know it was really Angela. For all I would know it could be you. No! Not acceptable at all. Only phone contact for that or no deal."

"I don't think you're in a position to bargain, Tommy. Maybe you should reconsider your situation before you start trying to make demands on me. I'm not fond of it."

"Bullshit, Carlo! Don't feed me that garbage."

Carlo's eyes went so wide, his face turned so red and his fingers gripped that chair so hard that Thomas was sure he might explode.

"You're pushing your luck," he screamed as he leaped out of his chair. "I should just end this all right now. Be done with both of you."

"Listen, Carlo," Thomas said as he stood to face him, "You aren't about to throw away over a million dollars. You aren't stupid. You harm me, or Angela, and you get nothing. I can't imagine that there's a million dollars worth of satisfaction in that, no matter what you say."

Thomas continued, "I'm doing what you want. Now humor me on that one issue. What can it hurt? It can only make me more eager to get the job done and get her home."

There was a long silence as Carlo finally relaxed and regained his composure.

"You try my patience. Fine! Your point is made. I warn you, though, don't assume so much in the future. One day you'll be very wrong, and the price will be very high."

"Understood! So, I'll talk to Angela every day for five minutes. Deal?"

"Every day? What the hell, sure, whatever! But two minutes. That's it. Take it or leave it. I am not going to negotiate."

"Fine, two minutes it is," Thomas relented, not wanting to argue over his unexpected victory.

"I hadn't expected to arrive at an agreement with you so soon. Thought you would hold out a little more. Your flight home isn't until tomorrow night. Antonio will return you to your hotel and pick you up tomorrow for the drive to the airport. Do your dear Angela a favor. Spend the time in your suite. Don't get any bright ideas."

"No problem. Right now, I'm damn tired, and I'll be very happy to sleep before that long trip home."

"I expect to hear from you the minute you arrive there. Then there are to be daily emails to tell me about your progress. You only have so much time. I want those trucks in the containers in no more than ten days."

"Ten days? Shouldn't be a problem."

"There's no such thing as shouldn't, Tommy. If I don't have proof that those trucks are there on time, Angela goes to Rico. Enough said?"

After that final warning, Carlo got up and left the room. Antonio, standing at the door the whole time, stuck out his huge hand and gestured with his finger for Thomas to follow him. As they were preparing to leave Thomas saw Paola standing somewhat behind the archway to the main living room and, once again, gave him that little smile, and a brief nod of her head. Once in the limo, the ride to the hotel was quiet. Neither Antonio nor Thomas said a single word. When they pulled up to the hotel, the doorman opened the limo door. As Thomas was preparing to get out, Antonio spoke, "Good luck, chump. You'll need it." Thomas would have sworn he sounded sincere.

Once back in his suite, he used his cell phone to call Sofia. Hopefully, she was not still in her meeting. He needed to tell her the truth about why he was in Brazil and ask for her help. He feared that it might be too much to ask of someone that barely knew him, but he had no choice. After a detailed explanation of the situation, Sofia was shocked and very distressed for both Thomas and Angela.

"Of course, I will help. But how can I? I have no idea how to help you in this."

"Sofia, you just might be the biggest help of all. You're a computer expert. Right? Computer security. Isn't that correct?"

"Yes, but…." Thomas cut her off before she could say more and gave her Carlo's email address.

"What is this? Is this your email?"

"No. It's Carlos," he said with a small chuckle.

"It is his? Really?"

"Yes! Really! I'm imagining that you may be able to do some very helpful things with it. I hope you are going to tell me that I am right about that."

She laughed and said, "Oh yes. With this, he is mine to do whatever I wish. I can gain entry to his computer with a virus attached to an email from you. I will be able to access all of his files."

"What about virus scans and firewalls?"

"New viruses arrive that fool existing antivirus programs. That is why they must constantly update them. In fact, I have a virus that I use in my demonstrations to companies that I am trying to sign up for our security program. It has never been released into the wild and is unknown to any current antivirus program. I am the only person in the world who knows of it. I wrote it, and it has fooled every known virus scan to date. I will have no difficulty getting past his firewall, if he even has one. People in Brazil are not always so careful when it comes to internet security. Yes, Thomas, with his email address we have control of him."

Thomas was pleased beyond belief. This was even more than he had hoped for. Now it was time for him and Sofia to apply a few more details to his plan before he had to return to Canada. He was beginning to think that this would actually be fun, even if there were still many worries that filled his mind. A high-risk challenge always managed to get his adrenaline flowing. They began by deciding that he would advise Sofia when the text of his first message to Carlo was prepared. He gave her the intended password for a new email account he would create with which she would access and attach the Trojan horse virus, and then send the email as if it originally came from Thomas. At that point, barring any surprises, she would have free access to his computer and be able to discover any secrets it might hold. From there, they would plan the next move. He could only hope that Carlo was foolish enough to keep information stored on his computer that would prove useful. In any event, they would know soon enough.

There were many details involved in setting up the scam on Carlo, most of which Thomas could not even begin dealing with until his arrival back in Huntsville. The remainder of his time in Brazil would be spent with this wonderful woman. He was still in a state of complete amazement at his good fortune in meeting her. He found himself wondering where it would ultimately lead. It was, however, premature to be thinking along those lines.

With his call to Sofia finished, Thomas sat on the balcony of his suite. It was then that he noticed a black Mercedes limo making its way slowly down the street, towards the front entrance to the hotel. While he realized there are several such vehicles in Sao Paulo, he still watched it closely. He was very grateful that he did. Suddenly, another car cut the Mercedes off and it slammed on its brakes. That was when he saw the unmistakable image of Antonio's head protrude from the driver's window, screaming obscenities at the offending motorist.

Thomas decided to head down to the lobby and find Antonio. He would just say that he was going for a drink in the bar. Maybe even invite him along.

When the elevator doors finally opened, he could see Antonio just arriving through the main entrance. After an evaluation of the situation, he made a point of simply waiting until

Antonio was halfway to the elevators before heading in the direction of the bar. They would have to pass each other before he reached it.

"Hey!" Antonio bellowed.

Thomas feigned a look of surprise when he responded, "Hey, Antonio. What are you doing here?"

"You didn't answer your phone."

"I didn't realize that you would be calling," he said with a sarcastic laugh.

"I wasn't calling. Carlo was. You didn't answer your phone."

"Yes, we've established that much. How long ago was that?"

"Half hour. Where were you?"

"I wanted to come down for a drink. I think I need one after all of this. Problem was, I forgot my wallet. Got all the way down here and had to go back up. Carlo must have called while I was in between."

"Carlo ain't happy you didn't answer."

"Well, if it will make him feel better, call him and tell him you found me. In fact, why don't you come and have a drink with me. You can keep a better eye on me that way."

Antonio looked almost stunned at the invitation. He didn't seem sure how to respond. Thomas took the liberty of trying to convince him. Spending time with this thug might give more clues to any chinks in Carlo's armor.

"Come on. I tried to sleep, and I can't. One drink with me, and then I'm going to bed for sure."

Antonio still had that stunned look as he rubbed his chin the way one might when posed with a dilemma. In the end, he agreed.

"OK. A drink might be good. I'll call Carlo and tell him I found ya."

Antonio took out his cell phone and called Carlo to give him the news. Once that was done, they went in and chose an out of the way table at which to sit. The waitress arrived seconds later. She was quite attractive, and Antonio was obviously impressed. Her hair was blonde, unusual in Brazil, and was permed in very tight waves, and extended well past her bare shoulders. She wore a micro mini and halter-top and had a striking figure. Antonio was looking over every square inch of it. His attempts at flirting were almost humorous. To her credit, the waitress smiled and remained polite, and even gave a wink or two in return. Thomas knew the routine. It was a very seductive effort to increase the prospects of a good tip. Antonio ordered scotch rocks, which surprised Thomas. He would have thought him nothing but a beer man. Thomas ordered his usual Bourbon and Pepsi.

As they waited for her to return with their drinks, Thomas decided to try and open a friendly dialogue with Antonio.

"So you're from Queens?"

"Yeah. Born and raised."

"Brazil is a long way from Queens. What the hell are you doing here?"

"I hada come here with Carlo."

"Do you like it here?"

"It's ok. Too damn hot sometimes! And the street crime is nuts. Worse than you could imagine."

The waitress returned with their drinks, and Antonio's eyes lit up. Thomas found it quite funny to see this big goon acting like a lovesick school kid. It just didn't fit. After a few more smiles, and winks, she left, and they continued their conversation.

"Well, Antonio, as for the crime, there are a lot of very poor people here. Desperate people do desperate things."

"Yeah, well not to me. Just bust the hell out of em if they try."

"So why did Carlo move here?"

The question prompted a curious look from Antonio. He was groping for an answer that sounded plausible, "Uh, he retired and wanted to live here. No arguing with him sometimes. I suggested Italy, but no. Had to be Brazil."

"It is a beautiful country. I'd live here. No doubt."

"I guess it ain't all that bad. There's worse holes. But gimme Italy, any day."

"So, what did Carlo retire from? What kind of work did he do?"

He gave Thomas quite possibly the most serious look he could muster up.

"You ask too many questions about Carlo. That ain't good."

"Hey, I'm just a little curious about the guy who has me by the balls right now. Can't blame me for that, can you? I didn't see any harm in asking."

"Yeah," Antonio chuckled, as he drained the last of his scotch from the glass, "He does have you by the balls pretty good, don't he?"

"Yeah, he does. But, what the hell, I'll do this thing and be done with it." Thomas signaled the waitress to bring them another drink.

"Hey, I thought we was havin one?" Antonio piped up.

"One, two, what's the difference. Besides, the waitress is pretty hot. Not bad to look at, don't you think?"

"Yeah," Antonio said as he smiled, "I gotta admit, she's something else." "Well, she seems to like you. You should go for it." "Nah, she ain't interested. She just wants a good tip."

"Hey, you never know. All she can say is no. You'll never find out if you don't try."

"You think so? Nah. No way."

"Well, you think about it. I have to go to the men's room. Be right back."

It wasn't really the men's room Thomas needed. He had an idea! He located the waitress and took her aside. Thankfully she spoke fairly good English.

"Hi, what's your name?"

"I'm Rosina."

"Well, Rosina, you know that big guy I'm with?"

"Yes. He is very big," she replied as she opened her eyes wide and then giggled.

"Well, he kind of likes you. Any chance that you would be interested in a date with him?"

"Oh, I am not sure he is my type. But he does seem to be nice. He flirts with me."

"Believe me, he's very nice. Would you consider trying at least one date with him? He's too shy to ask you himself. I'm just trying to help him along," Thomas said, as he slipped a fifty-dollar bill into her hand.

"Well, maybe, ok. If you say he is nice, I believe you. Maybe would be fun."

"Great. Now don't say that I talked to you. Not ever. He would be very angry. When you come back with our drinks, I'll start a conversation with you, and somehow, I'll get him to ask you. You just pretend we never talked."

"Sure. I can do that."

"Good. See you at the table in a few minutes. Thanks."

"Is ok. No problem. I think I will enjoy."

Once back at the table, Thomas kept pressing the issue.

"So, what do you think, Antonio?"

"What? Think about what?"

"The waitress! A date with her. What do you think?"

"Nah. No way she's goin out with me. I ain't gonna embarrass myself askin."

"Listen, when she comes back, just let me do the talking. Ok?"

"What are you gonna do?"

"Don't worry about it. It will all be good. Promise."

"You embarrass me, and I'll kick your ass."

"All the more reason for me to be sure not to."

Just then Rosina returned with their drinks. Thomas led off by asking, once again, her name. He was afraid she would blurt out that she already told him, but she didn't.

"My name is Rosina."

"Well, Rosina, nice to meet you. My friend and I were just talking about how beautiful you are."

"Oh, you will make me blush."

"Well, it's true. You're very attractive. Sadly, I'm a taken man or I would be very interested."

"Really? You are taken?"

"Yes, very much so. However, my friend Antonio here is very available." Thomas could see the redness creeping up Antonio's face as he directed her attention to him. Antonio was so convinced that she would never be interested in him that it must have been torture.

"He is single?"

"He really is. Just before you arrived, he was saying that he would be a very happy man if he could date someone like you." Thomas wasn't sure if the color in Antonio's face was embarrassment or anger. Either way, something good had to happen soon.

"Oh, that would be very nice. I would like that," she responded on cue, and Antonio suddenly went from red to completely pale. He had never expected that answer.

"Why don't you give him your number, and he'll call you to arrange a time."

"Yes, of course. I will like." She wrote her name and number on a cocktail napkin and handed it to Antonio. He was speechless. Thomas had to prompt him to say something.

"Antonio, when do you think you'll call her?"

"Uh, Uh, ok, uh, tomorrow? Is that ok?" he stammered with a tone of shyness in his voice.

Rosina smiled, "You are cute when you are shy. I will wait for you to call. I will be home all day tomorrow. Don't forget me."

Still somewhat stunned, Antonio managed to say, "OK," and Rosina went back to taking care of her other customers.

"You see? That wasn't so bad, was it?"

"Nah, not so bad." He looked at Thomas somewhat confused but with a sheepish grin on his face. "Why would you do that for me? I mean, with what's happening, and me working for Carlo and all?"

"Hey, you don't seem like such a bad guy. Just because Carlo has me in a box, doesn't mean I have to take it out on you. You're just doing your job. No hard feelings."

"You sure are a different kind of guy from what I usually deal with. I woulda thought you'd hate me. Ya know? But you're ok, Tommy. Kinda sorry I won't get to know ya better. Too bad you're in this mess. I kinda feel for ya. It's not fair you're in this jam."

"You never know how things turn out," Thomas said with a smile. It seemed he was establishing some rapport with this misplaced Queens giant. Truth is, he really didn't seem like a bad guy in some ways. If Thomas had somehow now gained his confidence, perhaps he could learn a little more from him. Every little bit he could discover about Carlo would help. By now, Antonio was on his fifth scotch, and he was much less guarded in his answers.

"So how long have you worked for Carlo?", Thomas asked a now somewhat tipsy Antonio.

"I dunno. Fifteen years I guess."

"That's a long time. How long have you been in Brazil?"

"That I can remember! It's like ten years tomorrow. Shit, I wanted to go to Italy. My family, ya know? Got relatives in Napoli. Never get to see them."

"Why don't you just go for a visit?"

"Can't do that. Carlo can't be seen there, and me either. People know I work for him."

"I don't understand. What's the big deal about being seen?"

"Let's just say there are guys that would love to find out where he is. Pain in the ass."

"I see. So how do you like working for him?"

"Carlo? Sometimes it ain't so bad. Usually, it sucks. He can be a real dick, if ya know what I mean."

"I got that impression. He seems to have quite a temper, too."

"Ain't that the truth! Crazy temper! He don't care about nobody but him. I mean, he pays me good, and takes care of lots of shit for me, but that's cause he needs me. For now, anyway. Not sure how much I trust the guy though. He ain't loyal to no one. Even me."

"I hate to say this, but you sound as if you could use a change of employers."

The big guy laughed an almost sad chuckle, "Ain't no leavin' Carlo. Ever! Not a good life decision."

"Well, things happen in life. One day you may find the opportunity when you least expect it. We can only hope you'll be wise enough to take it. Then maybe you can fulfill your dream of living in Napoli."

"Yeah. That'd be great," he said as he looked at his watch. "Hey, I gotta get back. Carlo will be pissed. I'll come to get ya at noon. Be sure you're ready," he said as he got up from the table, threw down a hundred-dollar bill, and headed, staggering slightly, towards the lobby.

Thomas was realizing that this big ox might just turn out to be useful. Now that he had planted the seed of freedom from Carlo in Antonio's mind, he hoped that it would sprout quickly.

CHAPTER 6

ANTONIOS SURPRISE

It was about eleven in the morning when Thomas finished packing and prepared to leave his room to wait in the lobby for Antonio. As he was about to open the door, the phone rang. It was Carlo.

"Just thought I would call and remind you how serious this whole thing is. Don't want you getting cold feet. It would be very bad for both of you."

"I'm not going to get cold feet. In fact, I've managed to get quite enthusiastic about it all. I think I'm going to enjoy the whole process. As for you, be sure you keep your word."

"Tommy, I keep telling you that you're in no position to make demands. If I tell you that I give my word, then that's all there is to it. Don't question my word. Not now. Not ever. Just do what you have to do."

"That's all I need to know," Thomas said as if Carlo's promise was worth anything at all. Better to let him think he trusted it. Let him feel secure.

"Remember, I expect to hear from you by email the minute you get home, Thomas. As promised, as soon as I hear from you, Angela will call to let you know she's ok."

"She'll call you every day for two minutes. But only after I receive your daily email. If I fail to hear from you, even one day, she goes to Rico. Understand?"

"I understand only too well. You'll hear from me every day, like clockwork. No problem."

"Good," was Carlo's only response.

With that abrupt end to their conversation, Thomas headed down to the lobby and found Antonio sitting there waiting for him. The minute Antonio spotted him, he stood up and grinned like a Cheshire cat. Thomas couldn't help but be taken aback by this change in his demeanor. Antonio never said a word as he turned towards the door and walked, in a somewhat buoyant step, out to the limo. He opened the back door and, as Thomas moved to get in, Antonio laughed and patted him on the back. Thomas was dying to know what the hell was up with him. Once they had pulled away from the curb, onto the Av Nocoes Unidas, Antonio spoke.

"You know that waitress last night? Rosina? The one you introduced to me?"

"Yeah. Of course, I remember. Why?"

"When I left you, I sat out in the limo for a while. An hour maybe! Just couldn't stop thinkin' about her."

"Really? She got to you that bad, did she?"

"Yeah, she did. I mean, Tommy, she was hot. Anyway, I went back in. You were gone already, so I asked her what she was doin' after work because I couldn't wait to call her. She wasn't doin' nothin'. So!"

"So? What?" Thomas was leaning forward in anticipation of what might come next.

"So, I got a room and we stayed here last night."

"Get out! No kidding? Oh, Antonio, my man! Awesome. I'm happy for you, you big ox," Thomas said with a genuinely cordial laugh. He actually seemed to be developing a liking for this guy.

"I owe you, Tommy. This gal is great. We're goin' out tonight. She ain't workin' tonight and were goin' out. I ain't had a girlfriend since we got to this place. And she really likes me. She ain't playin'. I tried to give her money and she got mad. She started to cry and said she was with me cause she liked me. I felt like shit. But we made up. It's all good, Tommy. It's all really good."

"You don't have to thank me. I told you before; you're not a bad guy. I hold no grudges against you. I'm glad I could help. I think it's great."

"Listen, we gotta have a talk. I gotta tell ya something important, and it ain't easy for me."

"Sure. What is it?"

Antonio pulled the limo over to the curb as soon as he could find a space. When he had parked, he turned around and looked straight into Thomas' eyes. It was obvious by the look on his face that this was something serious.

"I shouldn't be tellin' ya this, but you done a good thing for me. You got me thinkin', too. You're a nice guy. Not like the dirtbags we usually do business with. I can't let this happen to you. It just ain't right."

"Antonio, what the hell are you talking about?"

"It don't matter what you do. As soon as Carlo gets what he wants, Angela is dead. So are you. I gotta tell you that. You should forget this, and hide, Tommy. He'll send me to find you, but I won't. I'll just tell him I did."

Antonio had just displayed a heart Thomas never expected he had. It was time to let him know he wasn't so blind. How much he would dare to say, he had no way of knowing yet.

"Antonio, I'm aware of that. I'm not naive, my friend."

"You know? If you know, then you're gonna do what I said, right? You're gonna hide!"

"No way! Leave Angela to Rico? Not a chance!"

"But you gotta. Why the hell wouldn't you? It's suicide. You gotta know that."

"If I ever ran out on Angela at a time like this, I would never be able to live with myself. Every time I looked in the mirror, or when I looked at my kids, I would wish I were dead."

"Yeah, but you're gonna be dead. Can't you see that? You can't beat this! You can't beat Carlo! It's too big."

"Don't be so sure, my friend. You should never be so sure. You remember our conversation last night?"

"Which part? We talked about a lotta things."

"The part about how you know that someday Carlo will have no need for you anymore?"

"Yeah! What about it?"

"How about the part where you would like a new life in Napoli?"

"Yeah, yeah, I remember already. Why? What about it?"

"If there was even a remote chance that you could be out from under Carlo, have that life in Napoli, would you take it?" Thomas said as he slid forward in his seat.

"I dunno. Never thought about it that much."

"I have to trust you for the moment, Antonio. If you're just testing me, I'm dead now, and so is Angela."

"I ain't testing ya! I'm bein' straight here, Tommy! Give me a little credit will ya? I ain't never done this for nobody."

It was obvious he was actually hurt by the suggestion that Thomas didn't trust him. Thomas was now sure that Antonio was being sincere. There was no doubt in his mind.

"Carlo just might lose this one," he said. "I don't fold up so easily. I knew from the beginning that there was a death sentence for Angela and me. There's no way in hell that I can let that happen without a fight. Carlo is going to get a very big surprise."

"What the hell you gonna do? How the hell could you ever beat him? It ain't possible. He's got connections."

"I can't tell you everything yet, Antonio. You have to understand that. Remember when we were talking about the poor people here? And the crime and how desperate people do desperate things? Well, I'm desperate. What I'm going to do may seem even more desperate, but it has a good shot at working. I may need your help, if you're willing to take the risk and give it a shot for a chance at Napoli."

"My help? You wanna get me killed too?"

"Listen to me! You know that Carlo will never let you have what you want. You'll spend the rest of your life under his thumb, or at least until he does away with you for some idiotic reason. Take a risk for yourself! I'm taking one, and I may die in the effort. But that's better than living with the knowledge I did nothing. That would be even worse than death."

"You got a point. But I gotta think about it. That ain't so easy a thing to decide."

"That's fine. I know I'm asking a lot. You can think about it on the way to the airport, which is exactly where we need to get if I'm going to catch that plane."

"Holy shit," Antonio shouted as he threw the limo into drive and hurtled down the street toward the highway for the airport, "We gotta get movin'!"

"Let me know what you think when we get to the terminal. Whatever you decide, please, keep this to yourself."

The rest of the drive was very quiet. It was obvious that Antonio was deep in thought, and Thomas didn't care to interrupt. He wanted him to wrap his mind around the possibility of freedom from Carlo. He wanted him to dream of Napoli. The more he thought, the better the chance he might agree. Thomas couldn't help but notice that, occasionally, Antonio would glance at him in the rear-view mirror. It was as if he were trying to measure the possibility that he could succeed. Some twenty minutes later, they pulled up in front of the terminal. Antonio turned to face him and spoke, "What do ya want me to do?"

"You'll help me then? You'll help us, and yourself?"

"Yeah. I may regret it. But yeah! I got the feeling Carlo stepped on the wrong guy time. And you're right. I need a new life. this I hate this. I got no pleasure in life. I could take Rosina to Napoli with me! I'd love that. No more of Carlo's bullshit."

"Antonio," Tommy said as he patted his shoulder, "All you need to do right now is stay healthy until I get back.

"Get back? What are you talking about? You ain't supposed to come back. Carlo ain't expectin' that. I'm supposed to just go take care of you after the trucks get here."

"That's right! He isn't expecting me back. Won't he be surprised? It's when I'm back in Sao Paulo that I'll need your help. Will I have it?"

"Yeah! You got it. I don't want you to think this is stupid or nothin', but you're the closest thing to a friend I've had since I been here," he said as he reached back with his huge paw to shake Thomas' hand.

Once they had finished saying goodbye, Thomas was out of the limo and into the terminal to check in for his flight. He now had two people in Carlo's inner circle to help him. He hadn't told Antonio about Paola. No sense in risking a slip by him that could expose both of them.

Once on the plane, and settled into that comfortable first-class seat again, Thomas was beginning to feel the exhaustion creep over him. This time he wasn't so lucky in the area of traveling companions. He supposed that, after his good fortune in a seat companion on the trip down, it was poetic justice that he should end up next to an accountant who seemed determined to tell him all about the exciting business of staring at numbers all day long. It brought to mind a joke he had read, 'When does a person decide to become an accountant? When he realizes he lacks the charisma to succeed as an undertaker.'

The plane was finally in the air when Thomas turned to him and, somewhat politely, asked him to keep his business to himself so that he could sleep. He awoke only long enough to enjoy a sumptuous meal of surf and turf, accompanied by a shrimp cocktail and followed by a wonderful mile-high cheesecake. Once his appetite was fully sated, he slept for the remainder of the flight.

It was raining when he disembarked at Toronto's Pearson Airport. He grabbed the shuttle van to the Park n' Fly and retrieved his car. He would drive directly home. His sister-in-law expected that he might be gone a week or so, and it had been only three days. There was no need to let her know he was back. He would call her before he returned to Brazil, and extend the girls' stay at her home. The drive to Huntsville would give him time to re-hash his plan. He anticipated no difficulty in carrying out the first part of it, with the possible exception of Canada Customs. For that, he would need to call on his Ukrainian friends.

Fedir and Yuri were heavily involved in the sale of vehicles to Russia and other countries. They shipped used and new vehicles to numerous clients overseas. Their entire operation was, unlike some, totally legal and above board. They were well versed as to the ins and outs of shipping vehicles out of the country and, more importantly, they had contacts that Thomas would need to carry out a very critical part of the plan. Their place of operation was in Toronto, but he had no time to stop and see them now. It was necessary to get home and create the email for Carlo so that Sofia could enter his account, add her virus, and then send it on. Hopefully, if things went as planned, she would then have full access to his computer.

Thinking about that important task, he suddenly found himself worrying about Sofia. He had no idea if she had made it safely back to Chile. He pulled out his cell phone and called her. She must have been waiting, with phone in hand, because the answer was immediate.

"Thomas? Is that you?"

"Yes. It's me. Are you at home?"

"Yes, I arrived many hours ago. I have been waiting to hear from you. You did not call me from the plane?"

"No, I'm sorry. I slept the entire way. I was so tired. Is everything ok?"

"Yes. Now that I hear your voice, everything is fine. You are home now too?"

"I'm on the road, heading home. I'll be there in about two hours. I'll call you when the email for Carlo is written. Then you can work your magic."

"Yes, very good. I will wait for it. Call me as soon as you arrive home? Please? So I know you are safe."

"Of course. I promise." Her obvious concern for his safety had him wondering what feelings for him might be growing in her. Or even in him, for that matter.

"I will wait for your call. Sweet beijos for you."

Kisses? Now he really wondered, although in Latin cultures such comments between friends are not uncommon. He responded in kind.

"Beijos for you too. Bye."

Beijos was one of the very few Portuguese words that Thomas knew the meaning of. He was sure Sofia could teach him more, as well as Spanish, should the opportunity arise. She was fluent in both of those languages, as well as English.

Once back in Huntsville, he immediately went to task. He would carry out the bulk of the plan at the dealership and went there to write the email for Carlo, letting him know that he was home, and then saved it in the drafts folder. Sofia told him one other thing about the virus. It was programmed, after ten days, to destroy all information on the hard drive beyond recoverability and render the pc useless. Thomas liked that idea. He began to realize that Carlo's computer likely contained information that could lead someone to Angela, and to him if things didn't go very well. It was reassuring to know it would be destroyed.

Within half an hour, Sofia had sent the email to Carlo. Soon, she began downloading Carlo's files to her computer. Any useful items she discovered would be separated and forwarded to Thomas. From there, they would determine what further use access to Carlo's computer might provide before the virus shut it down for good.

The next step was to locate the trucks Carlo expected. Thomas logged onto the vehicle locator system and found several dealers with the appropriate vehicles in inventory. He then phoned and acquired faxed invoices and New Vehicle Information Slips which he would use to create the necessary paperwork for obtaining Ontario licensing and ownerships. The trucks would remain where they were. Once he had photocopied the ownerships, he would cancel all the licensing on the pretense that a major deal had fallen through. There would be no record of them ever having been plated. Now he had to wait for Carlo to provide him with information on the company he was supposed to establish in Ontario.

The Ministry of Transportation would require the first page of the incorporation papers in order to issue a registration number required to license vehicles in the company name. Hopefully, Carlo had this process underway. He had indicated that he would have a contact in Cornwall do the paperwork and fax him the documents. Thomas assumed the documents would be forgeries, but that didn't matter. They would work. Nothing further could be done on this part of the plan until he received the required papers. He hoped it would be soon, as any delay risked not being able to meet the ten-day deadline imposed by Carlo. Now, the time had arrived to call his Ukrainian friends, Fedir and Yuri, and bring them into the loop. He had known these two for about ten years and trusted them completely. He was certain they would be more than happy to help.

When he explained the situation, they were incredulous. They would have found the whole affair difficult to believe if it weren't for the fact that they were aware of the kinds of things carried out by the Russian mob on a regular basis. They weren't part of such things, but they didn't have to be involved in order to know what goes on in that circle. As expected, they offered to help in any way they could. Thomas asked that they set up a meeting at their office with someone they could trust within the customs brokerage they used. It was important that it took place as soon as possible. They succeeded in arranging it for the next afternoon. Thomas would drive to Toronto in the late morning in hopes that he could convince their contact to help with the documents that were critical to his plan.

There had been a great deal of curiosity around work as to why Thomas had returned so soon. Everyone had expected him to be gone for at least a week. He passed it off as a temporary return to close out some unfinished business and that he would be leaving again in a day or so.

True to his word, Carlo allowed Angela to call Thomas on his cell. It was a brief two minutes, but enough to determine that she was fine. Carlo seemed content, for the moment, to leave her to herself as he waited to see Thomas' progress. Thomas was relieved, and yet had not really expected Carlo to risk a million dollars by not keeping that end of the bargain. For today, all was well.

With explanations done, invoices acquired, Fedir and Yuri contacted, and the call from Angela arriving, Thomas' thoughts now turned to Sofia. He could feel something changing in him. Something called emotions. This woman, so truly beautiful in every way, had entered his life under the most unusual circumstance. It was time for him to admit that he was developing unexpected feelings. It was, on one hand, exhilarating, and yet a little frightening. He couldn't bring himself to be sure of where it might be headed. Only more time would provide an answer.

Thomas was still very tired and went home to rest. With the girls gone it was a very quiet house. As much as he missed his daughters, the silence was a very welcome thing for the time being. He took advantage of the opportunity to take a shower and lie down for a brief nap. He had been asleep for some time when his cell rang.

"Thomas? I have found some interesting things on our friend's pc. I will send them to you. I think you will like them a lot. I miss you."

"I look forward to seeing what you have found. I miss you too."

Those last four words surprised him, and they were sincere.

"You must look at what I sent you. You will find it very fascinating."

Thomas was jarred back to thinking of something other than his possible feelings for Sofia.

"Ah, yes, I'll check it right away. I'll call you after I've finished.".

"Yes. Please. I am curious to know how you may use it. We must plan things carefully, Thomas. We have to succeed in this."

"Yes, we do. If we don't, I may not be around to discover our future," he joked.

It didn't go over that well. It was obvious that even the thought of something bad happening to him was not a topic she cared to consider.

"Do not speak that way! I will not think of that! We will survive this! You will be safe! I will not hear you joke about it like that." There was some definite Latin temper in her words.

"Sofia, I'm sorry. I was just trying to ease the tension. Do you understand?"

"Yes, I understand. But no more! Please! I do not like to worry so much. I like to be positive."

"You're right, no more of that. You have my word."

"Thank you. Now go see what I have sent you and call me later. Muitos beijos."

"Ok. I'm going now. Sweet beijos for you."

Sofia's enthusiasm about what she had discovered on Carlo's computer had Thomas more than curious.

CHAPTER 7

THE MOTHER LOAD

As Thomas sifted through the items that Sofia had discovered on Carlo's pc, he was reminded of an old country song, 'She got the goldmine, and I got the shaft'. In this case, it appeared that Thomas was the one with the mother-load and Carlo might very well end up with the shaft he so richly deserved. There was no question that there seemed to be more than enough information to create serious trouble for that arrogant little man. Thomas imagined the pleasure he would derive from bringing him down.

Carlo appeared to be an avid keeper of a computer diary, a decision he would come to regret. One of the most valuable discoveries was a file, one of many that he foolishly kept in detail, outlining the source of his money. It appeared that he had, in previous times, been an accountant.

"Go figure," Thomas muttered out loud.

He certainly hadn't struck him as the type. Interestingly, it appeared that the only accounting he did was for a crime family in Queens. The Sabatini's. In his own detailed writings, Carlo explained how, over a period of less than two months, he managed to siphon over ten million dollars from these scions of organized crime. The event that precipitated this act of embezzlement, and disappearance to Brazil, was Carlo's receipt of a subpoena to testify at a Congressional hearing into money laundering by his boss. Carlo, no doubt correctly, feared that rather than let him testify it made more sense for Pauly Sabatini to dispose of him.

Unless lawyers had been able to squash the subpoena, there would have been only a brief three months before he would have had to report to Capitol Hill. That had left him with what he felt was only one choice. The money was diverted to offshore accounts for shell companies he created and would be transferred to Brazil later. He had the required false documents prepared that would allow him to move to Brazil permanently.

There were names of those in Brazil that he had bribed in order to gain entry, as well as names of those in the U.S. he had paid for his documents. His American participants were then murdered in order to secure his secret. If ever Thomas had doubted it, this proved that Carlo was indeed a cold-blooded killer when it served his best interest.

Antonio, quite surprisingly, was Carlo's cousin. That worried Thomas a bit. Blood isn't always thicker than water, but usually. In any case, it was too late to take back that conversation they had on the way to the airport. He would have to hope that in this case, blood didn't mean that much. Besides, there were some very interesting entries in this diary that could bring him back to Thomas' side if he began to waver. Carlo had always considered Antonio to be more of an annoyance than anything else. Even though he had served faithfully as his bodyguard, Carlo felt he had carried him throughout life and harbored some resentment of it. Carlo was not a man of any real generosity when it came to either money or spirit.

He also didn't know the meaning of the word loyalty, except as it pertained to his own survival. He didn't think Antonio very bright and was never sure how long he could trust him to keep his secret. Peppered throughout the years of entries were hints of having to do away with him. The last such comment was only a few months old and sounded more serious than the others. Carlo believed that once Antonio had taken care of Thomas, his time was up. Thomas decided to print some of the entries and take them with him on his return trip. They might come in very handy.

One question that cFedired Thomas' mind was why, with so much money already, would Carlo take such a foolish risk for another million dollars or so? It wasn't as if he was suddenly broke. Or was he? Among the files from his computer, there was banking information that allowed Thomas to access his online account balances. Upon close examination, it seemed that he was down to a little over two million dollars. While that doesn't qualify as being poor, his debts were more than his assets. He was in a bind. High living and the high cost of tribute and bribes, all detailed in his diary, had rendered him far less flush with cash than he could afford to be. In fact, the bank was calling in a loan of more than a million dollars. He only had two months to comply or risk losing that beautiful mansion.

Suddenly, everything began to make sense. Simply getting rid of Angela might have been safer, but it would not have helped his financial situation. Thomas recalled his own statement to Antonio, "desperate people do desperate things." Angela could be very grateful that Carlo needed money more than he needed her immediate death. His real goal was to have both the money and an end to Angela. His plan had just run into a major roadblock.

In a file entitled 'Carla', Thomas learned the final chapter in that relationship. Carlo's words left no doubt in that area. The entry was six years old and read:

September 12, 1996

"I still have recurring dreams about Carla. Even after five years. I can't erase those final moments from my mind. How she could have turned on me after I had given her so much, I'll never know. It's still impossible to believe that she was prepared to sell me out to the Sabatini's for a lousy quarter of a million. The only thing that comforts me is the knowledge that Pauly would never have paid. He would have killed her himself. Loose ends are not his style. We both would have been dead. My way, it was only her. The look on her face when I slit her throat still haunts me in the middle of the night. How surprised she was. Stupid bitch! How could she have done it?"

When Thomas finished reading that entry, he felt that same chill he had experienced the night Angela phoned. Today, there was no cool breeze to raise those goosebumps. Only the cold, calculating words of a murder confession.

Another file caught Thomas' attention. It was titled simply, "The man". What he discovered was a source of great interest. It seemed that Carlo had received significant assistance from this individual. Throughout these entries, no name was ever mentioned. He was simply referred to as "the man". Carlo appeared almost afraid to identify him by name, and from this Thomas assumed that he was very dangerous and someone that Carlo actually feared. Whoever this person was, he had, for the price of one million dollars, secured Carlo's entry into Brazil with false documents. Bribes were paid, services were bought, and Carlo ended up an unwitting partner with someone who appeared to be a very powerful, and corrupt element of Brazilian society. Perhaps even politically involved.

Aside from the million-dollar 'entry fee', Carlo was tied to an arrangement that required him to pay a twenty percent tribute to this person for any profits from his business of importing stolen goods for resale in Brazil. Angela had been correct. He was in the import business, but not the kind she had imagined. Shipments of stolen merchandise, in the form of high-end watches, like Rolex, as well as electronics, computers, and virtually anything of real value, were purchased for twenty or twenty-five cents on the dollar from fences overseas, and then imported to Brazil. Despite the shipping costs, duties, and the requisite bribes to customs officials who would understate the value for duty purposes, there was a very tidy profit to be made. Thomas was certain that this information would prove very useful.

In each instance, Carlo secured fifty percent of the purchase price from this individual. All communication was by email only. Carlo would forward the details and quantity of the items to be purchased, along with the cost and the potential profit. He would provide 'the man' with an overseas account number into which he would need to deposit half of the total required funds. Upon the arrival of the merchandise, and its sale to a string of distributors, Carlo would immediately repay the advanced money as well as the twenty percent tribute. It seemed an odd arrangement, as it did not totally deplete Carlo's resources, yet it gave a stronger measure of power to his mysterious partner. Throughout the entire file, it was apparent that Carlo never even dared to think of wavering from this agreement. He seemed aware that it would be a fatal decision. There were entries that lamented his situation and expressed some resentment of what he considered a form of indentured servitude. He complained but made it very clear that he wasn't certain he could ever dare breach that agreement.

Thomas now had the feeling that he could squeeze this little jerk in ways that he had never thought possible. What final help he would need to resolve this situation successfully would come from two sources who would have every reason to take vengeance on Carlo. One source he knew, the Sabatini's, and the identity of 'the man', he had to ascertain. The fates willing, Carlo would get his just reward, Angela would return to Canada, and Thomas would have the opportunity to discover what, if anything, was in the future for him and Sofia. He could only pray that his carefully thought-out plan did not go awry. Thomas picked up the phone and dialed Sofia.

"You were absolutely right, Sofia. This is fantastic. I'm thrilled beyond belief."

"I knew so. I was so happy to find such important things for you. How will you use them?"

"Well, first I need to know if there is a way you can take over Carlo's email and control the messages going in and out without his knowledge."

"Yes, of course. I can have his emails held up until I can copy them and then send them along."

"Perfect! This is a very critical element of the whole plan. Can you email from his account and prevent his receiving the reply? Can you ensure that only you will receive it?"

"Yes. Sure. What do you have in mind?"

"I'll send you the text of a message I want you to forward through his email. You must ensure that any response from that email address is diverted to you. If it gets to Carlo, we are in big trouble. Very big trouble!"

"No problem. It will be very easy."

"Wonderful! You are more help than you can imagine. I can't thank you enough."

"Don't make me so perfect. Maybe I am just selfish. I do not wish to lose you. So, I must help."

"Well, then I'm very happy about your selfish attitude," he said with a laugh.

"You do not object if my motive is that I wish only to save you?"

"Not at all. I think it's very flattering. I would have never thought I was worth it."

"Mmm, my sweet Thomas."

"When we are together again, Sofia, we will need to have an honest talk about us."

"Oh, please tell me it will not be a sad talk."

"Not at all. It is just one we need to have face to face."

"I will be waiting for that time, Thomas. But for now, beijos. We will talk again soon."

Thomas said goodbye and decided to try and find something to satisfy his now growling stomach. He opened a can of chili and heated it in the microwave. After finishing his meal, he retrieved the email address from his files for the one Carlo called 'The man' and began creating a message that would take on the same characteristics as Carlo's. He read over some of the previous ones Carlo had sent to this person to grasp the tone of his writing, and the manner in which he expressed the information and requests he was presenting. Thomas noticed that in every case of a money request, there was a different bank account used. The transfers seem to have been spread over several different banks in both Canada and the United States, and always in smaller cities. In fact, Carlo's trip to Cornwall was to close out an account there and transfer the funds to Brazil. This worked right into the newest wrinkle Thomas had injected into his plan.

Thomas would send an email, supposedly from Carlo, explaining the opportunity to acquire twenty trucks at fifty cents on the dollar. He would inflate the value of trucks in order to secure a larger advance of money. His email would include the description of the vehicles and the story that they were financed in the name of a phony company in Canada and that all proper ownerships were available. The lending institution would take the loss, and no one would ever know the vehicles made their way to Brazil. There would be a request that a deposit of two hundred and fifty thousand dollars be made to cover half the purchase price. There was no intention of keeping the money for himself, but rather to use it to cover expenses and reward Paola and Antonio for the assistance that they would provide in saving the lives of two people who would certainly be very grateful.

When the time came, it would be necessary to establish an account that could not later be traced to him. The need for identification would be a minor problem. The obituaries in the Toronto Star would provide a name with which he could obtain a birth certificate and the deceased's social insurance number, both of which would be needed to open an account. Once the funds were transferred, they would be used to purchase bearer bonds, or some other easily negotiable items that contain no identification of the owner. They are simply payable to whoever possesses them. That little scam would account for one person who would end up wanting Carlo's head on a platter. As for the other, at the right time, Thomas would provide anonymous information on Carlo's whereabouts to the Sabatini's, from who he stole his original ten million.

There would be nowhere for him to hide. As for what his fate might be, Thomas quite frankly didn't care. Whatever might happen, Carlo more than deserved it.

If all went well, and Thomas obtained the documents needed from Carlo's connection in Cornwall, he could be on a plane in two days. Before then, there was still much to do. He decided to make a quick drive to the corner store and purchased a Toronto Star with which to begin his search for just the right identity to open the bank account he needed. As he read through them, it seemed that things just kept going his way today. Among the numerous possibilities, he discovered the perfect choice. A forty-eight-year-old man had died from a sudden heart attack. Thomas, almost gleeful, wasn't being insensitive about his death. It was just that he desperately needed this man's identity to carry out his plan. He decided that once everything was successfully completed, his widow would receive a certain number of bearer bonds, anonymously, as a gesture of Thomas' appreciation and, in truth, an apology.

The most attractive aspect of this choice was that he was, like Thomas, a landed immigrant in Canada. He had been born in Pennsylvania and had moved to Toronto more than fifteen years ago. Even better, his only survivors were his wife and son. No relatives were listed from Pennsylvania. It was perfect! There would be virtually no possibility of anyone at the records office in Wilkes-Barre Pennsylvania, where he was born, being aware of his death. It also allowed Thomas to open a bank account in the United States, diverting attention from a Canadian connection. It would be a long drive, but worth the trip. A simple stroll into the records office and, perhaps ten or twenty dollars later, he would walk out again with a certified copy of his new birth certificate.

The more difficult task would be acquiring his U. S. Social Security number. For that, Thomas might need to do something that honestly made him feel very uneasy. It might become necessary to call the widow and pose as someone who could assist her in obtaining Social Security benefits from the United States. Thomas dreaded that prospect. It would be so much easier to acquire his Canadian Social Insurance number.

The newspaper disclosed where he had worked, and a simple phone call could provide an email address. Thomas was already aware of what Sofia could do with that. Accessing their computer's payroll records would easily divulge any information he required. Unfortunately, it was an American account he needed, and that might present a problem. In the end, he decided to have Sofia search his employer's payroll records anyway. Just in case. By now, it was after midnight. He took a quick shower and crawled into bed. Tomorrow would be a busy day.

CHAPTER 8

I NEVER DRINK VODKA

Thomas awoke at seven in the morning to the sound of his cell phone signaling a message from Sofia asking him to call as soon as possible. He brushed his teeth, made a pot of coffee, and settled down to call her.

He brought her up to date about his plans and indicated he would take a drive to Pennsylvania that day or the next. While they were still on the phone, she located the website for the company that had employed the man chosen from the obituaries. There was an email address posted on the site, and Sofia went straight to work. She indicated that she would call with what information she discovered as soon as was possible. He was hoping she would find something that would allow him to avoid that phone call to the widow. It didn't sit well with him to intrude on someone's grief for his own purpose.

Thomas only lived four or five minutes from work and was hoping to have something waiting for him when he arrived. He went to the fax machine and let out a sigh of relief when he found the letters of incorporation for Carlo's phony company. Over the next hour, he would prepare replacement New Vehicle Information Slips that would be required to license the trucks. Then it was on to the Ministry of Transportation to acquire the ownerships and license plates.

Once that was completed, he photocopied the ownerships and license plates and faxed them off to Carlo. Within fifteen minutes, Angela called.

"Thomas? Carlo received your fax. He's very pleased. So am I. I hope this is over soon. I want to go home."

"So far everything is going smoothly, Angela. With any luck, you'll be home within a week or so. Is everything all right there? No problems with Carlo?"

"No! None at all. I'm fine. You needn't worry about that. At least so far. I hope it stays that way."

"Me too. I'll get this done as quickly as possible." Thomas knew that Carlo would be listening in on the conversation and wanted to give him a secure feeling about how well things were proceeding, "I think I can beat Carlo's deadline of ten days and have these things in the containers in another two or three, tops."

"That's wonderful. I'm feeling very positive about getting home soon. I'm being told I must hang up now. We'll talk again tomorrow. Bye!"

"Bye, Angela. Keep a good thought. Everything will be fine."

Relieved that all was well with Angela, Thomas still had to deal with one more significant detail in his plan. Something had to go into those containers for Brazil. Without confirmed shipping documents for the loaded containers, the whole plan was useless.

There wouldn't be any new trucks, but there had to be something. It occurred to him that it could very well be trucks of some sort, just not good ones. He grabbed the phone and called Earl.

Earl was a pretty good guy that Thomas had known for at least ten years. He operated a small car lot and did quite a bit of wholesaling of used vehicles before he began to take life easy. He still did some, but not at his old pace. He spent the winters in Mexico, and the rest of the year messing around with his old trucks and cars. Earl loved to restore older vehicles and had recently purchased a fifty-five Chevy to occupy his time. He lived alongside highway eleven, in the small town of Katrine, in a nicely renovated apartment above his garage. Thomas was never sure how many people lived in Katrine, but he suspected that if a few dozen of them left for a week it would be a rather quiet place. Earl was an uncomplicated man, in a quiet little town, enjoying life in a laid-back and unhurried way.

Thomas jumped into his car and headed north towards his destination. It was only about a fifteen-minute drive. When he pulled into the driveway at Earl's place, he could see that he was working on that fifty-five Chevy. Thomas got his attention, and they sat down in the office so that he could explain his difficult situation. As with everyone else, he was in almost total disbelief, and yet willing to help in any way he could. Thomas explained that he needed something to put in those containers. "I need twenty trucks, Earl. Old! Barely running! Whatever! Doesn't matter what they are, as long as they can make it to the docks by transport. They need to run enough to get on and off the transport and into the containers."

Earl smiled through his graying beard and pointed to the gravel lot beside his garage. "Got five for you right there, buddy. No problem! None of them are worth much anyway, so they're yours if you need them."

They grabbed the keys so they could check and see if any of them would actually start and run long enough to get on and off a transport trailer. Each truck groaned to life with a little prodding, but they would all need some fine-tuning to help them get through their mission. Earl went right to the heart of it,

"I'll throw some new spark plugs in them and tune them up the best I can. You go ahead and arrange for the transport. I'll have them ready. No sweat! When do you think they'll pick them up?"

"I'm trying for tomorrow. Don't have a lot of time, and I still have to find fifteen more trucks somewhere. Any suggestions on that count?"

"Check out that wrecking yard down Aspden Road. You should be able to find whatever you need there. If they don't have fifteen trucks, I'm sure you can sneak some cars in the mix. Not like the boys in Brazil are going to know what is actually in the containers until it's too late."

"Good idea. Thanks, buddy. I can't tell you how much I appreciate this."

"No problem. You'd do the same for me. Hope this all works out. I would hate to find out you bit the bullet, so be very careful. You hear me? I'm not sure you really know what you're up against. And you're no kid anymore."

"I appreciate the concern, but I have a pretty good idea of what I'm doing. I'm sure everything will work out just fine. If not, at least I know I had to try."

After a cordial handshake, Thomas jumped back into his car and headed south. Once back at the dealership, a phone call to the wrecking yard Earl had suggested yielded the rest of the trucks he needed. Amazingly, they apparently were drivable. He grabbed Rick, the service manager, and explained the situation to him, in confidence. Once Rick was brought up to speed, they went to check out the trucks at the wrecking yard and determine what, if anything, they would need to make the trip. These trucks he had to pay for, but the total cost was peanuts at twenty-five hundred dollars. He might need to spend a few hundred dollars more to get them running well enough, but that was no big problem. He and Rick grabbed two that were not running too badly and drove back to the dealership. They had the shuttle driver take them back enough times to collect them all. An hour well spent.

With all fifteen trucks now back at the garage, a few of the mechanics performed some quick tune-up work and they were ready to go in less than two hours. Things were falling into place nicely. Thomas returned to the Ministry of Transportation to cancel the registrations for the new trucks and obtain ownerships for the ten junkers. Once that was done, it was on to Toronto to meet with Fedir, Yuri, and their customs contact. As he pulled back onto highway eleven, he got another call from Sofia. She had some news that made his day.

"Thomas, what is an IRA?"

"That's a kind of retirement fund in the U.S. Why?" He was suddenly feeling good about the possibility she may have found some magic in those payroll files.

"Your deceased friend was having deductions from his pay invested in them. There is something called a Social Security number. Do you need that?"

"Oh! Sofia, you've got to be kidding," he almost screamed into the phone. "Baby, I could kiss you a million times. That's exactly what I need. Thank you so much!"

"You need this number in order to kiss me a million times? You would not do it anyway?" she laughed that sweet; soft chuckle that always seemed to make him smile.

"I'm beginning to think that could be negotiated simply because you are amazing. But this information does make me very happy. It saves me from having to do something I would find very distasteful."

"You know I would do anything for you, Thomas. I want you safe and in Brazil as soon as possible."

"No worries, Sofia. Everything will be just fine. I think I may return to Sao Paulo in two or three days. I'll call you when I am there."

"Of course! I will be there tomorrow, waiting."

"I can't wait to see you."

"It is the same for me."

"Perfect. I'm on my way to Toronto now, and I'll continue on to Pennsylvania and finish what I need to do there before I return to Brazil. I'll call you later to have you send the email I prepared about the money transfer."

"Ok! Please drive safely and call me soon. Beijos."

It would take slightly less than two hours to get to Fedir and Yuri's. If the meeting didn't take too long, he would be in Wilkes-Bare that evening and finish his business there in the morning. He hoped there would be no delay in the transfer of funds from Brazil. If so, it would complicate matters. Not to mention that if anything went wrong with that part of the plan, things could get very dicey. At the moment, however, he was most enthusiastic about seeing Fedir and Yuri and bringing another element of this scenario into play. Thomas was now more into the excitement of the whole adventure, and less preoccupied with the possibility of failure. He knew that prospect still existed, yet he was becoming so wrapped up in the scam itself that he thought less and less about it.

The drive to Toronto was without incident and Thomas pulled into the parking lot at Fedir and Yuri's just after three. Entering the front door to their building was akin to entering a cave. There was a décor in the main stairway leading to their second-floor offices that reminded Thomas of stalagmites, but which were made of grayish plaster material. At the top of the stairs, to the left, was a lounge area complete with a big screen TV, a leather sectional, a large fish tank in a wall of artificial stone, and, of course, a well-stocked bar.

Around the corner of the stairwell, to the right, was a hallway leading to the secretary's office. She was a sweet Ukrainian girl, by the name of Svetlana. Just past her office was that of Yuri, and opposite his was where Fedir could be found, behind his desk, and with a phone perpetually attached to his ear. It seemed that no matter when Thomas might enter his office Fedir was involved in some overseas conversation or answering any number of calls on his cell phone.

Thomas gave a quick hello and smiled at Svetlana before heading directly for Fedir's office. As usual, he was in mid-conversation with someone overseas. Thomas sat in the leather chair nearest the window and lit a smoke. He was still cursing that pack he had stashed in his sock drawer, even though he had managed to smoke fewer than half of them over the past three days.

Within a few minutes, Fedir had finished his business and hung up the phone.

"Tommy, how are you? You have big problem, no?"

Fedir and Yuri were a few of those rare exceptions when it came to calling him Tommy. As much as he hated it from most others, from them it was genuine friendship and just their way of being cordial.

"All things considered, I'm fine. And yes, I have big trouble, but I hope this meeting will make it less of a problem. So far things are falling into place pretty well."

"I hope so, my friend. We will do what we can. You want drink? Have a nice Vodka?"

With a chuckle, Thomas reminded him, "I never drink Vodka."

Fedir never failed to ask; no matter how often Thomas declined.

"You know me, a coffee will be just fine."

Within moments, Svetlana appeared with his coffee and flashed her usual smile.

"Tommy, one day you will get drunk with me on Vodka. I know it will be," Fedir said with a mischievous smile.

"Don't count on it. I hate the feeling of being drunk. But, one day you might get me to have one or two. You never know. When this is all over and done, and everyone is safe, I may be in the mood for a few drinks to celebrate."

"We will celebrate together with some nice Ukrainian girls."

Thomas laughed slightly, "We may celebrate together, but there won't be any Ukrainian girls for me."

"What is that? You don't want a good woman to please you? Can't be true!"

"To be honest, I met an amazing woman. I have no clue where it is heading but I think I am ready to find out."

"What are you saying to me? You are in love? When did this happen? I don't believe! Such a change! Who is lucky woman?"

"The whole 'love' thing is what I am trying to figure out. Her name is Sofia, and she's in Brazil right now. In fact, she's helping me with this problem. I'm sure I would fail without her. When everything is taken care of, hopefully, we'll figure out if we are in love."

"Well, I hope you will have a long life together, Tommy. I would be very happy for you. She must be very wonderful."

At that moment Yuri walked in and gave his always gregarious smile and a firm handshake, "Tommy, how are you, my friend?"

"I'm fine, Yuri. And you?"

"I am good. You know me. Always good!"

Yuri sat in the chair next to Thomas.

"Now we must help you fix your problem."

At this point, Yuri heard someone on the stairs and got up to see who it was. It turned out to be the man they were waiting for. His name was Raymond, and he worked for the customs broker. The true test of Thomas' potential for success was about to begin. Yuri brought Raymond into the office where Fedir made the introduction to Thomas.

"Thomas, nice to meet you. Fedir has explained everything to me. I can help, but it will be tricky. I would never have thought I'd consider doing anything like this, but the reason is certainly a good one. I must tell you it wasn't that easy a decision. I had a pretty sleepless night."

"I can't tell you how much I appreciate it. You'll be helping to save two lives. I hope you know that."

"I do. That's what makes the decision the right one. I'm very happy to do what I can."

Fedir had been quiet to this point but then posed the important questions.

"OK, Raymond. What do we do now? You need information about both sets of vehicles, correct?"

"Yes. Exactly! I'll create customs documents and bills of lading for the phony trucks that Thomas can send to Brazil, and then the proper ones for the trucks that are actually in the containers. No one, other than I, and the people at the dock, will know what is actually being loaded on the ship until they arrive in Brazil. I can't do anything about the fees. I'm sorry about that, Thomas."

"Don't worry about it. I appreciate everything you're doing already. It's more than enough. Customs fees are, by far, the least of my worries."

"I hope you can get along with only photocopies of the bills of lading for the trucks you're not shipping."

"Why? Is there a problem with that?"

"Bills of lading are numbered. Every one of them must be accounted for. The best I can do is to prepare them, photocopy each one for you, and then void the originals out as a canceled shipment. Numbered bills of lading can't disappear. But the container numbers will be the same."

"I can understand that. I'll make do with photocopies. That should work just fine. I'll be faxing them, so he would never know they weren't the originals?"

"Good. Do you have the information on the vehicles?"

"Yes, right here," Thomas reached into his jacket pocket and handed him copies of the ownerships.

"Perfect. I'll get started today. You can have the photocopies tomorrow. I can't do the bills of lading for the trucks you are actually sending until they arrive here. Do you know when that will be?"

"I hope to have them here late tomorrow. How long to get them into the containers and on the docks?"

"I'll get them there by day after tomorrow. Not a problem."

"Perfect. I'll leave for Brazil as soon as they're in your hands. You're a Godsend, Raymond."

"Well, I wish you luck with all of this. I would hate to be in your shoes. I hope the rest of your plan is as creative as this part," he chuckled in an admiring way.

"Me too. My life depends on it. Not to mention Angela's."

With that detail taken care of so quickly, Thomas called the transport company to have the old trucks picked up at the dealership. It would take three trailers to bring them all. Thomas had already advised them that tomorrow would, in all probability, be the day, and they had slotted time for him. That done, he could head for Pennsylvania and put the final touches on the whole scam. One more hurdle to clear, and he would be on his way to Brazil, and back in Sofia's arms. He said his goodbyes and expressed his gratitude to Fedir and Yuri. Then he was on his way.

CHAPTER 9

TIME TO DO SOME BANKING

It would take him about four to five hours to get to Wilkes-Barre. He would get a hotel room and take care of business in the morning. As he settled into his car, he dialed Sofia's number.

"Ola? Thomas?"

"Yes. It's me. Everything is going well so far."

"Wonderful. Where are you now?"

"I'm on my way to Pennsylvania. I won't get there until late tonight."

"So tomorrow you will try to make the bank account?"

"Yes. Wish me luck. That's the part that's tricky."

"You do not need luck. You know what you are doing. It will all be fine."

Over the next thirty minutes or so they talked about how they looked forward to seeing each other again. Before he realized it, he was pulling up to the tollbooth at the Peace Bridge that cFedires the Niagara River into New York State. They said their goodbyes, and Thomas dug out the required change for the toll.

Now he would head east on the New York State Thruway to Syracuse, and then head south on interstate eighty-one and straight on into Wilkes-Barre. The southerly trip would take him through his old hometown, Binghamton. All he would get to see of it would be from the highway as he drove through the surrounding hills. He was sure he hadn't spent a total of twenty-four hours there in the last fifteen years or more. One day he would have to take the time.

It was then that he realized that he would not be at home to send Carlo's email the next day. Thomas decided that it would be easy enough to use a computer in the library in Wilkes-Barre. Assuming, of course, there was one in the library. If not, then he would call Sofia and have her send it or he would find a computer store with an online connection. If it hadn't been for the fact that it was past eleven, he would have called Sofia right then but better, he thought, to let her sleep and continue his drive.

It took about an hour to make the drive from Syracuse to Binghamton. Once past the flat terrain of the Syracuse area, it would have been a pretty drive during the day. At night, it would be just plain dark with no chance to see the rolling hills. A few hours later he passed through Scranton and would soon make his destination. He had only this one last hurdle standing before him, and he found himself somewhat nervous about carrying it out. This was the first link in the chain that he had to pursue with total strangers.

Thomas pulled into Wilkes-Barre just before eleven. He grabbed himself a room at the Holiday Inn and scoured the phone book for the nearest bank. He chose the First National and made a note of the address before jumping in the shower. Tomorrow he would get up early and be at City Hall to find the department of records. Then, if successful there, it was on to the First National with his fingers cFedired. He would make a small deposit and tell them that he was moving back to Wilkes-Barre, had sold a vacation property in Brazil, and was expecting a money transfer. He would express his desire to convert most of the money into bearer bonds and leave twenty thousand dollars in the account, awaiting further funds from Brazil with which to buy a house. It was a major stretch of a story, but he had to tell them something. Unless he could come up with a better tale, that would have to do.

Thomas looked in the yellow pages for somewhere he could use a computer to email Carlo. He gave up the library idea and assumed he could find a computer store with an online connection. There was one nearby, and he would hit there after City Hall and just before the bank.

The night was a stuttering of restless sleep. He would sleep for an hour, wake up and pace the floor for fifteen minutes or so, and then attempt to go back to bed. This went on throughout the night. Obviously, he was very nervous about the outcome of his morning activities. By six he had given up the prospect of getting back to sleep and simply stayed up until it was time to get dressed. At eight-fifteen he was out the front door of the hotel and looking for a doughnut shop to grab a coffee and a few old-fashioned plain doughnuts. He found one just around the corner and consumed the doughnuts while he drove to City Hall.

It took no time at all to find the records department. The somewhat crusty old gal behind the counter, seemingly bored with her job, barely asked a question other than his name, birth date, and the name of his parents. The obituary had provided the names of parents, including the mother's maiden name, and noted that they were deceased. Thankfully, he had made a point of memorizing them before his arrival there. Ten minutes later he had a crisp, notarized birth certificate. Now he was on his way to send Carlo his email before heading to the bank. With the email sent, he waited for Angela's call as he drove towards his next task. Ten minutes later, the call came. She was fine, Carlo was still pleased, and Thomas was relieved.

The bank, if they did their job right, would want more than just a birth certificate for identification. Thomas had managed to obtain a fake driver's license, complete with a photo, while he was in Toronto. It cost a hundred bucks but was well worth it. It would probably be easily spotted as a fake in Ontario, but doubtful here. At any rate, he was into it now and there was no turning back. It suddenly occurred to him that, if he were tripped up at the bank, he could end up in a jail cell in Wilkes-Barre. That was not what he needed to think about at that moment. He wasn't sure if early morning was a good choice for this. People tend to get sloppier later in the day when they look forward to closing. However, late afternoon was out of the question. He needed this account active today. The bank would have to report to the IRS about such a large transfer of funds, but Thomas wasn't too worried about it. The worst-case was they would be trying to collect taxes from someone who had died before the account was even open. The whole thing would be a dead-end for them.

The young woman who assisted him in opening the account was quite perky and pleasant. Thomas added to the authenticity of the whole thing by asking for her recommendation of a real estate agent. He even had her call and make an appointment for him for the following Monday. He guessed he wouldn't be showing up for it. The issue of the bonds was left out of the conversation for the moment. It would be dealt with later. With the account now open, and his free gift of a nifty pen and pencil set, his mind was now at ease. Once back in the car, he called Sofia, gave her the account information, and had her send the email request for the money to be deposited today. The time would be a few hours later in Brazil, and he hoped this mystery man would see the email in time to make the transfer before the banks closed there. He went back to the hotel to wait. The young woman at the bank had been given his cell number and was asked to phone him when the funds arrived. As he lay on the bed, the sleepless night caught up with him and he dozed off.

At about three o'clock Thomas awoke to the ringing of his cell. It was that bubbly girl from the bank to excitedly tell him that his two hundred and fifty thousand dollars were now on deposit. He told her he would be there in ten minutes.

By four-thirty, Thomas was heading north on interstate eighty-one with slightly less than two hundred and thirty thousand in bonds, after fees. So far, so good. He would be back in

Toronto by eight or nine and would stay there until tomorrow. He needed those bills of lading to fax to Carlo. Once that was done, and he knew the old trucks were in their containers, he would be on his way to Sao Paulo. The fact was the easy work had just been completed. It was in Sao Paulo that the greatest risk remained. Thomas couldn't trust Carlo to not lose control and finish off both him and Angela. With what he believed were two wild cards in his pocket, in the form of Angelo and Paola, he hoped to avoid that possibility.

He had pre-booked for the next day on the same flight that he had previously taken to Sao Paulo, although certainly not in First Class. He was scheduled to leave at the same hour as before and hoped to have the information no later than noon that his vehicles were in their containers. When he arrived back in Toronto he drove to Fedir and Yuri's. Fedir was still there, on the phone as always. He glanced up from his desk and motioned for Thomas to sit. Svetlana was gone for the day, so there could be no coffee. Instead, Thomas went to the waiting room and grabbed a Pepsi from the bar fridge.

When Fedir finished his call, he gave a big grin.

"Tommy here are copies of bills of lading and your trucks arrive just now. They will be in containers for the morning."

"Great. Things are going perfectly so far. I sure hope that they continue that way."

"When will you leave for Brazil?"

"Tomorrow night."

"My friend, this will be a dangerous time I think."

"No doubt. Say a prayer or two, if you think of it."

"God is on your side in this, Tommy. You will see. But be careful. God can only do so much. Then it is up to you."

"Yes. But I'll pray anyway. It'll be a new experience."

"So, you will go back to Huntsville and return here tomorrow for your flight?"

"No, not tonight. My bag has been packed and in my car, since the moment I knew I would be going back to Brazil. I don't feel like any more driving, so I have to find a hotel for the night."

"Hotel? What do you mean? No hotel! I have company tonight at my home, but you can stay here. There is sofa bed in the lounge. In morning you can have shower and get ready for trip. No question. You stay here," and then he chuckled "Drink Vodka."

"You never give up, Fedir. No Vodka. But I may clean out the Pepsi in the fridge."

"No problem. Drink all, is ok. So, you stay here then?"

"Yeah, that would be great. I appreciate it."

"First, we get something to eat. Then you come back here and rest."

Fedir got up from his desk and they headed down to his BMW and off to have some supper. It was a relaxing meal, punctuated by occasional conversation about what would happen in Brazil. Thomas laid out the rest of the plan.

Fedir shook his head and said, "Very good luck! You will need it, my friend."

When they had finished their supper, Fedir dropped Thomas off back at the office and he settled in to call Sofia. They spoke for at least an hour and never seemed to wish to say goodbye. Finally, they exchanged farewells and hung up. He opened the sofa bed and fell sound asleep the minute he laid his head on the pillow.

CHAPTER 10

CARE TO TRADE?

It was the soft voice of Svetlana that awoke Thomas from his slumber. It seemed she had arrived for work and, when she came in to make the morning coffee, was somewhat surprised to see him asleep on the sofa bed. With a smile, she said that coffee would be ready soon and directed him to the shower. Once showered, shaved, and refreshed, Thomas sat down with a cup Svetlana had prepared for him and called Sofia.

"Sofia? How are you?"

"I am hearing your voice, so I am well. And you?"

"Just as happy to hear you."

"Everything has gone well? I know you were very concerned about dealing with the bank."

"Yes! So far, no problem! The bank was a breeze, and the vehicles will be in the containers this morning. I fly out at four-thirty this afternoon, six-thirty your time. I'll be in Sao Paulo in the morning."

"Wonderful. I am so happy. I will make my flight today and be waiting for you at the hotel."

"That's perfect. Have a safe trip, and when you arrive call my cell with your room number. I'll need to find you without drawing the attention of the front desk."

"Yes, I will do it. No problem. I will be so happy to see you. I cannot wait for the moment."

"Me either. Can you bring your laptop with you?"

"Of course. I always have it."

"Great! I'll email Carlo this morning and tell him the vehicles are on the docks."

"Do you have an idea of what will happen when you arrive in Sao Paulo? Is your plan complete?"

Thomas hadn't told her about the dangerous part of all this, and couldn't bring himself to tell her now, so he just took the easy path for the moment.

"I have some ideas, but we can talk when I get there. Ok with you?"

"Yes, it is fine. I will call the airline now and make my flight before it is too late."

"Yes, we don't want you to miss that plane. Not a chance! I'll call you when I'm in the air. Have a safe flight."

"OK, Thomas. Bye for now."

"Bye. See you soon."

Once the conversation had finished, Thomas used Svetlana's computer to email Carlo. As usual, ten minutes later, Angela called. With enthusiasm, she indicated that Carlo was beside himself with satisfaction. Thomas was sure he had so many dollar signs in his eyes at this point that his judgment was quite likely to be impaired by greed. And at just the right time! He needed him greedy and not at the top of his game. If he had gauged Carlo correctly, the upper hand was Thomas's now. He certainly hoped he was right.

"Tommy, you are awake?" Fedir shouted as he came up the stairs. Yuri was following right behind him and smiling as usual.

"Wide awake, my friend."

"Fedir tells me you fly this afternoon?"

"Yes, have to be at the airport by two."

"OK, then we have lunch before you go. There is nothing you need to do this morning?"

"Nope. Everything I can do here is done. Now I just have to kill some time."

"I have cars to deliver to detailing shop. You can help if you like. Keep you busy."

"Yeah, no problem. It's the least I can do."

"OK, good. We go in twenty minutes."

Thomas finished his coffee as Fedir went about dealing with overseas calls, and Yuri prepared the cars they were to move from the storage area on the main floor. It took about two hours to finish up, and then it was time for lunch. They went to a nearby burger joint and had a good helping of greasy burgers and fries. Once they had finished, it was back to their office to get his car, and off to the airport. Thomas regretted that there was no first-class ride available on this trip. It would be a long haul to make in coach. He had booked his ticket with a return in ten days. If he didn't make that flight, then it would probably mean his plan had failed, and he was dead. He tried to erase those thoughts from his mind.

After parking his car in the usual Park n' Fly location, he was once again on a shuttle to the terminal. After a few hours of waiting around, he was seated on the aisle as he had requested. A repeat of the quick flight to Atlanta, the long wait for his connection, and then it was on to the final leg of the journey, armed with about four magazines to occupy his time. When the in-flight meal arrived, he could barely eat it. Mostly, he thought, this was because he remembered how good the food had been in first class and lost his appetite when seeing this offering. In any case, he forced it down and settled in for some reading after calling Sofia to verify her flight.

The trip, while tedious, was uneventful. He passed through customs in Sao Paulo with no trouble and grabbed the bus to downtown. In less than half an hour he would be in Sofia's arms. He couldn't wait. His mind and heart both raced with excitement. Once again, passing the favelas, he felt that disturbing pain for the poverty of the people there. He found himself recalling the story of Sofia's rise from such destitution. This remarkable woman had expressed in emotional words how much she desired to spend her life helping those no one wanted. She wanted so much to work with children, the old, and anyone that needed God's grace. Thomas wanted very much to join her in that ambition. He could imagine the two of them, joyously in love, and spending their lives devoted to the betterment of life for those less fortunate. For the first time ever, he truly felt he might have a calling, and the perfect partner to share it with.

When he arrived at the hotel, Thomas immediately moved past the front desk to the elevators. Within a few minutes, he was running down the hall to Sofia's room. He had barely knocked on the door when it opened enough for her to see it was him.

"Thomas," she whispered with a sultry kitten voice, "I have been waiting."

With that, she removed the safety chain and opened the door enough for him to enter. As she closed the door behind him, he could see that she was wrapped only in a towel. She took his hand and pulled him towards her as his bag dropped to the floor. He could hear the shower running as they approached the bathroom. Once there, she turned and dropped the towel to the floor. She began to pull his shirt over his head with one hand as she loosened his pants with the other. Thomas helped her along, and in seconds they were in a naked embrace in the shower. After a great deal of exploration and foreplay in that environment, they proceeded to the bed to make up for lost time in consummating a relationship that had finally proven to be their destiny.

An hour later, with pent-up passion sated for the moment, they discussed the rest of Thomas' plan as they sipped the coffee that Sofia had prepared in the room's coffee maker. The moment had arrived. It was necessary for him to let her know that the next step was risky. He knew it would worry her tremendously, and yet she had to know.

"It's time we discuss what will happen now, Sofia."

"What do you mean?"

"The next phase of my plan. It carries some risk."

"You worry me, Thomas. How is it so dangerous? I don't like the thought of you taking too many chances."

"I have to trade myself for Angela."

"What do you mean? I don't understand?" she said.

The sound of fear in her voice was unmistakable.

"I have to get Carlo to let her leave Brazil, and keep me instead, while he waits for the shipment."

"Thomas, no! You cannot do that! I will not let you!"

"I have no choice, Sofia! If she's not out of the country, she'll be dead. I have no doubt of that."

"But what about you? You will be dead when he discovers," she pleaded as tears filled her eyes.

"Honey, remember, I have Antonio and Paola on my side."

"But you cannot be sure. You do not know for sure they will be able to help you."

"I'm very confident of it. I wouldn't be doing this if I wasn't."

"I do not wish to lose you. Do not make me lose you."

Thomas took her in his arms and held her as she cried. Her tears, shed for any reason, were the one sure thing that could break his heart. It was best to let her have this release of emotion before he continued. Once she had calmed down a little, she spoke again.

"I am sorry, Thomas, but I cannot lose you now. I do not like this idea. It frightens me very much!"

"I'll be very careful. You're my reason to survive. I have to succeed because of you."

"I hope you are right. I know there is no point in trying to convince you to do it another way. You have made up your mind. I cannot change it. I can only pray."

"I know your prayers will make everything work out well. I depend on them."

"I will pray a lot. You can be sure."

"I know you will. Now let's talk about what you must do."

"Ok. We will talk about it then. What must I do besides worry, Thomas?"

"First, I need you to go to a bank and get a safety deposit box. I need you to put these in it," he said, as he pulled the bearer bonds from the false bottom he had created somewhat crudely in his carry-on bag. He had been very thankful that there had been no luggage search on this flight. Had the bonds been discovered, at either end of the trip, he would have been in a lot of trouble. There are serious laws concerning transporting financial instruments or cash from one country to another.

"This is the money? Why is it here?"

"I'll need it to reward Antonio, and especially Paola. She is just a poor woman who will be taking a very big risk for someone she doesn't even know."

"Yes, I like that idea. She deserves it, very much."

"She will have more than she ever dreamed of."

"And after I get this deposit box? What then?"

"Then I'll go to see Carlo, and I need you to wait here."

"What am I waiting for?"

"For me to call. I will call, one way or another, and you must wait for it. Then I can give you instructions about what you need to do from there on."

"I will wait, but I will worry. Will it be much time before you call?"

"It may be. I hope not longer than the day after tomorrow."

"Day after tomorrow? Two days? Why so long?"

"It's going to take time to get him to release Angela, and for her to get a flight home. I can't do anything about getting away from there until I know she is safely in the air, on her way to Canada."

"I see. Then I guess it must be that way. I do not like it, because I will be concerned every minute, but that is the situation. So, I can do nothing, except what you ask."

"Everything will be fine. We have to believe that."

"I do not think God brought you to me so that I would lose you."

"I'm sure he didn't. Now you have to get dressed and go to the bank. Be sure and hide the key to the safety deposit box. Somewhere very safe, but where we can get it easily if we have to return here."

"OK, I will do it. Let me get ready now."

Once Sofia had dressed, she left to make her way to the Citibank, just blocks away. She would return in less than an hour with the key to a safety deposit box. Thomas then dialed Carlo's cell number, which Sofia had copied from the phone records in his computer. It seemed he didn't like keeping paper around and scanned all his bills to store on his computer before destroying the paper copies. He answered the phone in somewhat of an aggressive tone, "Hello," he snarled, displaying his displeasure.

"Good morning, Carlo."

"Thomas? How did you get this number?"

"I bribed someone. That's the way it works, isn't it? Pay for what you want? Just like you do?"

"If I find out who, they won't live to make any more foolish mistakes. Now, what do you want?"

"I want to be picked up at the hotel. We need to talk."

"The hotel? What are you talking about?"

"I'm in Sao Paulo. Pick me up at the same place as last time," he said, and before Carlo could respond, hung up.

Assuming that Antonio would be pulling up within twenty minutes or so, he hastily dressed and said his goodbyes to Sofia. She was still very upset but tried to keep the tears at bay. He waited in the lobby no more than fifteen minutes before Antonio walked in.

"Son-of-a-bitch! You did come back! I don't believe it. Carlo is totally pissed! He turned so friggin red I thought he was gonna explode."

"Then we better get going. How are things with Rosina?"

"Things are great with her. Gettin' better all the time. So, what the hell you got in mind now, Tommy?"

"I guess that depends on you. I'm at your mercy now. I took your promise that you would help, and now I have to see if you do."

"I gave my word. I meant what I said. I just don't know what you got up your sleeve."

"We'll talk about it in the car, my friend."

As they were pulling away from the curb Thomas tucked his flip fold cell phone into his sock. He didn't want it taken away. It would be more than a little necessary.

"When the time comes, Antonio, I need you to get me out of the house safely. Then I'll tell you how you can have all that you wish for. That's a promise! I owe you huge for this."

"You don't gotta promise me nothin. I made a deal, I'll stick to it. Rosina and I have been seein each other every day. I ain't never been so happy, and it's because of you. Rosina and I want a new life, and this is the only way to get it. So I'm doin it for me and you both."

Thomas was happy, in more ways than one, to hear those words. He knew it meant he would have the help he needed, and that Antonio would have a new start in life. He wasn't sure about Rosina's motives though. He hoped they were honest. Thomas had come to believe that

Antonio was actually a pretty nice guy who got trapped in the wrong line of work and didn't like it so much.

"You also have to make sure Angela gets on the plane alright."

"What are you talkin' about? Plane?"

"She's going home. Carlo is going to get his chain pulled and he'll let her go home."

"I don't know what you got in mind, but I sure hope it works. For all of us."

"It will. I'm sure of it," Thomas said, not knowing if he really could be. Too many things could still go wrong. "You can bet that Carlo will hold me captive, probably in Angela's room. It'll be up to you to get me out. I'll let you know when. I'm really depending on you to free me so that the rest of the plan can play out."

"Carlo ain't gonna give up on finding you. You gotta know that. He won't rest until he gets you."

"He won't have to find me. I plan on telling him exactly where I'll be. That's the whole idea."

"What? Why the hell would ya do that? Do you wanna die?"

"I want him to come to me so that others can find him."

"I don't think I want to know no more, Tommy. I'll get you out. Just don't blow it. I gotta see Napoli before I die. I gotta. Me and Rosina."

"I can't afford to blow it. You'll see Napoli with Rosina. When all this is done, I have a pretty wonderful surprise for you."

"What? What kinda surprise?"

"A good one! You won't have any complaints about it. I promise. Listen, before we get to Carlo's, I need the answers to a few questions."

"What do ya need to know?"

"First of all, I assume Angela's room is bugged?"

"Yeah, of course. Since the day he put her down there."

"Can you disable it somehow?"

"Yeah, no problem. But not for long! He'll catch on."

"Do it when you're allowed to bring Paola to my room with my lunch tomorrow. You can fix it right after."

"Sure, no sweat! What else?"

"What time does he go to bed?"

"He's an early sleeper. Usually hits the sack by ten."

"Good. Are you in the house at that time?"

"Yeah. I'm always there late. Got my own place, but only started spending any kinda time there since I met Rosina."

"Does Carlo eat or drink anything before bed?"

"Yeah, it's like an obsession. He's gotta have a glass of warm milk and peanut butter toast. Like some sissy little kid. Or he can't sleep."

"Does he get it himself?"

"You kiddin? He don't do much of nothin for himself. That's Paola's job."

"Absolutely perfect!"

Thomas handed Antonio a piece of paper on which he had written the name of a very strong sedative.

"I need you to get this powder. Can you do it?"

"We already got it. We used it on Angela a few times to keep her quiet. It's in the kitchen cupboard."

Antonio, you're awesome," Thomas said as he reached up to give him a firm pat on his brawny shoulder. "We're going to do just fine with this. Wait and see my friend."

"Hope you ain't wrong about that. Cause if you are, we might all end up in the same grave."

"I have to keep faith. Everything will be just fine."

It seemed like only a few minutes, and they were pulling up to the gate at Carlo's. Antonio's last words as they drove up to the house were, "Good luck, Tommy. For all of us." They exited the limo and walked up the stairs to the front entrance. Paola opened the door and looked directly into Thomas' eyes. He reached out with his hand and softly touched the face of this obviously tender woman. He could only imagine the hell she must have gone through working for Carlo and fearing for her family should she ever fail to do his bidding. As his hand touched her cheek, she reached up, placed her hand on his, and smiled. Thomas would be so very happy to release her from what was, no doubt, almost a form of slavery. Paola once again led him to the library, with Antonio right on his heels. Carlo was already there.

"So, what the hell are you doing back here?" Carlo yelled from his seated position in what seemed to be his favorite chair, "I didn't tell you to come back!"

"I don't need you to tell me whether to come back here or not. I could care less what you think about it! I'm here! Now we need to talk."

His anger, as usual, was very apparent in the color of Carlo's face, and the grip of his hands on the chair as he screamed in Thomas' direction.

"I've about had all of your shit I'm willing to take. There's no reason not to kill your ass right now! Angela too!"

As Thomas sat down in the chair opposite Carlo, he fixed his eyes upon him in a steely glare that could only be interpreted as hatred.

"No, Carlo! It's your shit I'm not taking anymore. There are over two-million reasons you won't kill me now. Or, for that matter, Angela either! You know it, and so do I. So cut the crap."

"I warned you not to be so sure of yourself, Tommy."

"Stuff it. I'm not listening. You want those trucks? You play my way. They haven't left port yet and won't until I say so. There's no way around it. You need me, or you get nothing. So, relax, have a drink, and let's make the ground rules clear. Then we all get what we want."

It was obvious to Thomas that although Carlo was not in the least bit pleased with the situation, he knew very well he had no choice. The money was essential. Losing it was not something he could afford. Paola entered the room with a Pepsi for Thomas and bourbon for Carlo, who seemed, slowly, to be calming down. No doubt he was assuming he would humor Thomas for now and enjoy the thought of killing him when all was done. "Alright. I'll play along. For now! Fill me in. What's up your sleeve?"

"First, Angela goes home, safely, before the trucks leave port. Non-negotiable, so don't even ask. She's on a plane tonight. One leaves at eight forty-five. First-class ticket all the way. Period."

"You think I'm giving up my leverage with you? You're the one who's crazy."

"You have no leverage, Carlo, because if she isn't on that plane tonight, you can kill us both and I don't care. You were planning to anyway, no matter what I did. You couldn't possibly have thought I would believe otherwise. Two-million dollars, Carlo, that I happen to think you need quite badly. So, make your decision. Not much time for her to catch that plane. The trucks leave port when I talk to her in Canada and know that she is safely at home. End of story!"

Thomas could see Carlo's brow furrow, and his eyes squint, as his mind worked to come up with an answer to this new wrinkle. He really had to think there was nothing to lose. In his mind, he had to assume that he would just send someone to take care of Angela later. He could feel some certainty that she would keep her mouth shut in order to keep Thomas alive. It all had to seem so simple to him. Play along with Thomas and take care of the loose ends when the trucks arrived.

"I'm warning you, Tommy boy, if she opens her mouth to anyone, you die. There will be a lot of questions when she gets back to Canada. How is she going to answer them?"

"I'll make sure she has a good story. Just an hour with her and she will be more than prepared. She isn't going to risk my life."

"It appears I'm in a bind. You're right! The money is important. So, I guess we play your way for now."

"Good. Make the plane reservations right now, if you don't mind. Better yet, I'll make them, and you'll ensure they're paid for."

Thomas almost instinctively reached for his cell but caught himself at the last second and asked Carlo for his. He handed it to Thomas, and he called the airport, booked Angela's ticket for the evening flight, and had Carlo give them a credit card number for payment.

"Wise decision, Carlo. Now let's go tell Angela the good news so she can pack for the trip. I need a little time to condition her for what will happen when she gets home."

"I hope you like the décor of her room because it's your home now."

"I figured that much. A little less floral would be good. Can we change the sofa?" the sarcastic chuckle rolled from Thomas' mouth.

"You are one wise-ass. Do yourself a favor and quit while you're ahead."

"It was just a little humor. Lighten up."

They headed for the door behind the main staircase, and down to Angela's room. Thomas couldn't help but notice that Rico was nowhere to be seen. He didn't bother to ask why.

It was nice enough knowing he wasn't there. Carlo punched in the lock code and opened the door. Angela was sitting on the sofa and leaped to her feet the minute she saw Thomas. She ran into his arms and gave him a hug that could have broken ribs.

"I'll leave you to give her the good news, Tommy. Make sure she's ready in time. You only have about an hour before she should be on her way." He left the room and closed the door behind him.

"What's he talking about? Where am I going?"

"Home, Angela," Thomas said, with tears running down his face. "You're going home."

"We're going home? I don't believe it. I'm so happy."

"Not we, Angela, you. I have to stay in your place. At least for now."

"What? No! I won't let you do that. No! We both go or not at all."

"You're going! Don't worry about me. The trucks will leave port when you're safely home. They'll take about a week to get here, and then I'll be on my way." He pulled her close to him to remind her that they were being listened to. "Everything will be fine. When you get home you call Carlo's cell to let me know you're safe. Ok?"

"If you say so. But I don't feel right leaving you here."

"Don't worry! I'll be fine. Promise."

They sat on the sofa to arrange the story she would tell when she got home. That was purely for Carlo's listening benefit. Thomas had every intention of letting her tell her family the whole sordid tale. She just couldn't tell anyone else yet. They decided to let Carlo believe she would explain to them that she had just taken advantage of the opportunity to run away from everything, had spent the last five years living in the United States, and now wanted to come home. It was a pitiful excuse for a story, but he was sure Carlo wouldn't pay too much attention to its quality. They continued to make up details of what she had done during those five years until they felt enough ground had been covered to satisfy Carlo. Now it was time for her to hastily pack a bag and be on her way. Once she was packed, they stood at the door as Antonio waited to drive her to the airport. She couldn't help but cry out of concern for Thomas' safety.

"I am so worried. I hate leaving you here."

"I'm fine. I don't want you to worry. Just get home to our daughters."

"How can I ever thank you for what you've done for me?"

"The happiness the girls will feel when they see you is enough for me. Nothing else could compare to that. Now go! Catch that plane." He said as he kissed her forehead to send her on her way.

Antonio closed the door behind them, and she was gone. Now Thomas would wait patiently for the phone call that told him she was safely in Canada.

CHAPTER 11

THE ESCAPE PLAN

Thomas had lay down on Angela's sofa but hadn't slept for very long. It had been more of a quick catnap to gain back some lost energy. Once awake, he sat there and pondered the long wait ahead. Angela's plane would land in Toronto sometime around ten a.m. local time, or about noon Brazilian time. Then, with passing through customs and finally arriving at her sister's, Thomas guessed it would be closer to three p.m. when he finally heard from her. Once she phoned to report that she was home, there would be another wait of seven hours or so until Carlo went to bed. It was thought wise to wait at least an hour longer to ensure he was soundly under the effects of the sedative Thomas planned to have Paola slip into his warm milk. Then, hopefully, he would be free and meet Sofia to put the next stage of his plan into play. The rest of this mission would get pretty messy if he botched it.

Thomas realized that he needed a way to communicate with Antonio without Carlo eavesdropping over the bug in the room. He searched the desk for paper and pen but found none. There was a computer on the desk. There was no internet connection, for obvious reasons. He turned it on and opened the notepad. He would write questions and instructions that Antonio could simply answer with a nod of his head or a gesture. Thomas would then simply delete the information without saving it to the hard drive. He began typing the information very slowly, so as to minimize the sound of the clicking of the keyboard. He had barely finished, and turned off the monitor, when the door began to open. He resumed his position on the sofa in time to see Paola enter with his supper. Antonio was behind her. Thomas gestured for Antonio to come in and close the door. As Paola placed the supper tray on the coffee table, he pulled Antonio to the computer, making small talk as they went. Thomas turned on the monitor so that the information he had typed appeared on the screen.

Through this method, he learned there were two bugs, one in the lamp by the end table, and one in the bathroom ceiling. This left only one safe place to talk. The hallway was out of the question because of the risk of being seen. The closet was the only choice when privacy was needed. Thomas had also written that Paola was helping him. When he read that part of the message, Antonio looked at her and smiled. She didn't seem to know what to make of it and started to back towards the door. Thomas went to her and placed his hand on her shoulder as he put his finger to her lips to indicate that she shouldn't talk. He then leaned forward and whispered into her ear.

"Paola, there is a bug, a microphone, in the room. We must whisper. Don't be nervous about Antonio. He's on our side."

The look on her face made it clear that she still had her suspicions, but Antonio smiled in a way that seemed to relax her. Thomas told her that Antonio would give her instructions when the time came. She smiled, looked around as if trying to see the bug,

"Enjoy your meal, I cook for you myself," Paola said as she left the room. Thomas whispered to Antonio that tomorrow was when he would need him. He had to be sure he would be around, no matter what. Seconds later he was alone once again.

The sudden vibration at his ankle alerted him that he had a phone call. He had set his cell to silent vibrate mode to replace the ringing tone. Angela had his number and was told to call him a few hours after she was in the air. He went to the closet and pulled the phone from his sock.

"Hello?" he whispered.

"Thomas, I can't believe I'm actually flying home," It was clear from the cracking in her voice that she was crying.

"I'm so glad you're on the plane, Angela. This is a happy time. You're going home. Feel good about it."

"I know, but without you, it's very hard. I'm very worried you won't survive this."

"I'll make it. Promise! I won't accept any other alternative. You just get home and get to your sister's house. The girls are there. Call her when you get to the airport. Do you still remember her number?"

"Yes. I've got it. Please be careful, Thomas. We may not be a couple anymore, but it won't stop me from worrying and feeling a lot of pain if anything happens to you."

"I know. Maybe you can say a prayer or two, along with the others who are praying for me in this."

"I will. Believe me, I will."

"We have to make this quick. I'll wait for you to call Carlo when you get home. Don't call my cell anymore. It's much too dangerous. Have a safe flight."

"OK. See you soon. You had better not make me a liar about that either."

"I won't. Now go. Talk to you tomorrow."

Thomas closed the phone, stashed it back in his sock, opened the closet, and walked back to the sofa wondering what he would do for the many hours of sleeplessness that lay ahead. He grabbed the remote and turned on the TV. Carlo had a satellite dish, and there was an episode of The Sopranos on. How appropriate there would be a show on about the Mafia. And in Queens, no less. Thomas couldn't help but chuckle as he settled in to eat his supper. He began thinking of the final phase of the plan, the one where Carlo would get his just reward at the hands of people just like the ones he was watching on TV. The thought made him smile.

Once he had finished eating, and the Sopranos had ended, he decided to take a shower. Clean underwear would have to wait until the morning. Carlo had made him leave his bag in the library. Thomas was sure he wanted to inspect its contents before giving it back. He would find nothing but clean clothes, and a few magazines, so Thomas wasn't concerned. After a somewhat lonely shower, he grabbed a pillow and went to sleep on the sofa. He slept more easily than he had thought would be the case. It was apparent that the stress of the past few days had exhausted him to the point where sleep was not to be denied. It was probably all for the best. Sofia and he would be on a mad dash out of Sao Paulo in another day. Rest was well advised if he was to have his wits about him.

Morning almost seemed to come too early. The sound of Antonio and Paola entering the room woke Thomas from a very deep slumber. Paola had his breakfast, and Angelo had his bag. Thomas scrambled to cover himself with something, anything, in order to relieve Paola's embarrassment at seeing him in his underwear. He grabbed the blanket draping the back of the sofa, and pulled it down over him. Paola left his breakfast on the coffee table, giggled slightly, and left the room. Antonio was trying very hard not to laugh. Thomas got up and took Antonio by the sleeve and pulled him towards the closet. He was somewhat confused but then realized Thomas wanted to talk. Once out of range of the bug, Thomas told him the day's plan.

"This is the deal. When the phone call comes in from Angela it's my signal to set things in motion. You must talk to Paola and prepare her for what must be done tonight. First, you need to disable the bug before you bring Paola down with my lunch, so that we can discuss this more completely."

"Yeah. I'll take care of it. What exactly are we doing tonight?"

"We'll talk about it later."

They left the closet and Antonio headed back upstairs as Thomas settled in for more waiting. It was just after eight a.m. now, and Angela would not get to her sisters for at least another six hours. They would doubtless be the longest hours of his life. He decided to go back into the cramped space of the closet and call Sofia.

"Hi, sweetheart."

"Oh, Thomas, I have worried so. Is everything ok?"

"Everything is fine. There should be a call from Angela in about six hours. I'll be out of here at about midnight. Be ready to leave for the airport. I need you to call and book two tickets to Manaus."

"Manaus? We are going to Manaus? It is beautiful there."

"Yes, we are going to Manaus. There is still work to do, but we'll have some days alone together before I can put the finishing touches on my plan."

"As long as we are together, I will not worry. I will check on flight times right now."

"Good. We may have to spend some time in the airport. Hopefully that won't be a problem. If the flight is too late, we must find another way out of Sao Paulo. We can't stay here past the morning. If we're gone by eight a.m., or soon after, it would be perfect."

"OK, then. I will check now. If the flight is too late? What will I do?"

"If we can't be on a plane no later than nine a.m., then rent a car and have it ready at the hotel."

"OK. I will do that. Shall I call you back?"

"No, baby. Too dangerous! I'll call you."

"I understand. I will await your call. Beijos!"

"Beijos. See you soon."

"Yes, and I will be very happy."

Thomas was hoping there would be a flight early enough for them to be in the air before Carlo was up and about. The odds were good he would be asleep until after eleven a.m., but there was no guarantee. It was one detail Thomas wasn't able to check. They couldn't afford to be sitting around the airport when Carlo discovered he was gone. It would surely be the first place he looked for Thomas. On the other hand, there was no thought of trying to travel the huge distance to Manaus by car. He wasn't the least bit sure it was even possible. He had no idea if it was accessible from the east by road. After all, he knew the city was almost in the middle of Brazil, on the Rio Negro, near its meeting with the Amazon, literally carved out of, and surrounded by, Brazilian rain forest.

Thomas wouldn't mind a leisurely drive to Manaus. The problem was that only about ten percent of Brazil's two million kilometers of roads are paved, and it makes for some very interesting, but often very risky driving. Thomas knew nothing about the roads to the north, in the direction of Fortaleza. In fact, he knew little of Brazilian geography itself. He had always traveled by plane when he was during his two visits there. He wouldn't know the answer regarding driving options until he called Sofia again. She was his guide to Brazil. Whatever direction they had to take; they would travel it together. She would be his roadmap through any part of this journey that must be made by car.

At the moment, Thomas was very much looking forward to lunch. Not because he was hungry, but because it would assure him that everything was still on track. It would be another opportunity to confirm things with Antonio and Paola. What he needed was for Antonio to successfully disable the bug so that they could all talk freely. As he sat quietly on the sofa, he heard the door open. In walked Paola and Antonio.

Antonio smiled and said, "I took care of the bug, Tommy. We probably got ten minutes before Carlo figures it out."

"Great! We should be able to cover everything by then. And you Paola? Are you worried?" he asked.

She looked at Antonio and didn't answer. He asked again, "Paola? Are you worried? Everything is fine, I promise. Antonio is helping me. Helping us! You can trust him. I promise you."

"But he work for Carlo."

"Not after tonight."

"What is happen tonight?"

"Tonight, we work together to be free. Free from Carlo."

"I don't dare hope. It is all I wish."

"It will all be fine. It's very important that you follow the instructions I give to you. Understand? Then everything will work out well."

"I will do what you tell me. I trust you. Enough I have had of him," the look of disgust on her face made it clear what she thought of Carlo. "I don't care if I die. Better than this life. I will do anything to be free."

"Paola, you're not going to die. Don't worry. You're going to be safe and have a good life from now on."

The look on her weathered, yet attractive face was one of desperation, "I hope, I pray." This woman, Thomas was sure, meant it when she said she preferred death to suffering any more of what she had been through with Carlo.

As they sat there on the sofa, Thomas spelled out the activity for the night.

"Paola, when you are preparing Carlo's milk and toast, Antonio will put in a teaspoon of a sedative powder. You will deliver it to his room as usual. You understand?"

"Is a sleeping powder?"

"Yes. It's very strong. This is important. You need to stay, quietly; outside his door to be sure he drinks it. Once you are sure that he has finished the milk, you must let Antonio know."

"Yes! But how will I see if he drinks?"

"The old doors in this house have keyholes. Hopefully, you can see him that way."

"Ah! Yes. I have done so before," she answered with a mischievous laugh.

"Good! Perfect! Antonio, it's your job to go to Carlo's room one hour later and make sure that he's sound asleep. Once he is, you get me out of this room."

"Gotcha! No problem, Tommy."

"We can do the rest of this one of two ways. First, no matter which way we choose, Paola must be here in the morning, and continue with her work as usual, until I get Carlo to leave Sao Paulo. Then she will leave and never return. You need to decide which you think is best regarding you." It was at this point that Paola looked at Thomas and voiced some concern.

"I must stay? Why I must stay? Why I no leave with you?"

"Because it's safer, Paola. If you're gone, he will know you helped me and he'll do everything to find you. If you're still here, he will never suspect you. I don't want him looking for you when I'm gone. It's better. Believe me."

"But when I go then?"

"I'll have Carlo out of Sao Paulo within five days. I'm sure you can make it that long. When he leaves Sao Paulo, you take the money I give you and go wherever you wish."

"Money? What money? I do not wish your money. I do not do this for your money."

"It's not my money. It was taken from someone as bad as Carlo. You don't need to feel guilty about it. There will be money for you, and also for Antonio. I want you both to have a new start. You will have saved my life, and Angela's. You deserve it."

"I do not know how to thank you," she said as she held her hands to her eyes and cried. Thomas put his arm around her shoulder and gave her a gentle kiss on the forehead. She really was a sweet woman, with a good heart. He was so happy that she would be free from Carlo at last.

"OK, Antonio. Now for you! I think the best thing is to disappear when I do. If you stay, he'll want to know how I got away and why you didn't prevent it. It would be helpful to have you still inside the house, but I won't make you take that risk if we can't come up with something that gives you a good cover. I haven't been able to think of anything."

"Ain't no way you could get outta here without help. And there ain't no story I could tell Carlo that he would believe. He'll know I helped ya, no matter what I say."

"Then it's settled. You and I go together. How do we get past the gate?"

"Let's just say that you'll be the first guy that ever rode in the trunk while he was still breathin," he said with a laugh that displayed pleasure with his little joke.

"Oh, thanks. I really needed to know that," Thomas chuckled. "OK, then. You get me out of here as soon as he's out cold. No later than midnight, I hope. Paola always brings breakfast at eight-thirty or so in the morning. Tomorrow she'll do no differently. I want her to be sure and prepare the breakfast as always. She'll wait for Carlo to wake up and tell him that she couldn't find you to take her down to deliver my food. She'll ask what she should do. It's really important, Paola, that you don't appear nervous and that you act very surprised by the whole thing. He'll never suspect you, I'm sure. He knows you can't go to my room without Antonio."

"I will do. Not to worry."

"OK. Paola, I'm going to give you my cell phone when I leave. Hide it very well so that only you can find it. When Carlo is gone, take the phone and carry it in your pocket. I'll call and tell you where to go to get the money that I leave for you. OK?"

"Ok. Yes. You must show me how to use. I never use before."

"No problem. I'll teach you how before I leave. Antonio, you'll drive me to the hotel. I'll get your money for you, and you can take Rosina and get far away. I would suggest that you don't use the Sao Paulo airport. Get rid of the limo and take the bus north to Fortaleza, or somewhere, and catch a plane there. You have to know that Carlo will have someone looking for you in Sao Paulo. I doubt they would ever expect you to be on a bus. Are we agreed on that? I don't want you getting caught."

"Yeah, sounds about right. Good idea, Tommy."

"Alright then, we have our plan, and we all know what to do. Now you better get back upstairs and fix that bug before Carlo gets wise."

Once they were gone, Thomas decided to check out the contents of the computer. He began to search for files on the hard drive. Somewhere in the back of his mind, he wondered if Angela had written anything there that would give any insight into what she had been through these last weeks. There were a few entries in the documents file, and he set about reading them. They weren't dated, only identified by the day of the week.

Wednesday

I have been in this room for two days, ever since I regained my memory and went after Carlo with a butcher knife. I can't explain the overpowering feeling of grief, fear, and anger that overcame me within minutes of my discovery of what had happened to me. Carlo, having avoided my attempt with the knife, wrestled me to the floor. Antonio covered my face with a cloth soaked in what must have been chloroform, or something similar. I know that I was unconscious almost instantly. When I woke up, I was alone in this room. I never knew this room even existed. Carlo later told me that he had built it with the possibility of this day in mind. I have no idea what will happen to me. Sometimes I hear Rico in the hallway, and it scares me a lot. This awful, and disgusting pervert leers at me whenever he's around. I'm afraid that Carlo won't feel the need to protect me from him any longer. I can't sleep. I am constantly afraid.

Thursday

Sweet Paola brought me my breakfast this morning, as always. She brings me all my meals and, though she seems afraid to even talk to me, I can see in her eyes that she is feeling my pain. I have always just adored her. She is nothing in Carlo's mind, but this woman is filled with compassion and love. I have no idea why she remains here. Carlo must have some hold on her. I am going crazy wondering what will happen to me. Will I be a prisoner here for the rest of my life? If so, then I will find a way to end it.

Friday

Today Carlo came to my room. Now I know what he wants. He is thinking he will get some ransom from Thomas for my release. I have no idea what he thinks Thomas has because he has nothing that Carlo could possibly need. All I know is that he will have me call Thomas. I can't imagine his surprise to hear my voice. I know how wonderful it will be to hear his, so deep and masculine. I am worried about what I will find out. It's been five years. Maybe there is someone else in his life now. I know that our relationship had some serious problems, but maybe they can be worked out if he hasn't moved too far on with his life. I have been trying to avoid thinking about the girls. Whenever I begin to think of the years, I have lost with them, it hurts far too much. I try so hard to block it from my mind. I need to find my strength and enjoy the memories I have of them. I pray that I see them soon.

Saturday

I have not seen Carlo since our short discussion yesterday. I have no idea when he is planning to have me call Thomas. I hope that it's soon. Antonio surprised me today. He is always with Paola when she brings my food. Today, after she had brought me my lunch, Antonio handed me a note. In it, he warned me that the room was bugged and to be careful what I say out loud. It also said he was sorry. I never could understand Antonio being so tied to Carlo. I always thought him to be a big teddy bear that tried so hard to act tough. I hope tomorrow I get to call Thomas. I'm very anxious. I need to hear his voice and to find out what Carlo wants from him. Antonio came back to the room and handed me a piece of paper. He said that Carlo wanted me to memorize it for my conversation with Thomas. When I read it, I almost fainted. He wanted me to get Thomas to come to Sao Paulo. That scares me. It's bad enough that I am in this situation, but I don't want Thomas to be in any danger. I think I may refuse to make the call.

Sunday

Carlo and Antonio came to my room at five thirty in the morning. For some reason he wanted me to call Thomas then, even though it would be three hours earlier there, and he would certainly be asleep. I told him that I refused to make the call, and that Thomas could not have anything he needed. He had no money to pay ransom. Carlo said nothing. He just walked to the door. When he opened it, Rico was there. He told me if I didn't make the call he would lock Rico in the room with me and, in his words 'let him have the fun he has always wanted with you'. I was scared to death. There is nothing I am more afraid of than that beast. I agreed to call Thomas and felt so guilty for thinking only of myself at that moment. It was six a.m. when I called him. I followed the script that Carlo had sent to me, even though I wanted to say so much more. I was stunned when Thomas agreed to come to Sao Paulo. I was both happy and very worried for his safety. When Carlo and Antonio left the room, I cried for an hour.

Monday

I spent the morning a bundle of nerves. I knew that Thomas would be in Sao Paulo today, and wondered when, or even if, I would get to see him. I wondered how different he would be. I wondered if he still loved me. I wondered what I would do when I saw him. When Antonio brought him to my room, I fell apart. He really hadn't changed much, and I was so happy to see him. Even though he was affectionate and attentive, I didn't see the feeling I had hoped for. Perhaps I was expecting too much. We slept side by side and I woke up in the night asking to make love. That was when he told me that we had separated before I had disappeared. I couldn't believe it. Why didn't I remember that? I knew now there was someone else in his life. What I didn't know was why he would come all that way for me. He made me understand that he could never refuse. It was important for the girls. He wanted to give them their mother back.

Tuesday

Thomas and I had breakfast, and he told me that I shouldn't worry. He promised that he would get me home. I can't imagine how he can, but I at least hope he gets home safely. Soon, Antonio came to get him, and he was gone. I'm left here to wait and wonder. I'm almost out of hope. I feel more depressed now than I was before. I am worried for Thomas. I don't think I will eat today. I have no desire for food.

For some reason, the entries stopped there. Angela had appeared thinner than on Thomas' first visit, and he imagined that she was in such a state of depression that she ate very little. He assumed that she spent most of her time sleeping to avoid having to think about her situation, and his. He was so very happy that she was safely on her way home. It was one less worry to occupy his mind. He had only one wish at that moment, to see the faces of his daughters when she walked in the door.

CHAPTER 12

IT'S ONLY JUST BEGUN

For more than an hour, Thomas had been in a very restless state. So much so, that, when Carlo and Antonio came to his room, he nearly leaped from the sofa. Carlo was carrying his cell phone and handed it to Thomas.

"Hello? Angela?"

"Yes, Thomas. I'm at Theresa's," she said as she cried into the phone, "I'm home, and I can't believe it."

"I'm so happy that you're safe. That's what's important." Thomas' said in a voice filled with relief.

"Yes, but I am so worried for your safety. I can't stop thinking about what might happen to you."

"I told you, don't worry. How did the girls react to seeing you?"

"They haven't stopped crying or asking questions. They have no idea that you're aware I'm alive, so they don't know I'm calling you!"

"I'm glad you're home. Now please, try not to worry too much about me. Everything will be fine."

"I'll try. If I could only reassure myself."

At that point, Carlo grabbed the phone, told Angela the conversation was over, and abruptly hung up.

"OK, Tommy. Now do your part. Get those containers released," he said as he handed him the phone. Thomas dialed the number for an answering service that would bounce the call to Fedir' cell phone. When he answered, Thomas spoke two sentences.

"You can release the containers, but don't let them unload until you hear from me again. They're not to leave that ship until I say so."

He then hung up and handed the phone back to Carlo.

"What the hell was that shit?" Carlo fumed.

"You must truly think I'm stupid, Carlo. Those containers may be on their way here soon, but they won't make it off that ship until I say so. That's my protection. Isn't life a bitch?"

He had finally pushed just a little too far. Carlo jumped at him and swung wildly at his head, connecting with Thomas' jaw and sending him sprawling to the floor. Before he could react, Carlo was kicking him everywhere his foot could find. It was only Antonio that saved him from a continuation of the furious assault.

"Boss, you gotta stop. If anything happens to him there won't be no trucks. You need them trucks. You gotta stop."

Carlo, now breathing heavily, face as red as a beet and hatred in his eyes, finally ended his attack. He straightened his tie and jacket, stood over Thomas and laughed.

"Fine, smart-ass. One more time we play it your way. You mess with me again, and I'll find Angela and those kids and kill them all. You got it?"

"Yeah, I got it," Thomas said through a swollen jaw that he feared might be broken. Carlo and Antonio left the room as he lay there, blood dripping from his mouth, his body racked with pain.

"That bastard has one hell of a punch. And he kicks like a damn mule," he muttered to himself.

He didn't need to be in a crippled-up condition when the time came to leave, so he slowly dragged himself to the bathroom and started to draw a hot bath in which to soak his aching body. As the tub filled, he examined his face, weathered enough at the best of times, and now swollen from the punch delivered by Carlo. It didn't seem to be broken, and he hoped the swelling would subside fairly quickly. With his face cleaned up, he lowered himself into the tub and let the water do its magic. After more than an hour of soaking, in continually running hot water, he felt some degree of relief. He dried himself off and limped his way over to lie on the sofa. With the pain he was suffering, the next seven hours would feel even longer.

The threat Carlo had made towards Angela and the girls was still ringing in his ears. Were he not in a heap on the floor, he was sure he would have tried to kill him right then. Within a few minutes, the door opened, and Antonio appeared. He made a deliberate point of speaking in the direction of the bugged lamp.

"Carlo sent me to make sure you were still alive, asshole," and with that remark, he winked at Thomas before he continued, "He figured there was a chance he just mighta done some damage to your insides. What do ya think? You gonna live?"

"Yeah. I'll live. Fortunately for him," Thomas replied as Antonio handed him a bottle of Tylenol and an ice pack for his jaw.

Thomas was sure Carlo never told him to provide those. He patted Thomas on the shoulder and left the room. He was beginning to really like this guy. After a cold glass of water to wash down about six Tylenol, Thomas lay back on the sofa and put the ice pack to good use. He was hoping that everything would feel a lot better by midnight. If not, it would be a very uncomfortable night on the run. How he was wishing that he could be with Sofia. Her gentle hands would soothe every ache and pain. Still, it was certainly better that she didn't see him like this. She would be overcome with fear and sadness.

Thomas found his mind attempting to cover every eventuality for the coming night. What if Carlo didn't drink the milk? What if he woke up and discovered the whole thing? He had told Antonio that if there was a problem, he should find a way to call his cell and let him know. If it came to that, Thomas wanted to be freed from the room, any way possible, and then, if need be, he would kill Carlo himself. That wasn't anything he looked forward to or wanted to contemplate, but if it was necessary, he knew he would. It was certain that one way or another he was getting the hell out of there, and no way he would allow Carlo to take revenge on Angela and his kids. There was no chance he wasn't going to make it back to Sofia. He could no longer consider the possibility he might not succeed. He would! No matter what it took.

Eventually, Thomas dozed off giving his body the rest it needed from the beating it had taken. He woke up a few hours later and was disappointed that there were still some four hours to wait. He had no idea what to do with the time, other than pace and suffer the racing of his mind with every worry and detail of what could possibly go wrong. Fortunately, the Tylenol was doing a remarkable job of relieving his pain. He wasn't sure any doctor would recommend taking six of them, but then they wouldn't be feeling as bad as he had been. He decided to make one more trip to the closet. He needed to call Sofia and find out what the situation was concerning flight times. Getting out of Sao Paulo quickly was paramount in his mind.

"Thomas? Is it you?"

"Yes, Sofia. It's me."

"What is wrong? Your voice sounds different." She had obviously noticed the difference it makes speaking through a swollen jaw.

"Everything's fine. Just a toothache! I took something for it." He wasn't ready to tell her what had really happened. She was already worried enough.

"OK. But Thomas, I have bad news about the flights."

"I was afraid of that. It would have been much too easy."

"There is a flight at seven-thirty, but it is fully booked. We would have to wait for someone to not arrive for the flight. What is it called? Standby?"

"No way! We can't take that risk. Did you arrange a car?"

"Yes. I knew you would not wish to take such a chance. The car is downstairs now. I am packed and waiting for you."

"Good. I hope to be there not much past midnight. Then I suppose we'll head to Fortaleza or Rio. Which is best? Which is closer to Sao Paulo?"

"Fortaleza is very far. Thousands of hard kilometers! Better to take the good highway to Rio. We can arrive there by morning. There are flights in the mornings at seven-twenty. I checked for that when I knew we could not fly from Sao Paulo. There is a stop in Brasilia and then arrive in Manaus at five-fifteen at night. It's ok?"

"It's perfect. I had no idea Fortaleza was such a long drive. This is better. Maybe we'll stay two nights in Rio."

"Two nights? With my Thomas? Wonderful. We can do it?"

"You bet. We deserve it. Listen, I had better go. I'll phone you when I'm on my way. Beijos."

"OK! Please be careful. I'll be waiting."

The remaining time passed more quickly than Thomas would have imagined. At almost midnight, Antonio opened the door and gave him a smile.

"It's all clear, Tommy. Time to go."

"Where's Paola?"

"She's upstairs. She's got a panic thing goin on."

"She's upset?"

"Sorta. Well, more than sorta. She's a wreck, I think."

Thomas headed up the stairs to find Paola standing in the foyer, literally shaking from head to toe. He took her in his arms and just held her for a minute or two until he felt her body become more relaxed.

"Paola, shh, shh, it's ok. Please, you have to calm down. Everything will be fine."

"I cannot stay here. I can never pretend I had nothing to do with it. He will know. He will kill me. I am so afraid. Please, no leave me. Please. I must go with you."

It was obvious that she was never going to survive even one day with Carlo. He would have the truth out of her, and then kill her for sure. That was something Thomas could never let happen. This sweet woman had risked everything for him. He must now do all he could to protect her.

"Do you have family in Sao Paulo?"

"No. I have none. I am alone here. My only family is in Brasilia. I must get to them. You will help me?"

There was not a moment's hesitation in Thomas' voice as he told her, "Then you'll come with me. I'll get you to Brasilia." and once again he wrapped her in his arms to comfort her. "You don't have time to pack anything, Paola. We must go right now. Is there anything that you feel you must take with you?"

"Yes. Please wait," and she rushed off to her room. Within a few minutes, she returned with a small, somewhat tattered scrapbook. "This is all I have. It is my family." It was then that Antonio spoke.

"I guess there's gonna be two of you in the trunk. Better take out the golf clubs," and headed for the kitchen.

Thomas and Paola followed and used the back door to avoid being seen.

The limo was parked at the side of the house, and Paola and Thomas settled into the trunk. When they were somewhat tightly squeezed in, Angelo closed the lid. He climbed into the driver's seat and headed towards the gate. Paola was actually giggling, like a kid playing a game. It seemed that her fear had suddenly turned into youthful excitement. Thomas had to cover her mouth and tell her to be very quiet, or they would be discovered. He was extreWalty pleased that he had not left her behind. One thing he knew for sure, Sofia's kind heart would look forward to helping her get to her family. It looked like they would have some company for a few days.

Thomas could hear Antonio talking to the guard at the front gate, and then the limo pulled onto the street. When they had traveled a few blocks from the house, Antonio pulled over and let the two of them out of the trunk. They climbed into the back seat, and Thomas called Sofia to let her know he was on his way. She had gone to the bank and emptied the safety deposit box, as he had instructed her before he left for Carlo's. His plan had been to return to Sao Paulo, when all was finished, and leave Paola's bonds for her to pick up. Now, she would take them with her to Brasilia. She had no idea how wealthy she was to become. He briefly told Sofia about the situation with Paola. She was very pleased that Thomas had not left her behind, although she wanted to be assured, they would have their privacy at the appropriate times. Thomas promised her that he had every intention of securing them all the alone time they could want.

Within twenty minutes they pulled up in front of the hotel. Antonio and Paola accompanied Thomas to Sofia's room. Fortunately, Thomas realized that he should call and let her know they would have company. He wasn't sure how she might answer the door for him. Apparently, it was a good thing he called. She mumbled something in Portuguese that sounded an awful lot like frustration, and then said, "Bye, I must get dressed," and hung up the phone.

Thomas decided to take the long way to her room, down a few extra hallways, in order to give her enough time to make herself presentable. When he knocked at her door, Sofia answered wearing a beautiful red sweater and black pants. She looked amazing, as always. They entered the room, and Thomas introduced Antonio and Paola. Sofia had tears in her eyes as she thanked them both for their help. She had prepared two packages of bonds, one for each of them. If Antonio was surprised to be handed a hundred thousand American dollars, Paola was dumbfounded. Thomas was sure she would faint any second. Her mind was undoubtedly thinking of all the good things she could do for her family. Antonio couldn't wait to call Rosina and tell her. She was waiting for his call with her bags packed. Thomas' parting with Antonio was bittersweet.

"Tommy, I can't say nothin. I got no words for this."

"There's nothing you need to say. I've really grown to like you, and I owe my life to you. I hope one day to visit you in Napoli."

"Yeah," Antonio said as his eyes widened, "You gotta come, Tommy. You and Sofia! I'd like that. You'll love Napoli."

"I'm sure we would. I'll plan on it one day. First I have to finish what I've started."

"Tommy, I keep telling ya, you gotta go. You gotta get out of Brazil. Let the cops deal with it."

"Are you kidding? By the time they got around to even investigating, we could all be dead. I'm not taking that risk."

By now Sofia was displaying a very concerned look on her face. Thomas thought he may have been less than candid about the remaining danger he might be in.

"What is he saying, Thomas? Are you still in danger?"

"It'll be fine. You'll see. Someone else will take care of Carlo for me, and then our life goes on."

Thankfully, Antonio realized she needed some reassurance and chimed in.

"Tommy will be ok. He's got this thing planned good," he said without having a clue if he did or not. "You shouldn't worry none. Just listen to him. He's doin good with this."

"See, Sofia? Antonio knows things will be fine when we get to Manaus. Try not to worry so much."

"I pray it is so. I want everything to be fine, but as long as I am with you, whatever happens, I accept. As long as we are together, I don't care."

Antonio had called Rosina and was ready to leave to pick her up and catch a bus out of town. On his way out the door, he turned and shook Thomas' hand, followed by a somewhat painful bear hug. "So, you are going to Manaus?"

"Yes, we are. Should be there in three days."

"Be careful. I gotta tell ya, Carlo has people working for him that are friggin scary. Other guys from the favelas, the slums, who are almost as evil as Rico. I mean they're bad. You got no clue how bad."

Thomas stepped into the hallway with Antonio and asked, "What else can you tell me that will help? Who should I expect to come looking for me?"

"There's six guys out of the slums he uses for real dirty work. One time, some dumb schmuck stole one lousy watch out of a shipment of maybe a thousand. Cartier watches, I think. They gutted him, Tommy! Cut him open and spilled his insides all over the street. Over one lousy watch! These guys will hunt you like an animal. That's why I told ya, you should just get out of Brazil. Fast!"

"I can't do that! You know that he would never give up trying to find us. No matter where we went. I have to finish him. No other choice in the matter."

"I guess you're right. Good luck. Sure hope you got this figured out good," he said as he walked down the hallway towards the elevator and, ultimately, Napoli.

As Thomas closed the door and returned to the room, he noticed Paola just sitting on the bed looking at the bonds, a stare of total amazement on her face. It was a shame that such a pretty face had been weathered with age before its time. Thomas could only smile. Sofia led Paola to the sofa, made her some coffee, and then sat and talked with her briefly in Portuguese. There was no time for conversation of any length. They needed to get on the road as quickly as possible. Very shortly, bags in hand, they headed down to the parking lot, and the car that Sofia had rented. They were on their way to Rio, and Thomas was feeling relieved to be saying goodbye to Sao Paulo.

Sofia had rented a sedan, an Opal made with a Chevy nameplate for sale in Brazil. A nice Mustang would have been his choice, but he supposed beggars couldn't be choosers. At least they were on their way, and the Opal blended in with the traffic better than a Mustang would have. With the bags tucked in the trunk, and Paola comfortable in the back seat, Thomas let Sofia drive. As much as he would have preferred to drive, he had no idea where he was going. When they got out of the city, and on some straight highway, Thomas would take his turn at the wheel.

There was some concern about being stopped at one of the many Police stations along Brazilian highways. He knew that they would pull cars over, often at random, examine their papers, and maybe even search the vehicle. With Paola carrying a hundred thousand in bonds, and another thirty thousand stashed in Sofia's luggage, Thomas wasn't interested in being stopped. That was the kind of thing difficult to explain to seriously underpaid policemen. The thought worried him so much that he had Sofia pull over once they were on the highway. He pulled the rear seat loose and stashed all the bonds under it, before putting it back in its place. If they did get stopped, perhaps they would only search the luggage. Once back on the road, Sofia began to talk at length in Portuguese with Paola. It was a very animated conversation. More than once, in fact, very often, Sofia would express what, even in Portuguese, Thomas could recognize as surprise and disbelief. The conversation was still going on when they approached the first of the police stations they would probably see. Thankfully, the two officers out in the night air were leaning against their car having a smoke. They passed by without incident.

The other concern that filled Thomas' mind was the problem of organized gangs of highway robbers. These individuals make use of the route from Sao Paulo to Rio, and often set up obstacles in the road that force a driver to stop his vehicle. At that point, he is robbed, and certainly runs a significant risk of being killed. The middle of the night was certainly the riskiest time to make such a drive. Thomas decided to have Sofia pull over and trade places with him. He had somewhat more confidence in his driving skills in the event of that sort of trouble. She had no objection, as it made it easier for her to continue her conversation with Paola. Not an hour had passed from that point until they came upon another police station. This time the car was waived over. Thomas could feel the knots in his stomach. The mustachioed officers, one on each side of the car, were reasonably polite. Sofia advised them that Thomas was a tourist and did not speak Portuguese. They all presented their documents to one of the officers as the other searched the trunk. Within no more than ten minutes, after a warning from the officer concerning a recent robbery about ten kilometers ahead, they were on the road again.

There had been some concern about what might await them down the road. Happily, the remainder of the drive passed without incident. It was early morning as they pulled into Rio.

When they decided on Rio as their destination to catch a flight to Manaus, Thomas had asked Sofia to reserve a suite in one of the finest hotels available.

"Sofia, I forgot to ask. Where are we staying in Rio?"

"The Hotel Copacabana Palace. It is so beautiful and faces the beach. It is a landmark in Rio. Almost a hundred years old. You will love it, I am sure."

"How much is it a night?"

"Don't forget, you told me the best hotel," she teased.

"Yes, I remember," Thomas laughed. "But how much is it?"

"The suite is six hundred and fifty American dollars."

"Well, I can't imagine anything more expensive than that," he said with a laugh.

"Oh yes! The best suite is eight hundred and fifty American. Do you prefer that?"

"Uh, no! I think the one you chose is just fine." Thomas was smiling at the thought of spending that kind of money for one night, but still carrying the bank debit card issued to him in Wilkes-Barre, and having twenty thousand available in that account, he decided price was no object. After all, it was only "The Mans" money, and he had just given two hundred thousand of it away with another thirty thousand waiting to be sent to the widow whose husband's identity he had stolen. He wasn't feeling guilty using some of the funds to add a little comfort to their journey. After all, on the off chance he might not live through this experience, he might as well enjoy the time. Besides, he thought, they could have gone for the eight fifty per night suite, but no point in being totally decadent.

Thomas and Sofia had decided, prior to leaving Sao Paulo, that they would share a suite together in Rio. It was time for them to discuss what feelings they have for each other. They needed to make a decision together about where it would go from here. Thomas felt pretty sure that things were going to become very serious between them.

They pulled up in front of the hotel just after eight in the morning. There was a certain beauty about the place that seemed enhanced by the still-rising sun. Thomas was impressed. With their bags in the care of a bellman, they took in the view of the surrounding area, while slowly making their way to the main entrance. This was going to be a pleasant two days to spend with Sofia. They checked in at the front desk and arranged another, somewhat less lavish room, for Paola. She would certainly spend a great deal of time with them, but when it was appropriate, she would have her own room, and Sofia and he would have their much-desired privacy. She was quite content with that arrangement.

Poor Paola had been stuffed into the trunk of the limo, hustled into a hotel, rushed back out to a car, and then driven for hundreds of kilometers in the middle of the night. She had nothing but the very plain and simple clothes on her back, her photo album, and a smile. Sofia and Thomas agreed that the first order of business in Rio was for Sofia to take her to the boutique in the hotel and buy her a few outfits and some shoes. They would get her hair done, a facial, and maybe even a manicure. Then she could join them for a wonderful supper in one of the amazing restaurants the hotel offered. Paola's face lit up like a kid when Sofia told her they we're going shopping, and then out for supper. Giddily, they went off to carry out their mission as Thomas prepared to take a much-needed nap. How, he wondered, could they still have the energy to shop after an all-night road trip? Within minutes he was sound asleep on the sofa.

CHAPTER 13

GOOD MORNING, CARLO

Carlo was finally stirring to life. As he yawned and glanced at the clock on the end table, he bolted upright with a shout of disbelief.

"Holy shit! Eleven o'clock? That damn Paola knows not to let me sleep that late. Damn it."

He bounded from bed, grabbed his robe from the closet, and fastened it as he stalked out of the bedroom calling for the little maid.

"Paola? Paola, where are you? You better hide, damn you," his tirade continued as he proceeded down the stairs to the foyer, "Why the hell did you let me sleep so late? Where the hell are you?"

Carlo was rapidly turning that shade of red that came so easily to his face. He went directly to the kitchen, still looking for Paola, and now for Antonio as well.

"Paola? Antonio? Where are you?"

As he looked around the kitchen, he saw no sign that there had been any activity there. Antonio ate like a horse, and it was an accepted fact of life that he always had breakfast at Carlo's. Yet there was no sign at all that anything had been prepared for him, or Paola, or Thomas. The very moment he thought of his captive in the basement, he got a very uneasy feeling.

"Shit! Thomas," he yelled as he trotted his way to the door behind the stairway in the foyer. He made his way down the stairs and to Thomas' room, quickly punched in the security code, and threw the door open. There was no Thomas, no carry-on bag, nothing. Carlo stood staring at a room devoid of any indication that Thomas had ever been there.

"Son-of-a-bitch! You rotten bastard! How the hell did you get out of here? Paola! Had to be her," he muttered as he paced the room. "I should have killed that bitch long ago."

Carlo was certainly perplexed over the whole situation. He found himself wondering how Paola could have gotten the lock code for the door. It was in the back of his mind that she couldn't have done it alone. He was unprepared, however, to accept any thought of betrayal on Antonio's part.

Carlo slammed the door behind him as he raced down the hallway to the stairs. Once in the library, he grabbed the phone and dialed Antonio's old cell number. There was, of course, no answer. He left a voice message, demanding that Antonio call him as soon as he heard it. He slammed the phone down on its cradle and went to the bar at the other end of the room. Still cursing, he grabbed a bottle of bourbon, put it to his mouth, and took a very large gulp. He wanted to call Rico, but he never was able to teach the moron to use a cell phone. Limited intelligence was an asset in situations where Rico's services were required, but it was a serious inconvenience at times. Anyway, Rico always showed up at noon, so nothing for Carlo to do but wait for him. He sat in his favorite chair, a bottle of bourbon in hand, and pondered this very serious dilemma.

This was certainly a very bad situation for him. He needed those trucks. He needed that money. He could not afford for this whole plan to go bad. At one point, he considered calling his Brazilian mentor, "The man", but ruled it out because he would be in even more trouble for hiding this transaction from him, and therefore depriving him of his percentage. No! Better to leave him out of it. He would use Rico and his minions to find Thomas. Once he was found, he would deal with him mercilessly and he couldn't help thinking out loud:

"I wish I knew where to find that damned Angela."

Thomas had been wise enough to tell her to buy a prepaid cell phone when she returned to Canada, and then use it for the call to Carlo. It was untraceable, and fortunately for Angela, Carlo had no idea where she was.

As he took another slug from the bottle of bourbon, Carlo heard the front door open. He jumped to his feet and raced, robe fluttering behind him, to the foyer. It was Rico.

"Rico! Glad you're here. I need you to gather up a few of your boys," he slurred, now slightly drunk, "Thomas escaped, and we have to find him."

Rico, looking stunned and stupid, as usual, responded, "Escape? How do that?"

"How the hell do I know, you moron? Just get a few guys together. Fast."

"How many guys you want?"

"I'm sure two more is enough. Now move it and get back here as fast as possible. I'll give you instructions when you get here."

Rico responded with a guttural, "Yes, boss," and left.

Carlo returned to his bedroom and flopped limply on the bed.

"Damn, why did I drink so much? This isn't good."

Eventually, he forced himself to get up, take a shower, and get dressed. When Rico and his men went on their search for Thomas, Carlo would go back to the room in the basement and look for any clue to his whereabouts. Just one slip up! That's all it would take, and he could find him. Once dressed, Carlo returned to the library to wait for his thugs. It didn't take very long before the three of them came barging through the front door and into the library.

"We here boss," Rico mumbled.

"This is the name of the hotel he stayed at. The three of you go there and see what you can find out. I'm sure he's gone, but someone may have seen something. Do whatever it takes, but don't get violent. We don't need trouble. Money talks. Take this," Carlo said as he handed three hundred American dollars to Rico, "Pay for the information. And listen, make it quick, and get back here. I want to find this bastard."

"I do it. We find him. No worry."

"Yeah! No worry. Easy for you to say. Now get going."

With Rico and his partners gone, Carlo went back to Thomas' room. After a thorough search of every nook and cranny, he noticed the computer monitor was on. There, lit up on the screen, was a message.

"Not to worry, Carlo. I'll let you know where to find me. When the time is right. As for now, the containers are on their way. Be patient. You really didn't think I would risk staying there, did you? I told you. I'm not stupid. You'll get what's coming to you. No worries."

Carlo picked up the monitor and tossed it on the floor.

"Oh, Tommy, you are definitely stupid if you think I'm going to let any of you live after this. Killing you is going to be a pleasure. I'll even do it myself."

Carlo headed back upstairs to await Rico's return. Within an hour, he walked in the front door with disturbing news.

"I find out, boss."

"What? Did you find out where they went?"

"No, boss. But man on desk saw him come in last night. Antonio and Paola with him."

Carlo gasped at hearing the news he had dreaded, "Antonio? Was he sure it was Antonio? How could he know?"

"He tell me what he look like. It Antonio."

"Son-of-a-bitch. My own damn cousin," Carlo exclaimed, forgetting that he had made his own plans to do away with him when this was all finished.

"I have more boss."

"More? Tell me."

"Antonio leave alone. Thomas leave with Paola, and other woman."

"Other woman? What other woman? Angela?"

"No. Not Angela. Too young. She very beautiful, man at desk say. Looked like Brazilian woman."

"Brazilian? Who the hell did he know here?" there was frustration in Carlo's voice as he wondered who this mystery woman could be. "We have to find out who she is. Go back and find out. Now."

"No can, boss. Ask already. She sign by company name."

"Company name? What company?"

"I have man write down," Rico said as he handed a piece of paper to Carlo.

"Ultimate Security? Who the hell are they? Never mind. I'll find out myself. You get to the airport and see if they took a flight. Check all the airlines. Check the bus depot. Check car rental agencies. Check everywhere. Do you hear me? Everywhere!"

"Yes, boss."

"But first, you go to Paola's family and find her. If she's there, bring her back here."

Once Rico and his men were gone, Carlo went to his computer and did a search for Ultimate Security. All he discovered was that there had been a website for the company, but it had shut down.

"Bastard. Can't I get one damn break?"

There was nothing to do for the time being, except wait for his men to report back. Carlo was frustrated that Rico was so dense that he didn't know how to use a cell phone. Unable to contact him, he simply had to wait it out. He sat in his overstuffed leather chair, sullen and depressed, wondering if there was any hope at all of finding Thomas and getting his revenge.

Almost two hours later, Rico finally reported back. Carlo, still moping and glued to his chair, asked almost hopelessly, "Well, what did you find out?"

"Paola's family gone. No live there three years now."

"What? Shit. What else?"

"No plane. Rent car. Thomas, Paola, and other woman."

Now Carlo was feeling his spirits lift.

"They rented a car? Did you get her name this time?"

"No. Just company name again."

"Damn it. What good is any of it then?"

"They say return car in Rio."

Now Carlo's eyes lit up with delight.

"Rio? They were going to Rio? Wonderful. I'll book a flight for the four of us. We're going to scour every hotel until we find them. And no weapons, you morons! No guns, no knifes, not a thing! I don't need you getting nailed at the airport. We'll get what we need in Rio. I was going to suggest you go and pack something, but what the hell was I thinking? I'm not sure you ever change clothes," Carlo winced in disgust at the thought. "Just wait downstairs."

Carlo picked up the phone and booked four tickets to Rio on the ten-p.m. flight. It was the only one with available seats, and he could only hope it wasn't going to be too late to find Thomas. He was relishing the thought of discovering their location and surprising them in the middle of the night. At eight o'clock, they headed for the airport to check-in for their flight. The chase for vengeance was on.

As they waited to board the plane, Carlo was deep in thought. Where would they look for them? There must be a thousand hotels in Rio. It was a safe bet, at least in Carlo's mind, that they would stay low profile and because he assumed Thomas was not flush with cash, inexpensive. To him, that meant that they would opt for the more basic of accommodations, rather than one of the luxurious hotels near the beach. He would pick up a brochure with hotel listings at the airport in Rio and they would begin their painstaking search. He could only hope that Thomas was still there and would remain there long enough to locate him. There had always been a great capacity for hatred in Carlo. This time, it was more than hatred. This time it was an obsession to cause maximum pain and suffering to this man who dared create such a problem for him. No one had ever stood up to him before, and it couldn't be allowed to pass without grave consequences. The more he thought about it, the more violent were his thoughts of revenge.

Carlo's greatest dilemma was exercising self-control long enough to obtain the trucks he desperately needed. If Paola and this mystery woman were still with Thomas, they would be the key to forcing Thomas to do whatever Carlo wanted. Thomas didn't seem the type to allow the rape, torture, and murder of innocents in order to save himself. It could all be very bloody, very inhumane, and very necessary. The prospect didn't trouble Carlo in the least as they finally boarded the flight for Rio.

While Carlo and his crew were getting airborne in Sao Paulo, back in Rio, Sofia and Paola finally returned from what ended up an all-day shopping and spa spree. Paola was a different woman. What an amazing metamorphosis. Like some colorful butterfly emerging from its cocoon, Paola was, without question, beautiful. Sofia was beside herself with happiness to have given this sweet woman such a wonderful change of appearance. She could see that the years of Paola's servitude and despair had washed away with the results of this makeover. Paola could simply not stop giggling. Thomas totally loved it. He knew in his heart that she deserved every ounce of happiness she could experience.

It was now eight in the evening, and they began deciding where to eat. There were some wonderful choices in that amazing hotel. They could choose the Hotel Cipriani Restaurant, which specialized in Italian dishes and was frequented by Rio's jet set, or perhaps the Copacabana Palace or the Copacabana piano bar. With his taste running to Italian, Thomas managed to win the debate without much convincing. To see Paola's excitement at the prospect of dining in such a classy restaurant was worth whatever the price might be. They decided to rest up for a few hours and go for supper at just after ten.

Thomas had grown accustomed to the fact that Brazilians tend to dine late in the evening, so it wasn't unusual that they would eat at that hour. Right now, a few hours of rest for the women would be more important. They were very tired, and a nap wouldn't hurt either of them at this point. Paola retired to her room, and Sofia and Thomas lie in each other's arms, falling sound asleep in a matter of minutes.

When he awoke, Thomas finally took in the beauty of the suite. It was decorated with Brazilian mahogany, inlaid with Brazilian agates. The whole décor was luxurious, yet not overdone. The suite featured a large bedroom, separate living area, dining area, and desk. There was a wonderful view of the ocean and the beach. He couldn't have asked for a better choice. The bathroom was a wonderful display of classic fixtures, dressed in Brazilian marble and a very welcoming-looking shower.

As they were dressing for supper it was beginning to creep into Thomas' mind that Carlo should be well on his way to trying to find them by now. He never expected that he would just sit and wait it out.

"Sofia?"

"Yes, Thomas?"

"I'm a little worried that Carlo may identify you from the hotel register. That would be a problem."

"No, my love. I used a company name."

"Yes, but he can trace you through the company. The address, a website?"

Sofia walked up to Thomas, wrapped her arms around him, and gazed into his eyes. "Dear, sweet, Thomas. You are talking with a woman who knows what she is doing."

"The company name I used was for a temporary corporation that closed two years ago. The website is shut down, and the company address is no good. No way to trace me from that."

"Oh, baby. You do have skills," Thomas chuckled, "But then I always knew that. You're smarter than I am. That's for sure."

"Well, maybe just a little," Sofia giggled as she kissed him again, "But I can live with it if you can."

"No problem! I need a smart woman to keep me from making all those mistakes I seem to be so adept at. Interested in the responsibility?"

"It will be my pleasure to keep you out of trouble," she purred, as she rested her head on his shoulder.

"Then I'm a very lucky man. Especially if those kisses keep coming. But listen, we need to assume that Carlo has found out about the rental car by now. He probably even knows that we would be returning it in Rio. So, I have to believe he'll be on his way here soon if he's not already. Caution is the watchword from now on."

"I know. We must be very careful."

"I think that soon it will be time to send Carlo on a wild goose chase. Might as well preempt his actions and muddy up whatever plan he has in his angry little mind."

"What will you do?"

"I'm going to call him," Thomas said with a laugh.

"Now?"

"Right now," Thomas said as he took out his phone and dialed Carlo's cell number. He answered almost immediately.

"Carlo, my old buddy. How are you?"

"Tommy! How nice to hear from you. It reminds me of how much I hate you, and how enjoyable it's going to be taking my revenge."

"Now, Carlo, business first. Are those jet engines I hear humming in the background? I do believe you're in the air, and on your way to, oh, let me guess, Rio?"

There was a hesitation at Carlo's end before he answered, "Yes. Rio. That's where you're returning your rental car isn't it? Carlo chuckled sarcastically while wondering if he was on a fool's errand to the wrong place.

"The car part is right. Although I'm not sure why you think I went to Rio with it. But that works fine for me."

"So, then it was Paola and the woman you left the hotel with?"

Even though Thomas was well aware that Carlo would know about Sofia at this point, he was still struck with a sense of dread over the prospect.

"Paola is long gone, Carlo. Forget about her. As for the other woman, she was just someone who kindly offered a little assistance, and then went on her way."

"Somehow, I don't believe you, Tommy. From what I hear she was very beautiful, and the two of you looked to be very enamored with each other. No! She's still with you, or at least in contact with you. That I'm sure of."

"Suit yourself. Far be it for me to convince you of the truth."

"And Antonio? Is he with you?"

"Antonio is long gone, too. Out of Brazil by now for sure."

"How did you turn him on me? Just curious."

"I didn't. You did."

"What do you mean, I did?"

"Nobody likes being a slave to a self-centered jackass who treats him like dirt.

Besides, you were planning on taking care of him when this business was finished anyway,"

Thomas realized the minute those words left his mouth that he had said too much.

"Now where would you get that idea? I've never expressed that desire to anyone."

Thomas groped for an answer, "All I can tell you is that somehow Antonio knew. So, it was you who turned him, not me. You've been the maker of your own dilemma."

"Well, we can discuss it when I get to Rio, Thomas."

"That might be hard to do. I won't be in Rio. But we'll get together soon. Promise. As soon as you get back to Sao Paulo."

Right then, Thomas hung up, and Carlo was left to wonder if he was on a wasted trip. Could it be possible that Thomas was still in Sao Paulo? It might make sense. A diversionary tactic! It might have only been this mystery woman making her departure by car, and not Thomas at all. This was a serious problem.

Thomas picked up his cell again and called the hotel in Sao Paulo. He had left the girl at the front desk, Marta, a rather large tip of two hundred American dollars when he departed. He suggested that he might need a favor from her in the near future. Now was the time. He was happy to hear that she was on duty and gave her the instructions he had in mind. Then, it was time to call Carlo again.

"Is that you again, Tommy? You're disturbing my rest."

"Yes. Me again. I forgot to tell you, when you get back to Sao Paulo, call me at the hotel. Same place as usual. Kind of like it there."

Thomas hung up the phone and cFedired his fingers that Carlo would fall for his little trick. The minute the line went dead, Carlo got the hotel's number from information and dialed it. Marta answered with her usual cheerful voice, and Carlo got right to the point.

"Can you tell me if there is a Thomas DeAngelo registered there?"

"Yes. Mister DeAngelo check in a few hours ago."

"Connect me with his room please."

"I am sorry, but Mister DeAngelo just left the lobby for outside. He said would be back very late tonight. Maybe not until after midnight."

"Where did he go?"

"I do not know. He did not say. Such a nice man! We like him very much here. Would you leave a message for him?"

"No. That's fine."

Carlo was not in a very good mood when he hung up.

"Son-of-a-bitch!" he said out loud. He turned to Rico, who was sitting acFedir the aisle. "We have to go right back to Sao Paulo. The bastard is still there. It must have been part of his plan to have me leave town. What the hell does he have up his sleeve?"

Carlo was beginning to develop an appreciation for Thomas' creativity. He was also developing an even greater animosity towards him. The rest of this flight would be nothing short of frustration. He called the airport in Rio and booked a return flight on the very same plane. They would be on the ground for less than two hours, and then on their way back to Sao Paulo. The chase was about to take an unexpected u-turn.

CHAPTER 14

THE QUEENS CONNECTION

When it came to Pauly Sabatini, there was one cardinal rule. You didn't bother him at supper hour without a life-or-death reason. When he married his wife, Marie, thirty years ago, it was her cooking that sealed the deal. Pauly was proof that the adage about the way to a man's heart being through his stomach was sometimes true.

His endless passion for her lasagna, manicotti, veal parmesan, homemade meatballs, and any number of other Italian favorites, had added over a hundred pounds to his five-foot nine-inch frame over the years. Food was Pauly's one true passion.

When the doorbell rang, as Pauly stuffed his mouth with one more of those wonderful meatballs, Marie knew what was coming. After a quick swallow, he looked acFedir the table at her, "Go tell whoever that is that this better be damned important. If it ain't, they better run."

"Oh, Pauly, missing out on a few minutes of stuffing your face isn't gonna kill ya," Marie said as she got up from the table. She was certainly the only person in the world who could get away with talking to him like that. No one else would even dare think of it. As the head of the Sabatini crime family, he was notorious for his brutality.

"Pauly, it's Gino. He says it couldn't wait. He says he would have been more afraid of not coming here right away. He's in the den." Marie said as she sat down at the table.

Pauly pushed his chair back and struggled, breathing heavily, to get to his feet.

"Better be damned important."

He walked to the foyer, and into the library where he found Gino, looking nervous, and standing in the middle of the room.

"Hope you got a good excuse for this, Gino. You know the rule."

"Boss, this you want to see, now. It's a letter we got today."

"What? What is it? Who's it from?"

"You better just read it, boss," he said, as he handed him an envelope. Pauly opened it and began to read.

"Mr. Sabatini."

"You don't know me, but I'm the guy who can give you something you've been wanting for ten years. I believe you're missing a large quantity of money and the man who took it. If you wish to discuss this further, call me at the number at the bottom of the page. Have a nice day."

Thomas had mailed the letter from Toronto before he left. The only address he had was for a Pizza shop that was mentioned in Carlo's computer files as belonging to Pauly. He had hoped the letter would arrive at the appropriate time to involve the Sabatini crew in his plan. The number he had indicated to call was for a prepaid, throw-away, untraceable cell phone.

"Where did this come from?" Pauly demanded.

"It's postmarked Toronto, boss."

"So, the son-of-a-bitch is in Canada?"

"I don't think so. The phone is an overseas number.

I looked up the country code. It's Brazil."

"Brazil? That's interesting! But who the hell is this guy?"

"Got no idea. Maybe you should just call him."

"Yeah, guess I should," Pauly said, as he sat behind a massive oak desk and dialed the number. Thomas, knowing it could only be one person calling, picked up his phone and answered.

"Mister Sabatini, I assume?"

"Yeah. That would be me. Now, who the hell are you?"

"Doesn't matter. What matters is what I can give you."

Thomas had learned from Sofia's painstaking search of Carlo's computer files that his real surname was DiPietro.

"I'm assuming you would like to know where you can find Mr. DiPietro. No? And don't let the postmark fool you. He's not in Canada."

"I already figured that out, wise-guy. This is a Brazilian phone number. So, what do I need you for? I know he's in Brazil. I'll find him myself."

"Yeah, maybe you're right. Brazil is such a small country. Just takes up half of South America. Oh, and of course you speak Portuguese. Should be a snap. You think?"

Pauly was getting a little agitated but knew he likely had no real chance of finding Carlo on his own. Especially after ten years of trying and failing.

"Yeah, I guess you got a point. I'll set up a meet between you and me in Queens. Just the two of us. There'll be something in it for you if your information is good."

Thomas couldn't help but laugh, "Are you kidding me? Do you think I would walk into Queens and let you grab me? I'm not stupid, Pauly. I don't plan on being tortured for the information, and I sure don't plan on letting you kill me when you get what you want."

"Not a very trusting guy, are ya?"

"Not in the least. I know who I'm dealing with."

"Do ya now? So, what do you suggest? And what are you lookin for? What's your price for this?"

"We can get to what I suggest later. As for price, I'm not interested in your money. This is vengeance. I owe Carlo this. All I ask of you is that no one bothers me, or mine, when it's over."

"No money? Free is always good. Vengeance? Seems we both want that. So now what happens?"

"I'll contact you with further information when the time is right. What you need to do right now is arrange visas to visit Brazil for four or five of your men. Better send some with no serious criminal records. Might make the visas a problem if you don't"

"Where in Brazil? Might help to know that."

"For visa purposes, you might as well say they're going to Rio on vacation. It's a common tourist spot. It's not their ultimate destination, but that comes later."

"Fine. When should they be ready to leave?"

"A matter of days. Can't be exact yet. Just get the visas. And no weapons. You don't want them getting busted before they even get here. It's no problem getting what they need where they're going."

"You need to know that if this is some sort of trick, I'll personally cut your heart out. That's a promise."

"It's no trick, Pauly. It's just your fondest dream come true. Now give me a number to reach you."

He gave Thomas his cell number, and the conversation was over. Pauly then hung up the phone and sat quietly behind his desk. It was Gino who spoke first.

"What have you got in mind boss? You think this is for real?"

"How the hell do I know if it's for real? What I do know is that I can't ignore the possibility. I want you to pick a crew of three more guys. No criminal records. We're going to Rio. I'll put a fast hustle on the visas"

"Rio? Wow! Now that's somewhere I've always wanted to go. The women there are totally hot."

"Hey, this ain't a vacation. You better keep your mind on business there. You understand me?"

"Yeah, Pauly. Sure. No problem. When do we go?"

I dunno. Have to wait for another call. Get your crew together and we'll get the travel visas done so we'll be ready when it comes."

"Right. I'll get right on it." and Gino started to leave.

"Gino! If we find Carlo? We make sure to do this guy too. He seems to know more than I like. No loose ends. You understand?"

"Yeah. No problem. Do them both."

"And anybody that's with them. Nobody who knows about stays alive. We make damn sure of it."

"Right, boss. No sweat."

Pauly, it seemed, was already thinking about possible means of disposal.

"I hear they got these little fish down there that can eat people. Big, razor-sharp teeth on these little fish."

"Yeah, piranhas, Pauly. Really vicious little bastards."

"Yeah, that's them. We'll feed them to the piranhas."

"I don't think they got those in Rio, boss." "Sharks

then. They got those don't they?"

"Yeah. I'm sure they do."

"Good. Now get outta here and let me finish my supper."

With Gino gone, Pauly returned to the dining room table. Marie always asked, even though she knew he wouldn't tell her anything.

"So? What was so important?"

"Nothin. Just business. Bring me some more of those amazing meatballs. I love your meatballs, Marie."

When Thomas answered the call from Pauly Sabatini, Sofia was in front of the large bathroom mirror, applying what little makeup she actually used. She had listened as best she could and had the urge to ask Thomas about it.

"You got a call from that Sabatini man Carlo stole from?"

"Yes. He's a critical part of the plan."

"I am afraid you involve too many bad people in this, Thomas. Now they will want to find you too."

"I'm sure they will. What's important is to have them find Carlo. I still have a few other tricks up my sleeve."

"I'm not sure I want to know. But maybe you should tell me anyway."

"I need you to dig into those files of Carlo's and see if you can find anything that can identify this guy, he refers to only as 'The Man'. He could be a critical issue in this. I need to know something about him. Anything. He's the only uncertain entity in this whole plan. I don't feel comfortable not knowing his connections."

"I will see what I can do. I will work on it later tonight."

"Thanks. I could never get through this without you. You know that?"

Right at that moment, there was a knock at the door.

It was Paola, dressed very beautifully in a knee-length knit dress that clung quite nicely to every curve. This woman had a figure that Thomas never would have guessed she possessed. It had been well hidden underneath the cheap, and loose-fitting maids clothing she wore working for Carlo. Her hair, dark brown and shoulder-length, was quite stunning. He had only previously seen it tied in a bun at the back of her head. Her face, a very sculptured and pretty one, was softly and subtly enhanced by a good balance of eyeliner and very pale lipstick that highlighted her full lips. It was difficult to believe that this was the same woman. Thomas actually did a double take when he first saw her.

"Paola? You look absolutely beautiful. You have been hiding your beauty from the world," he said, as she blushed and smiled in embarrassment.

Sofia had the slightest hint of a tear in her eye as she looked at the change in this woman that she had become friends with. It made her very happy to have contributed to Paola's discovery of her own beauty.

"You make me shy," Paola said with a slight giggle. "I am not so beautiful. But thank you."

"I think I must be careful that Thomas does not become too attracted to you," Sofia smiled, and glanced at him with a sly wink.

Thomas had just given this woman a new life, a fortune in money, and tender affection. It wouldn't be beyond the realm of possibility that she might build romantic notions around those things. That wouldn't be a good idea for her. It was certainly best that they would have her back with her family in another few days. Let her start her new life and, no doubt, someone will recognize the sweetness and beauty of this woman and she will find her true partner.

Thomas' eyes had been constantly on Sofia since she entered the room. Her hair glistened as it fell in gentle curls below her bare shoulders. Her deep brown eyes, always so soulful looking, were softly highlighted and, as always, held him in an almost hypnotic state. She was wearing a strapless, off-white dress that molded to the shape of her wondrous body from her shoulders to just about an inch above her knees. She wore a simple gold necklace and matching earrings that, along with the dress, made a wonderful contrast with her tanned body. She was amazing. To Thomas, she had become that much and more. It wouldn't matter whether she was dressed like this, or wearing jeans, or walking around in a towel with her hair wrapped on top of her head. To Thomas, in every moment, she was the most beautiful woman in the world. He could never take his eyes from her without feeling the need to look at her again. The feelings he had been resisting were now impossible to ignore.

As they made their way to the Cipriani Restaurant, they could feel the eyes of everyone upon them. These two beautiful women certainly drew a lot of attention and, no doubt, some envious looks. Thomas was sure his chest might have puffed up a bit at the idea of being seen with two such attractive ladies, one on each arm. Throughout their meal, they were always aware that everyone in the room was taking the occasional opportunity to look their way. They didn't mind. To them, it was fun to see the looks of envy on the faces of the men. As for the women, they gave a very different look. If they weren't glaring at their partners as if to disapprove of their glances, they were often looking at the three of them as if they found the whole thing annoying.

The happy trio remained in the restaurant until after midnight. Once they had been well fed, and with a few drinks in them, they made their way back to the suite. The three of them sat on the large sofa, Paola on one side of Thomas, and Sofia on the other. They had opened the bar fridge and had another few drinks as they sat quietly watching "Something about Mary" on television, in English. Once the movie was over, Sofia politely suggested that they were tired and wanted to go to sleep. Paola looked at Thomas as she said something in Portuguese to Sofia. They both laughed, the way one does when there is something of a certain nature in the comments, and then looked at Thomas and smiled. Paola got up, thanked them for such a nice evening, gave them each a hug and a kiss, and bid them goodnight. Tonight would be a night for Thomas and Sofia to further explore their passion for each other. Once they were alone, he had to ask.

"Ok! What did she say that was so funny?"

"Hmmmm, well she knows it is not sleep that I wish."

"Ah, I see," he said, as he nodded in agreement. "I suppose she's right."

"Yes. She is."

"I never want to be without you."

"Sure? Very sure, Thomas?"

"Very sure, Sofia. I couldn't even imagine it!"

"Mmmmm, that is what I truly wish to hear. Always. Make it be so forever."

"Forever is a long time, but I honestly feel that if anyone can make it be true, we can." Thomas replied and held her in his arms as he placed a kiss upon her forehead.

He had thought many times of making this journey, starting with her forehead, then her eyes, nose, cheeks, chin, lips and onward down her entire body. He especially enjoyed the idea of starting to undress her as he went. This would be a night of great passion between two people who had fallen so very much in love. Over the course of the next few hours, they never left the living room of the suite. They managed to make use of the sofa, the chair, the floor, the coffee table, the wall, and even the picture window. It seemed they were determined to leave no place in the room unused. They never did make it to the bedroom, eventually falling asleep in each other's arms on the sofa. The last thought on Thomas' mind, before sleep overcame him, was how much he loved this woman. The thought that had occurred to him prior to that one, was that he should start taking vitamins. Soo

CHAPTER 15

PAOLA'S STORY

Thomas and Sofia didn't stir from the sofa until almost ten a.m. When they awoke, they took a shower and dressed in the amazingly soft cotton bathrobes provided by the hotel. They ordered breakfast from room service and sat together on the sofa. Sofia snuggled up against him and began a conversation about Paola.

"Thomas? Do you know about Paola's life?"

"No, sweetheart, I don't."

"She told me everything while we were driving here. It is very sad. I can't believe what she has been through."

"Well, now I understand why there was so much Portuguese chatter during the trip, he said with a chuckle. "I'm pretty sure she didn't have a very good life working for Carlo."

"It is much more than Carlo. You know how she came to work for him?"

"I have no idea."

"Let me start from the beginning, ok?"

"Sure! Go ahead."

"Paola was, like me, born very poor. Unlike me, she came from a very large family. Her parents had six children, including her. They were fortunate, in a way, because they never suffered the indignity of living in the favelas. Still, they were not much better off. The entire family lived in three rooms in an old apartment building in one of the poorer sections of Sao Paulo. The older children, four of them, all slept on the floor in one room. The younger ones slept on the floor in their parent's room. The third room was nothing more than a small living area with a tiny refrigerator and a hot plate."

"That's a pretty crowded situation. Still, better than the favelas."

"Yes, that is true. But still difficult! Food was scarce and the family lived mostly on rice and, maybe every few weeks some meat, potatoes and fresh vegetables. Most of the food came from one of the food banks in Sao Paulo. Most of their money went to pay rent and electricity."

"Did any of the children work? Or go to school?"

"Yes, they had some schooling, but not much. When most of the children were old enough to do some form of work, they managed to afford a slightly larger apartment. It still included only two bedrooms but had a living room and a separate kitchen. Some of the children would then sleep in the living room."

"So how did Paola come to meet Carlo?"

"It was when she was thirty years old. She worked as a very low paid clerk in a shoe store. She had never been married or even had a close boyfriend. She had led a very sheltered life and devoted herself to helping support her family. It was there that Carlo discovered her. He seemed, at first, to be attracted to her in a romantic way. One day he asked her if she would like to go out for dinner. She accepted. It turned out to be the day in her life that she regrets most. After dinner, Carlo convinced her to come and see his home. Once they were there, he became an animal. Paola, frightened for her life, cried as she was sodomized, raped and forced to engage in every form of degrading sex that Carlo could imagine. When he had finished, she lay in a cowering fetal position on the floor. She was forever traumatized. She was also in fear for her life."

"Oh my God! That poor woman! But then why was she working for him?"

"Carlo gave her a choice. She would be silent about what had happened and remain in the house as his maid and sexual plaything, or she would die along with all of her family. If she ever tried to leave, he would hunt down and kill them all. Paola's fear for her family forced her to submit herself to almost ten years of servitude."

"What a rotten son-of-a-bitch. As if I needed another reason to hate him! She's been abused all that time?"

"No! After about three years, mercifully, Carlo lost interest in sexually abusing her. It was then that she became nothing more than the housemaid. She told me that, despite Carlo's verbal abuse, the past seven years were easy, compared to before. He actually paid her a small amount every month. Fifty dollars American! Throughout her time there, Carlo had allowed her to make weekly visits to her family, but she was always supervised by Antonio. Better to avoid any suspicion. Of course, Carlo always had the threat of death over them all should Paola make the mistake of talking. For the past seven years she gave every penny of her pay to her parents, which they saved faithfully in hopes of leaving Sao Paulo.

Paola insisted that they should do so and use the money to move to Brasilia where they might have a better life. She had assured them that she would join them one day, although she felt in her heart she never would.

"So that's why her family is in Brasilia! But how would Carlo not know?"

"Antonio! When Paola's family moved to Brasilia three years ago, Antonio helped her to keep it a secret. They still made the supposed weekly visit with her family in order to keep Carlo unaware that he had lost his leverage over her. She still feared for her life, and so never made the attempt to leave. Antonio would take her, once a week, and they would go for a drive, have lunch, and then return to Carlo's. From what Paola told me, she had developed a bit of a crush on Antonio. He had no idea. He had been truly kind to her. He could do nothing about the early years of sexual abuse at Carlo's hands. He had apologized to her many times for not being able to help her during that time."

"I knew the big guy had a heart. I still wish he had stopped it somehow. I wish he had killed the bastard."

"Paola forgave him for that. She knew there was nothing he could do and was very grateful for his kindness. Her biggest fear was of perhaps being given over to Rico. She knew what he did with young girls from the favelas. She lived every day in fear that Carlo would hand her over to him. Thankfully, Rico showed no interest in her, and Carlo never appeared to consider it."

The conversation was interrupted by the arrival of room service with their breakfast. Thomas had heard enough anyway, and now had even more compassion and affection for Paola as well as more hatred for Carlo.

"You know, Sofia, it's hard to explain the feeling of knowing you've helped someone to escape such a horrid life. It feels good! Almost a cleansing of the spirit."

"I know, my Thomas. We have done a very good thing."

About midway through their breakfast, Paola arrived and joined them at the table. She was all smiles and asked a few questions of Sofia in Portuguese. Thomas had a fairly good idea of what they might concern. The schoolgirl laughter was hard to disguise. The conversation between them hadn't latest long enough for Sofia to have given many details, but Paola no doubt knew that they had enjoyed a wonderful night.

After breakfast they decided to get dressed and go for a walk down by the beach. It was a beautiful sunny day, and they had no desire to remain cooped up in a hotel suite. The three of them walked leisurely along the sand as they listened to the waves crashing against the shore.

There were several people enjoying the sun and water, even at this early hour. Exotic-looking women in extreWalty small bikinis were everywhere. It seemed that these people showed no concern for the hazards of too much sun. They were all so tanned as to make Thomas think they never spent a minute of the day in the shade. No matter, this was a lively and carefree people. No time to worry about such things as skin cancer.

As they continued their walk, Paola talked almost non-stop with Sofia. Thomas could tell it was a very intense conversation and his curiosity was killing him. He would wait until he and Sofia were alone and she would be able to tell him what else she may have learned about Paola. Gradually they found themselves back at the hotel, sitting by the pool with a nice afternoon drink.

Paola kept dipping her toes in the pool and finally she and Sofia decided to take a swim. They went to the boutique, bought two bikinis and went upstairs to change. It was Thomas' pleasure to sit and enjoy watching the two of them laugh and frolic in the pool. They were like two schoolgirls having an afternoon out. It was very nice to see them both so happy and smiling. By tomorrow they would be on their way to Brasilia after which he and Sofia would continue on to Manaus. Thomas had a feeling that they would never lose touch with Paola. She had become family in the truest sense of the word. There was no doubt they both loved her, not only as a friend but as they would a sister. It was a very nice feeling. They were to catch a flight in the morning and, after a brief discussion, decided to all share a quiet dinner together in the suite before they retired for the night.

It would, in all likelihood, be the last night the three of them would be together until, perhaps, they could connect again when all of this business was finally finished. It seemed very important to be alone with each other and enjoy their last hours together in privacy. Paola went to her room to change, and Sofia and Thomas went back to the suite. As he watched Sofia drop her robe and remove her bathing suit, it was difficult for him to concentrate on what she was telling him about Paola. Suddenly, when he heard the word baby, he was jolted back to attention.

"Baby? Baby? What baby?"

"Were you not listening, Thomas?"

"It's a little hard to concentrate when I'm watching you undress, my love. What can I say!" he said with a shrug of his shoulders, "Now what about a baby?"

"Paola had a baby three years ago. Carlo made her send it to an orphanage."

"My God! Poor Paola. But, Carlo's baby? She might be better off with it out of her life. I hate to say that, but…"

Sofia cut him off before he could finish.

"It was not Carlo's baby."

"Not his? Whose then?"

"Antonio. But he does not know it is his. They had one occasion of sex and she got pregnant. He thinks it is Carlo's, but Carlo had not touched her for almost two years."

"Good Lord. I can't believe this. I wonder what Antonio would do if he knew? Surely Carlo must have wondered whose it was?"

"He knew it was Antonio's. He threatened Paola if she ever told him. I want to find her baby for her, Thomas. It is her son. I am sure she would like to be with him. We must find him."

"How can we do that? Where would we start?"

"I do not know. We must think of something. We must."

"Well, I have no ideas, so I hope you can come up with something worthwhile. It may be hopeless."

Thomas truly didn't have any ideas at all. He wondered how they could possibly find this child. Where would they even look? This would be a problem that, at first, he had his doubts they would ever solve. Then he remembered that Antonio had bought a new cell phone and had given him the number. Antonio had gotten rid of the old phone. He didn't want to worry that he might answer it one day and it would be Carlo. Thomas decided to call him and see if he could remember where the baby had been taken. Antonio answered the phone with a somewhat hesitant tone in his voice.

"Hello? Who is it?"

"Antonio, it's me, Thomas. How are you?"

"Oh, Thomas, you're ok! Good. I'm fine. Here in Napoli."

"I'm so glad you made it. Is it everything you hoped for?"

"Yeah, sorta. It's kinda big, and very dirty here, but at least it's Italy. I might try to find a small town somewhere to live. I think I'm gonna like that better."

"Well, you can live wherever you like now."

"Yeah, it's great. So, are you outta Brazil yet?"

"No. Still a bit more to do before I can leave. Right now, I need your help."

"Yeah? What do ya need? Anything you want."

"I just discovered that Paola had a baby. I would like to reunite them. Do you remember where he was taken?"

There was a long pause on the other end before he answered.

"Yeah. She did. A son. It sucked that Carlo made me take it away from her. I dropped it off at a church near Paulista Ave. I don't remember the name. Catholic church. I figured the Nuns would know what to do with him."

"I wish you could remember the name. There must be a lot of Catholic churches there."

"Not much around Paulista Ave. Maybe someone can find it. I wish I could help more. I'm sorry, Tommy. How is Paola? She's a good woman. I hope she's ok." There was a real tenderness in his voice as he asked about her.

"Paola is fine. She's very happy to be going home. And don't be sorry. You've been a big help. It's a place to start anyway. Thanks, Antonio. I'll call you when everything is finished here. You take care of yourself, and Rosina."

Once again there was a hesitation at the other end before Antonio answered.

"Yeah," he said with a somewhat downcast voice. "I'll do that. You and Sofia get out of Brazil as soon as you can. OK? Make sure."

"Doing the best that I can, my friend. Should be out soon. You take care."

They said their goodbyes and the conversation was finished. Thomas told Sofia what Antonio had said about the church. She began to rub her chin, obviously pondering this riddle.

"Let me call someone, Thomas. Maybe I can find this church."

"Of course! Call anyone. I hope you can find something. This would be a great gift for Paola."

Sofia went into the bedroom and, after about twenty minutes on the phone, she returned. There was a smile on her face, and excitement in her voice.

"I have a friend in Sao Paulo. She works with orphans. She thinks she knows the church. She will go there tonight and see what she can find out."

"Great! I hope she finds something helpful to us."

"Yes, me too. Now let's take a shower," she reached out and took Thomas' hand to lead him towards the bathroom.

Needless to say, he followed along cheerfully. When they were satisfied that their passion was sated, they dressed for dinner. Paola would arrive soon, and they didn't want to be caught undressed. Tomorrow they would leave, as scheduled, for Manaus. They sat on the sofa and Thomas called room service and ordered three surf and turf dinners, which would be delivered within a half hour. He had no sooner hung up the phone than Paola knocked at the door. Shortly thereafter, they were all seated around the table enjoying a wonderful meal and making small talk. Paola was constantly offering her appreciation for their efforts to get her to her family in Brasilia. Her gratitude seemed never-ending. Though they assured her it was their pleasure, and she didn't have to thank them anymore, she would say 'Obrigado' again.

She was still overwhelmed by the gift of so much money. With it, she would take care of her parents, and brothers and sisters. Thomas supposed he might do the same in her position.

About halfway through dinner, Sofia's cell phone rang. She went to the bedroom to take the call and was gone about fifteen minutes. When she returned, she had a big smile on her face. She was becoming good at coded messages.

"Thomas, my friend is amazing. She has found the package already," she said with a smile of happiness and surprise spreading acFedir her face.

"You're kidding? Really? So fast?"

"Yes. I am amazed. But she is sure it is the right one."

Sofia and Thomas smiled at each other knowingly and went back to enjoying their meal. Before they took on the significant responsibility of returning this child, Thomas would have Sofia do a little more delicate prying on Paola to be sure it is what she would want. He was certain it would be, but better to be sure. After dinner, he went to the bedroom and a few minutes later called Sofia to come in.

They decided that he would go down to the lobby on the pretense of needing cigarettes, at which time Sofia would engage Paola in conversation about her son. She would not give away any secrets; only find out more about Paola's feelings and how her family might have reacted to her having a child. Her family would certainly be an issue, and their acceptance would be important to her. Thomas was confident that Sofia would be very tactful, and they would know the answer without giving anything away.

Once down in the main lobby, Thomas decided to sit and have a drink and a smoke as he waited a reasonable amount of time for Sofia to speak with Paola. He found himself wondering how Antonio would react if he knew. Somehow, he had the feeling there had been some emotion in the big guy for her. Here, in Brazil, he had a son he was not aware of, and a woman who, Thomas had the feeling, truly cared for him. None of it mattered much, he supposed, with he and Rosina off in Italy.

Their brief conversation did seem a bit odd, however. He didn't seem to have the same infatuation with Naples and, when Thomas mentioned Rosina, he wasn't his usual gushing self every time the subject of her came up. Perhaps, he thought, he was reading something that wasn't there. No doubt all was fine, and Antonio was just nervous at the possibility Carlo might find him. Thomas passed about an hour at the bar running more thoughts through his mind before heading back upstairs. When he entered the suite, Sofia was alone and had obviously been crying. It was apparent that their conversation had been very emotional.

"Sofia? Is everything ok? Where's Paola?"

"She has gone to her room. Oh, my Thomas, she wants her baby so much. She longs for her son. She is tormented over it," she said as she nestled in his arms.

"Well! Then I guess we know what we have to do."

"Yes. We must get her baby to her. And do you know something?"

"What, honey?"

"She was in love with Antonio. Can you believe it? She said he was always so good to her. The time they made love was one of those days he pretended to take her to see her family. They went for a picnic. She spoke so romantically about it. Poor woman. What will we do?"

"Gee, sweetheart. The baby I think we can take care of. Antonio, that's another story. He's in Naples with Rosina. I don't think it's such a good idea to complicate things for him."

"Yes. You are right. It is so sad. Poor Paola."

"I feel bad for her too. She deserves so much right now. Let's just be happy with getting her son back to her. Ok?"

"Yes. It is all we can do. But Thomas, I must tell you something."

"You have that look on your face. What are you up to?"

"My friend Johanna already has the baby," she said, as she looked into Thomas' eyes, almost afraid of his reaction.

"She has?" he blurted out.

"Yes. You are not angry that I told her to get the baby?"

"Oh, Sofia. No! Never! I think it's wonderful. It saves us a lot of trouble. It's better we didn't have to go back to get him."

"Yes. Thomas?" she said with a look in her eye that implied that the other shoe was about to drop.

"What? Why are you looking at me like that?"

"I must go back to get the baby," there was an instant tensing of her body as she said those words. It was obvious that she knew he wouldn't like the idea.

"You? Why? We're flying to Brasilia tomorrow. Can she not bring him there? You can't go back to Sao Paulo. It would be too risky."

"She cannot leave Sao Paulo now. I must go. I will only meet her at the airport and be back on a plane in only a few hours. It will be fine. Promise."

"Why do I get the feeling that I would be wasting my time arguing with you? Fine. Then I will go with you."

"No. You will not go. Carlo may still have people looking for you at the airport. You cannot take the chance. Then we would both be in real danger. You must stay in Brasilia and wait for me."

Thomas saw no point in debating it. She was right about the possibility of him being seen at the airport. He hated the idea of her going alone, but it was the only way.

Sofia phoned to book a flight back to Sao Paulo for the morning. She would also book a same-day return to Rio and a connection to Brasilia. She then phoned Johanna to make arrangements to meet her at the airport. She and Thomas would concoct a story to tell Paola, probably about the missing package, and she and Thomas would continue on to Brasilia. He would get a room there and Paola would be back with her family. Then the wait for Sofia would begin. They still had elements of the final phase of his plan to work out and he needed her to help him with it. He would be in limbo in that respect, not to mention worried sick about Sofia, and more than lonely without her. He went to sleep with a very uneasy feeling in his stomach.

CHAPTER 16

THE NOT SO LITTLE BUNDLE OF JOY

Thomas and Sofia were up and ready to leave for the airport when Paola knocked at the door. Sofia explained that she would return to Sao Paulo for the package she had lost. Paola would go on to Brasilia with Thomas, where he would await Sofia's return. Paola had no problem accepting that story and expressed happiness that Thomas would be in Brasilia for at least an extra day. It was her fondest wish for her family to meet him and Sofia. She was like an overexcited child at the prospect of seeing her parents and siblings for the first time in three years.

They checked out of the hotel and grabbed a shuttle to the airport. Sofia's plane was departing after theirs, so Paola and Thomas said their goodbyes to her and boarded the flight to Brasilia. It would be only a two-hour flight and during that time they spoke a little about how surprised her family would be to see her. They had no idea she was coming. Two of her brothers and one of her sisters were married now and had children. She had never seen any of her nieces or nephews and was so looking forward to it. She had no idea Thomas knew about her son, and he didn't bring up the subject. Over the course of the next few hours, he tried but failed, to remember all that she told him about her family. By the time they reached Brasilia, he couldn't even remember one of the dozen or so names she had mentioned.

This wasn't an unusual problem for Thomas. He had never been much good with names to begin with. When you add to that little memory problem the fact that Brazilians talk a mile a minute, Thomas was lost during most of the conversation. What he did remember was that Paola asked at least five times if he would come with her to meet her family. It seemed that she feared he would just dump her at the airport and that would be the end of it. Of course, Thomas assured her that he would be very happy to meet them and, in fact, looked forward to it.

When the plane landed, Paola was like some restless cat as she waited to disembark. Thomas knew that feeling of being so near to something he wanted so badly and yet not able to get to it quickly enough. For her, he was sure, minutes seemed like hours as she alternately fidgeted, got teary-eyed, and giggled. It was as if her body wasn't sure which emotion it should display, so it covered them all. Once off the plane, it was all Thomas could do to keep pace with her as she raced to the terminal exit. He was actually finding it quite amusing and enjoyable to see her so wound up with youthful exuberance.

When they exited the terminal, he hailed a taxi. Paola pulled out a piece of paper with the address of her parents on it and advised the driver where they needed to go. She never spoke a word during what was a thirty-minute drive. She just sat there with tears running down her cheeks. Thomas began to realize that he was in for a very emotional reunion. He had actually begun to feel that he might even be in the way. Yet it seemed so important to Paola for him to be there that refusal was not an option. He would just try to stay on the sidelines and let them enjoy the moment. Finally, after what seemed like an eternity, the taxi pulled up in front of a ten-story apartment building.

"Thomas, this is the home of my parents and my young brother and sister. The married ones live in another place."

They left the taxi and entered the lobby. After climbing two flights of stairs, they stood in front of the door to her parent's apartment. Thomas waited for her to knock, but she just stood there sobbing and shaking from nervousness. After a few moments, he reached out and knocked on the door before standing off to the side as Paola waited for someone to answer. Within a few seconds, a young woman, appearing to be in her twenties, opened the door. There was a brief silence before she literally screamed, "Paola?" The torrent of Portuguese that issued forth was so rapid and loud that, even had Thomas spoken the language, he would never have understood. Within seconds, Paola's parents, as well as her sister and brother surrounded her. Everyone wanted their hug and kiss, and all were talking at once.

Some minutes had passed before anyone seemed to notice Thomas standing there. Paola's mother said something that caused Paola to laugh and blush a great deal. His curiosity was killing him.

"Why are you laughing so much and looking at me?"

"I am sorry, Thomas. My mother asked if you were my boyfriend," she responded with a giggle. "I told her that you were not, but that your girlfriend would be here tonight."

Paola explained who he was, and the result was to be surrounded by these four grateful people wanting to smother him with hugs and kisses for bringing their Paola home. He had never felt quite so appreciated. Not one of them, except Paola, spoke so much as a word of English. Thomas was very much out of his element and at the mercy of Paola's occasional translation. Still, there was an amazing feeling of love and family that surrounded him with a warmth that knows no language barrier. The only thing missing was Sofia. Being without her was like torture. Thankfully, she would be in Brasilia later that night.

After a few cups of wonderful Brazilian coffee, and a superb breakfast prepared by Paola's mother, it was time to check in to a hotel. Thomas had Paola phone and book a reservation for a suite at Earlia Confort Park, a four-star hotel near the downtown area. After a somewhat drawn-out goodbye to everyone, he grabbed a taxi and was on his way. He had assured Paola that in the morning they would call her. She would come to the hotel and then take them to visit her family. She made him promise as if she wasn't sure he was telling her the truth. Finally, he had managed to convince her and was on his way.

If all went well, Sofia's journey to Sao Paulo would be a quick roundtrip. She would have a wait of a few hours for the return flight and her arrival in Brasilia should be at about eight that night. Thomas settled into the hotel suite and called her cell. It was killing him not knowing if everything was fine.

"Hey, my Thomas. Do you miss me?"

"Yes, I miss you like crazy. Everything alright there?"

"Yes. Wonderful. I am at the airport in Sao Paulo. The baby is with me, and we are waiting for the return flight. Such a beautiful baby, Thomas! Well, not so much a baby," she laughed, "He is so big for three years old. You can't believe it. A big boy just like his daddy."

"I'm sure he's a very beautiful child, sweetheart. Have you seen anyone suspicious around the airport?"

"Well, you know Sao Paulo's airport. Full of suspicious-looking people," she laughed, "So many people all the time. How to know who is doing what? There are two men that are walking around as if they are looking for someone but could be just a coincidence. They pay no attention to me."

"Nevertheless, be careful. I want you to get back here safely."

"Not to worry, I will be fine. The plane leaves in one hour. I will call you when we are in the air."

"OK, baby. I love you. See you soon."

"I love you too. Bye for now"

With the knowledge that Sofia was, at least for now, safe and in no danger, Thomas could lie down and have a much-needed nap. He called the front desk and put in a wake-up call for five-thirty, after which he would have a light meal before going to the airport. It was only one in the afternoon now, but he was more than tired enough to sleep until the evening. Besides, if he knew Sofia, he was certain that he would need his rest for that night. Then again, they would have Paola's son with them, and so he imagined it might possibly be a quiet occasion. Thomas was looking forward to seeing the little guy. He was confident there would not be any dry eyes when Paola's family met her son for the first time. That night and the next day promised to be something very special.

His wake-up call came in right on time. He passed on ordering from room service, freshened up, and dressed for the ride to the airport. He called the front desk and arranged a taxi for nine-thirty. Then he went to the bar for a Rum and Pepsi, a quick smoke, and a mental run-through of what they needed to do when they arrived in Manaus. It was imperative that he didn't lose sight of the final objective. As important as this stopover might be, there was still a great deal to take care of if he planned to survive this whole ordeal.

While he was in mid-thought, the desk clerk arrived to tell him that his taxi was waiting. He downed the rest of his drink, butted his smoke, and made his way out of the hotel. As the taxi careened its way to the airport, Thomas was still running over every remaining detail in his mind. It seemed that the more time passed, the more restless he became. This whole situation was beginning to take its toll. He could only stifle fear for so long before it raised its head to remind him of the danger. He didn't object to the warning. Better that than to become complacent and lose the intensity of the desire for survival. Tomorrow they would be on their way to Manaus and the final stages of his plan. Within a matter of days, hopefully, they would be safely on their way to La Serena, Chile, where Sofia's parents lived. That thought carried with it a new concern altogether. Meeting Sofia's family for the first time!

Thomas paced the arrival area of the airport like a man on a razor's edge. Sofia was truly his strength in this situation, and he needed her support and, most of all, her comfort. He also needed her to dig into the files from Carlo's computer and see what, if anything, might identify "The Man". Time was running out and he needed to determine what adjustments to his plan might be necessary to deal with this mysterious person. With good reason, it had been a nagging question for the past two days. Like a bad omen!

As a literal sea of people began to crush their way through the arrival gate into the waiting area, Thomas strained to get a glimpse of Sofia. It seemed that two hundred people had walked through that door with no sign of her. His heart was beginning to pound and his breath become short as he worried whether she had made it at all. Suddenly, running on youthful legs and laughing continuously, a little boy burst into the waiting area. Behind him, in a trot and with a somewhat flustered look, was Sofia calling out almost hopelessly, in Portuguese, to that wayward child. She looked frazzled beyond belief.

Laughing hysterically at the sight of her chasing frantically behind a very large three-year-old, all the concerns that had been troubling him were washed away. This was one of those priceless moments in time that would be the subject of future memories. He moved quickly to intercept the exuberant lad and lifted him into his arms.

"Hey, little guy. Where do you think you're going?"

He held the boy out at arm's length, which was no easy task since he was about twice the size of a normal three-year-old.

"You are one heavy little man. Stocky! Just like your daddy. Look at that black curly hair, those steel-blue eyes. You are definitely your old man's kid. No doubt about it."

As this adorable little boy stared at Thomas, with a pout that clearly displayed his confusion, Sofia rushed to his side. She was out of breath, pulling her carryon bag behind, another bag over her shoulder, yet still managing to laugh.

"Oh, Thomas. I am so happy to see you. Isn't he wonderful? But so active! I am exhausted."

"Yes. He is quite something. Can you imagine Paola's face when she sees him?"

"I am sure whatever I imagine will not do it justice. I think there will be much crying."

"Yes. Including me," Thomas replied as the tears began to well up in his eyes.

"His name is Victor. Is a nice name, I think! Don't you think so, Thomas? It is the name that Paola gave him. It was so good they kept that name with him."

"It's a wonderful name. I think it suits him very well,"

Thomas' arms were aching from having held the little heavyweight for so long. He laughed as he put him back down.

"Let's get him to the hotel and feed him something. I get the feeling he eats a lot," and off they went to catch a taxi.

Settled into the suite, and with Victor running around exploring every nook and cranny, Thomas called room service and ordered steak dinners for him and Sofia and a burger and fries for Victor.

Room service arrived thirty minutes later, and Victor tore into his food as if he had not eaten in a week. Thomas spent more time joyously watching him than he did eating his own meal. When supper was finished, they found a cartoon channel on television and Victor lay on the sofa to watch. Hopefully, Sofia would now have uninterrupted time to check Carlo's files for what Thomas needed. She took her laptop to the desk and began a painstaking search. Thomas settled on the sofa next to Victor and watched cartoons, in Portuguese. He was deriving great pleasure out of the little guy's periodic laughter, even though he had no idea what he was laughing at.

Almost an hour had passed when Sofia called Thomas to the desk.

"Thomas, I have found something, but I'm not sure I like it."

He stood over her shoulder as she opened a file that contained some news clippings.

"What is it that you don't like so much?"

"If this is the person Carlo refers to, he is very dangerous. I know very much about him. He is Luiz de Salvo. This is a copy of a newspaper story about the murder of a poor, hardworking man who dared to speak out about the corruption in the city government. De Salvo was attempting to run for Mayor of Sao Paulo at the time. This man was saying publicly many things about de Salvo's supposed criminal ties. Things that most people suspected but remained silent about."

"What does that have to do with it? Was he involved in the murder?"

"There were suggestions that he was. This man was shot in the street, in front of his family. His wife and children saw it all. Some people called the police and the newspaper to say that they recognized the killers as people they had seen in de Salvo's company."

"So why didn't they arrest him?"

"The people who called could give no names for these men. They themselves were too afraid to give their own names or to testify. So, it went nowhere. Tragically, that is often the case. At least, with the scandal and suspicion about the murder, he did not get elected Mayor. He did not lose by very much, though. Luiz de Salvos' men used threats and violence to try and get votes. It was all very horrible. He is still very powerful in Sao Paulo."

"Well, I think it's a safe bet that he's Carlo's connection then. It all fits very well. Criminal and political connections like those add up to some good evidence."

"And the police, Thomas. It was suggested that de Salvo was very close with some of the high-ranking police in the city. How else could he escape every investigation?"

"Well, that does open up a new dimension to this situation. I'll have to be sure I isolate him from the rest of this plan. Don't need him on my back too."

"Yes, but you took two hundred and fifty thousand of his money. He will be after you."

"As far as he will know, Carlo took it. Not me. He might logically assume that Carlo ripped him off and then fled Brazil. You can be sure he'll investigate Carlo's finances and discover he was having difficulty. Plus, undoubtedly, he knows that Carlo did the same thing to Pauly Sabatini. Why would he doubt that Carlo would steal from him too?"

"Yes! We do hope."

"I guess we'll see in due time. What I find strange is that he has never emailed Carlo about these trucks since he sent the money. You've been checking Carlo's email every day before you send it on to him?"

"Yes, of course. There has been nothing at all. Not from anyone. He does not seem to get many emails."

"Well, I imagine he uses it only for certain activities. You are living proof that email can be a dangerous thing with someone like you on the case." Thomas smiled and winked.

"Anyway, keep checking. We don't want to miss anything."

Thomas glanced over at the sofa to see that Victor was sound asleep. There would be a quiet night after all.

"Sofia, look. It seems that Victor wore himself out while he was running you off your feet," he chuckled as he placed a kiss on her forehead, "Maybe it's time we went to bed too. Tomorrow is going to be pretty amazing."

"Yes! I am so excited about it. Paola will be so very surprised. I am afraid she will faint."

"Could be. We better have the sWaltling salts ready," he laughed. "Now let's go to bed."

"We are going to sleep?"

"Eventually," Thomas said, smiling that knowing smile as he took Sofia's hand and led her to the bedroom.

CHAPTER 16

MOTHER AND CHILD REUNION

Morning came early, and with a thud. Victor had awakened and found the bedroom. In his attempt to climb up on the bed to be with Sofia, he had fallen backward and crashed, with a resounding bang, on the floor. Now it was apparent that not only could he eat with gusto, but he could cry with it as well. The fall alone was enough to wake Sofia and Thomas, and the crying instantly erased any remaining sleepiness that existed. Sofia picked Victor up, groaning mightily at the weight of him, and cradled him in her arms as she softly sang a lullaby in Portuguese. Soon enough he was finished with his tears, snuggling against her shoulder, and making his own effort to sing along. Thomas could only smile at such a sweet and tender sight.

"I should call down and order some breakfast. I'm sure the hamburger he had last night has worn off by now," he said as he reached for the menu so that Sofia could make her selection before he called.

Sofia held the menu in front of Victor and jokingly asked, "What would you like for breakfast, sweet Victor?"

"I'm sure he'd like the whole menu, honey," Thomas called out as he made his way to the bathroom to brush his teeth. He found himself unable to resist humming an old Paul Simon song, 'Mother and Child Reunion'. How appropriate on this day.

It was only seven in the morning, and a little early for Thomas' liking, but it would give them time for a leisurely breakfast and the opportunity to get Victor cleaned up and looking perfect for his mother.

"I'm going to jump in the shower, Sofia. I hate to say it, but you better stay with Victor," he chuckled. "We'll make up for it later."

"You can be sure. I will make you keep that promise. I will give Victor a bath when you are finished. Then you can dress him while I take my shower."

"Sure. I can handle that. We'll call Paola after we eat. I can't wait to see her face."

Sofia was having a good laugh at the sound of Thomas singing over the noise of the running water. The song 'Mother and Child Reunion' was still in his mind, and he did a fairly good job of doing it an injustice. Less than an hour had passed before everyone was showered, bathed, dressed, and ready for the food that Thomas had ordered. Victor, with his usual enthusiasm, dug into his eggs, sausage, toast, and juice as if he hadn't eaten in a week. When his plate was clean, he gleefully went after Thomas' eggs benedict.

"Good heavens, Sofia. It'll take all of the money I gave Paola just to feed this kid until he's fifteen," he said with a joyous laugh. "God love him, he's a healthy little guy."

"Yes, he is. I think when he finishes your eggs, he will want mine too."

"Mmm, nope. I think that's enough cholesterol for this boy today."

Victor pouted and sobbed in the most pitiful way when Thomas took his plate away from him.

"You're not going to starve, buddy. So lose the cute little pout. Here, have some fruit cup. It's better for you."

"Thomas, you are so cute with him. I think maybe you wish you had a son to go with all those daughters."

"The thought has cFedired my mind once or twice, wondering what it would have been like. But I don't regret having daughters at all. Not sure I would know what to do with a boy. I'm so used to spoiling girls with affection. Probably make a sissy out of him."

Thinking of his girls caused Thomas to realize he had never called Angela to let her know he was safely out of Carlo's. She was probably frantic with worry. He dialed his sister-in-law as he paced the floor.

"Hello?" Theresa answered with concern in her voice.

"Hey, Theresa, how are you?"

"Oh my God, Thomas. You're safe. Everyone has been frantic to hear from you. I can't believe this whole thing. This family couldn't possibly thank you enough for what you did for Angela. Now get your butt home, please! We're all worried about you."

"You know that I could never have turned my back. As for coming home, it'll be a while yet before that can happen. Is Angela there?"

"Yes, she's outside with the girls. They still don't know."

"Well, best not to let them know I'm on the phone. Just tell Angela that I'm fine and I'll call again in a few days."

"If that's what you want, but why can't you come home now?"

"Still some loose ends to tie up if I don't want trouble following me back to Canada. In a few days, I'll be in Manaus, and shortly after that, with a bit of luck, everything will be fine, and I'll go to Chile for a week."

"Manaus? Where's that?"

"Halfway up the Amazon," Thomas chuckled, "Jungle country."

"Oh, really! Well, I suppose you have a good reason for going there. But what's the deal with Chile?"

"Well, I'll explain that one later."

"It's a woman, isn't it," Theresa laughed knowingly.

"Yeah! It is. Quite a wonderful one too."

"I think that's great, Thomas. I know that Angela was suspecting that was the case. She seems to remember now that you two weren't together anymore. She wants you to be happy. So go for it."

"I was planning on it. No matter what she thought! What's over is over. Life starts anew for both of us."

"True enough. Well, please be careful. I hope to see you soon."

"Me too. Take care and don't let on to the kids."

"No problem. Bye."

Thomas hung up the phone as Sofia asked, "Is everything alright there?"

"Yes. Everything is fine. Everyone is worried, but fine."

"Well, I choose not to worry now. I choose to call Paola. What do you think?"

"Good choice. Give her a call now. I can't wait to spring this surprise on her."

Sofia dialed the number Paola had given to Thomas and spent only a few minutes in conversation before she hung up.

"She will be here in less than an hour. I am so excited." Sofia said as she began to cry. Thomas took her in his arms and gently swayed back and forth as he kissed her forehead.

"It's a happy thing, Sofia. You should be smiling, not crying."

"I cannot help it. Whenever I think that she has missed three years of Victor's life it makes me so sad. When I think that had we not found him, she may never have seen him again. She would have lost her son forever."

"All the more reason to smile. We were fortunate to find him and give her the chance to enjoy life with her son."

Victor, sensing something emotional going on, toddled over and began to hug their legs as he looked up with a pout on his face that cried out "pick me up". Thomas reached down and lifted him into his arms. Victor put one arm around each of their necks, giggled, and then kissed them both.

"This kid is a sweetheart. He doesn't seem to talk very much though. Maybe because of the new surroundings? I wouldn't understand him anyway, but I would love to hear him talk more. Poor kid. Three years in an orphanage."

"You are probably right. This is all new to him. He was in a home with many other children, and now he is with two strangers. I am sure he is confused and so quiet. I think that will change soon enough."

"You know, if he wasn't Paola's boy, I'd adopt him myself," Thomas laughed softly as he nuzzled his face against Victor's, causing him to giggle and throw his arms around Thomas' neck and lay his head on his shoulder.

"This boy longs for a father, Sofia. Damn, if Antonio wasn't in Napoli."

"I prefer not to think of it. I do not wish to be sad on such a happy day."

Thomas called room service and had them clear away the breakfast dishes. He then sat on the sofa with Victor to watch a few more cartoons. There was an episode of The Simpson's on, and Thomas found it quite interesting to hear his favorite characters in Portuguese. Victor sat on his lap and giggled constantly. Thomas was beginning to realize that having to leave this sweet kid behind was going to be somewhat painful.

"Sofia, do you think Paola will let me be in Victor's life in some way?"

Victor had stolen his fatherly heart. It was something he had never expected but wasn't the least bit unhappy about.

"I cannot say, Thomas, but if I had to guess, I think she would be thrilled. She adores you and I am sure she would be so happy that you take such an interest in Victor."

"I hope so. I would be very proud to be an uncle to him." The very moment he uttered the last word there was a gentle knock at the door.

"Oh! Sofia, it must be Paola. Take Victor into the bedroom. I'll call you when to bring him out."

Sofia uttered a few words to Victor and took him into the bedroom and out of sight. Thomas opened the door to find a smiling Paola standing there with her sister. He hadn't expected her to have anyone with her, but no matter.

"Good morning, Paola. How are you today?"

"I am fine. So happy to see you. Where is Sofia?"

"She's in the bedroom. She'll be out in a few minutes. I have something to tell you first."

"Yes? What is?"

"Well, we have a very big surprise for you. I think you'll like it."

"You have surprised me very much already. So much money, clothes, bringing me to my family. What more surprise could you do?"

"This is a big one. Bigger than all the others put together."

By now Paola's sister was looking left out. Not understanding any English, she had no idea what was going on and just stood off to the side. Thomas couldn't help but wonder what her reaction would be.

"Are you ready, Paola? Very ready?"

"Thomas, you are making me so nervous. What is it? Please tell me."

Thomas gave her a hug and called out to Sofia.

"Sofia? It's time. Send out the surprise," at which point the door to the bedroom opened, and out came Victor, running full steam ahead and straight to Thomas.

Paola smiled and looked somewhat confused and almost afraid to ask,

"Who is? He is a very cute baby. But who is?"

"He's your son, Paola. It's Victor," Thomas said with tears running down his face.

She looked visibly shaken as the tears welled up in her eyes. She stared, with a look that carried the pain of lost years, at Victor clinging to Thomas' leg and acting very shy. She was in total disbelief. Her face began to go pale, and her sister had to prop her up to keep her from falling to the floor in a faint.

There was a torrent of Portuguese taking place between Sofia and Paola's sister who, now aware of who Victor was, developed her own problem with turning pale and crying. Finally, Paola recovered enough to kneel in front of an ever-shyer Victor and speak softly to him in Portuguese. As she spoke through constant tears, combined with a motherly smile, Victor began to loosen his grip on Thomas' leg and smile ever so sweetly back. Within a few moments, he was in her arms, babbling softly and fidgeting with her hair. Somehow, almost amazingly, the mother and child bond seemed to be so natural as to cause Thomas to think that, even in young Victor, it had existed just beneath the surface, waiting all this time for them to be reunited.

Everyone, including Paola's sister, who was in total and yet delighted shock, was crying. This was a moment that none of them would ever forget. Even poor Victor, seeing everyone else doing so, was shedding his own tears.

After what seemed like an hour, Paola stood and threw her arms around Thomas and Sofia, sobbing uncontrollably as she said "thank you" over and over again. When she finally released her grip on them, she spoke.

"Now we must go to show my parents their grandson. We must all celebrate. We can go now, please? Come, come, we go, please."

Thomas chuckled and said, "Of course, Paola. I can't wait to see your family's reaction. Are you ready to go, Sofia?"

"Yes. You know Paola's sister is so thrilled. She cannot believe that we have done such a thing. She says her whole family will be so pleased."

"One more very good thing out of all of this. First, I find you, and then this wonderful reunion for Paola. Sometimes very good things come out of difficult situations."

"Yes. Thanks to God for every wonderful gift."

With all five of them stuffed into a taxi, they proceeded to the apartment of Paola's parents. The whole family would be there, including her married siblings and her nephews and nieces. Thomas could only imagine the frantic chatter in Portuguese combined with the crying and the joy that he was about to witness. It would have to be a quick visit for Thomas and Sofia because they needed to return to the hotel and get ready for their flight to Manaus. Despite the joy of this occasion, there was still much in the way of dangerous work ahead for them.

When they arrived at the apartment, Paola went inside with her sister to prepare her family for what was about to happen. Shortly after, the door was flung open, and the entire family came surging into the hallway to find Victor.

This large group of overly exuberant people frightened him to the point of his hiding behind Thomas and crying profusely.

Paola crouched down beside him, spoke some soothing words into his ear and then groaned from the weight of him as she picked him up to further calm him. Soon enough, Victor realized that he rather enjoyed all of these kisses and caresses and was smiling happily as everyone went back into the apartment for lunch.

Throughout, Sofia was almost constantly translating the many expressions of appreciation being offered to Thomas by everyone in the room. This was a very typical Brazilian family, very close and very expressive. Thomas was almost embarrassed by all the attention but, nevertheless, somewhat enjoyed it. Suddenly, Victor came running over and jumped on his lap, gave him a hug around the neck, and a kiss, and then settled against his chest to rest. Paola noticed the obvious affection he held for Thomas.

"Victor shows much feeling for you. I think he loves you very much."

It was then that Sofia began speaking to Paola in Portuguese. When their conversation was finished, Paola looked at Thomas and with tears in her eyes.

"I would be very proud for you to be an uncle to Victor. I am so happy you want to." She walked over to Thomas and gave him a gentle kiss and then spoke to Victor in Portuguese. "Este é seu tio Thomas e ama-o muito muito."

Victor turned and gave Thomas another big hug as Thomas asked, "What did you tell him?"

"I said you are his Uncle Thomas and that you love him very much." Thomas could feel the tears running down his cheeks. What a wonderful feeling as he heard Victor speak for the first time,.

"Eu te amo, tio Thomas." That, Thomas understood.

A few hours had passed with much excitement and emotion and now it was, sadly, time to leave Paola and her family behind. Thomas and Sofia had to prepare for their flight and found the need to say their goodbyes. Paola surprised Thomas when she asked:

"If you speak with Antonio, will you tell him I say hello? He is a good man. No matter what else. He was so very good to me."

There was a look in her eyes that spoke volumes about the emotions she obviously still held for Antonio. Thomas had this feeling that it might be difficult, if not impossible, for her to think in terms of any man other than the father of her son. It was truly awkward.

"You bet I will, Paola. I promise. I am sure I'll be talking to him sometime soon." He took her in his arms and gently kissed her forehead. Looking into her eyes, he pleaded: "Please, Paola, take very good care of yourself. Here is my cell number. If there is ever any trouble, of any kind, call me. Promise?"

"Yes! I promise. Please take care of yourself too. I worry for you and Sofia. You must get to a place that is safe from Carlo."

"Don't worry. We'll be fine."

All the goodbyes having been said, Thomas and Sofia were on their way back to the hotel. There was excitement over the prospect of spending time in Manaus. There was also some trepidation over the fact that it would be the most dangerous part of this entire situation.

"Sofia, when we get back to the hotel we need to send a few emails and I have to make at least two calls. It's time to set the wheels in motion for the final phase of this thing."

"We will do that and then leave for the airport?"

"Yes. Tonight we will be in Manaus. We should have a day or two without interruption. I'm looking forward to it. I have always wanted to go there. To me, that's Brazil."

"You will not be disappointed. It is truly beautiful. But it rains a lot. Every day." "Well, I'm sure we can find something to occupy us during the rain," Thomas laughed as he placed his arm around Sofia's shoulder.

"I can always count on my Thomas to say just the right thing."

The taxi pulled up in front of the hotel and they went directly to their room. Sofia took out her laptop so that Thomas, using Carlos' account, could compose an email to Luiz de Salvo providing the container numbers to make arrangements to secure the trucks from the docks. He anticipated that they would arrive in two days. That would give de Salvo time to arrange travel to the port in Fortaleza. Thomas planted a reference to the quarter of a million dollars that allegedly went towards the purchase of the trucks, and suggested that de Salvo would be somewhat surprised at how much he actually got for his money. Just a little hidden gem of sarcasm to whet de Salvo's appetite. What a surprise would be in store for him when the containers were actually opened and he saw how little he had really received for his cash.

He also indicated in the email that there was business to attend to in Manaus and he, Carlo, would not return for approximately one week. So, de Salvo would discover the ruse in Fortaleza and then, no doubt, head directly for Manaus to deal with Carlo. Manaus would be a very busy place with the convergence of the various factions wanting Carlo's head on a platter. Now it was time to call Pauly Sabatini and have him send his men to Rio. Thomas pulled out the disposable cell and dialed his number.

"Yeah," Pauly answered in his usual fashion.

"Mr. Sabatini. It's time to get your boys on their way."

"Been wondering when I would hear from you. Where they going?"

"Rio! You already have this cell number. They can call me when they arrive and I'll give further instructions."

"You're being a little too secretive for me. I need to know more than that."

"Then I guess the conversation is done. Bye."

"No! Wait! Fine. I want that bastard, so I guess I have to play by your rules for the time being."

"Good plan."

"What about my money?"

"Your money?"

"Yeah! The ten million the son-of-a-bitch stole from me."

"Well, I hate to be the bearer of bad news, but Carlo is down to his last million. Seems he's not so good at managing his finances. Or should I say, your money," Thomas couldn't resist a chuckle.

"I'm not laughing. Are you shitting me? That dope went through nine million in ten years?"

"I would never kid about something like that. However, when all is said and done, I can help you get the money that's left."

"Tell me now and we can leave him broke until we get him."

Thomas chuckled again, "Nah, I don't think so. Let's just call it insurance. You want it? I and mine have to come out of this whole thing safe and sound. Got it?"

"Yeah! I got it. Fair trade I guess."

"Glad you agree. I'll expect to hear from you in two days. I hope they're smart enough to not get nailed for something stupid. Like trying to sneak weapons on board the plane."

"They won't. I've made it very clear to everyone. Besides, I'm tagging along. You I gotta meet."

Thomas was caught by surprise. He never expected to get the big fish in his net too. He was beginning to hope he hadn't gone after too big a catch.

"Good to know, Pauly. You'll have no problem finding a contact to get what you need in Brazil. Talk to you soon." When Thomas hung up, Pauly leaned back and lit up a Cuban cigar.

After a few deep draws of smoke he mumbled out loud.

"It ain't worth a million to let you live, dumb ass. The hell with the money. You're gonna have to die. Sorry about your luck,"

CHAPTER 18

THE RIVER RUNS DEEP

Carlo and his men had returned to Sao Paulo and headed directly for the hotel looking for Thomas. Marta, who had proven to be a very faithful aide in Thomas' deceit of Carlo, was working the reception area as usual. Carlo rushed up to the counter.

"Thomas DeAngelo! What room is he in?"

"I'm sorry sir, but I could not give out a guest's room number if he was still here."

"If he was still here? What the hell are you talking about?" Carlo's face was beet red at this point.

"Mister DeAngelo checked out, sir. He is gone."

"What? When? He was still here when I called eight hours ago!"

"Oh yes, was you who called? I tell him someone called. He said to say he would contact you soon. He asked that you please wait for his call."

"Damn it! I can't believe this shit," he erupted as he pounded his fist on the counter.

"Sir! Please, I must ask you to control yourself."

"Oh, go to hell," Carlo spewed the words out like venom, turned away from the counter and barged out of the hotel with Rico and his men right behind him. Now he had nothing to do but wait. Again! He sent Rico and his men on their way and then took a taxi home. Once inside, he went directly to the library and that bottle of bourbon he had made a dent in a few days earlier. He was approaching a state of depression, and only a good drunk was going to ease the pain. Settling into his favorite chair, he drank straight from the bottle. Within an hour he was more than slightly tipsy. When the phone rang, he picked it up and blurted out a "What?" as he swallowed another gulp.

"Carlo? How are you? I'm happy to find you at home."

"Tommy? You son-of-a-bitch. You are one tricky bastard," Carlo slurred through a somewhat sardonic smile.

"Why, Carlo, I do believe you're drunk."

"Yeah, just a little. Damn, Tommy! What the hell are you doing to me? First, you're here, then you're not. You're like a friggin ghost. Where the hell are you anyway?"

"I'm afraid I can't tell you that quite yet. Soon enough! Did you know the containers would be in port in two days? Just as I promised."

"Yeah? Two days?" he laughed, "You trying to tell me I'm still getting my trucks, Tommy?"

"Of course. I promised trucks, you're getting trucks."

"You're shitting me. I can't believe that."

"Not shitting you at all. The containers will be there. You'll see. Then our business is finished. Right? Everything is done."

"Yeah. If those trucks are there, we're clean," Carlo lied as he took another slug from the bottle.

"Good! I'll call you again in a few days. And listen; try going easy on that bottle. Not good for the liver," Thomas said as he hung up and left Carlo to his thoughts.

With the effects of the bourbon making it nearly impossible for him to get up and walk, Carlo simply leaned back in the chair and fell sound asleep. The full meaning of his conversation with Thomas had been lost for the moment. The morning would no doubt bring many questions to his mind along with a deeper hatred for this nemesis.

With the email and phone calls now completed, Thomas and Sofia began their preparation to catch the flight to Manaus. Once they had finished packing, Thomas called down for a taxi and they were on their way. The flight to that city would depart at nine forty-five and arrive at eleven-thirty. The trip would be less than two hours, and they would be settled in their hotel by twelve-thirty at night.

Once they were in the air, Sofia leaned against Thomas' shoulder and asked, "Why did you choose to go to Manaus? Why not just leave Brazil."

"I guess there are two reasons for that. For one thing, I've always regretted not having gone there on my last trip to this beautiful country. I always wanted so much to see it. Everything I hear about the place excites me."

"Yes! That I understand. So, what is the other reason?"

"Well, that one I think you won't like so much."

Sofia lifted her head from his shoulder and looked into his eyes.

"Why will I not like it so much? What is so bad?"

"Sofia, I know what a tender and caring person you are. I know the values you have. We share the same ones. The problem is that I have to be realistic about the outcome of this whole situation with Carlo."

"Thomas! Do not be so evasive with me. Just tell me."

"Sofia, my love, you must know that Carlo, if he is still alive, will never rest until he finds me. In fact, he'll never rest until he finds Angela. Worse yet, if he finds me, he also finds you. None of us will be safe. The same goes for de Salvo. With his connections we would never find a safe place to hide."

"What are you telling me, Thomas?"

"I'm telling you that the Amazon is the best place for them to die. It's the safest place, upriver, in the jungle, without worries about the police."

"Oh my God! Thomas, you are going to kill them?"

"Actually, my plan is for them to kill each other. With the help of the Sabatini's, of course. I'm somewhat worried about them too, but the rest of Carlo's money may buy us out of any problems with that crew. Can never be sure."

"Thomas, now you make me worry too much." Sofia returned her head to Thomas' shoulder and began to cry softly. Thomas brushed away her tears and kissed her forehead.

"Baby, I'm so sorry. Maybe it's better you go on to La Serena. They'll never find you there. I can follow later when everything is finished, and we're safe from any possible reprisal."

Sofia's response was swift and firm:

"I will never leave you. Never! We are in this together. What must be done, I cannot argue it. I don't like it, but I know the truth of what you say. May God forgive us for what we must do for our own survival!"

"You are amazing, Sofia. I am a very lucky man."

The remainder of the flight was without further conversation. They were each, it seemed, in deep thought and not without worry about what lay ahead. When the plane landed in Manaus they disembarked silently and proceeded through the waiting area to hail a taxi for the hotel. Sofia had made reservations at the Tropical Manaus Resort. Thomas had read about it in his research for a possible trip to this city. Nothing he had read, however, could have adequately prepared him for what his eyes would see when they exited the taxi.

It wasn't merely the façade or the sheer size of the place that created the impression. No, that was secondary to his reaction. The hotel sat on property cut out of pure Brazilian rainforest. It was surrounded by acacias, orchids of all colors, chicle trees, which he knew were the original source of chewing gum, Cercropias, the most abundant trees in the Amazon, and countless ferns.

"My God, Sofia! This is amazing. I'm stunned."

"Wait until morning. Then you will be astounded. When you are not in the dark, with only these few lights to show you your surroundings. Yes, wait until morning."

They checked in at the front desk and were escorted to their suite by a bellboy. When they closed the door and put their bags down, they looked at each other and simultaneously began to smile and laugh. They both obviously had the same thought at the same moment and, with clothing strewn behind them, made their way to the shower.

This night's session of making love was more emotional than any other had been. Thomas felt that each knew in their hearts they faced a terrible risk that could put an end to their happiness. The thought caused them to savor what each feared might be one of their final memories. No words of any such concern were spoken, but they weren't necessary. Thomas instinctively knew what was going through each of their minds. In the end, they lay in each other's arms for an hour before finally falling asleep.

At some point in the middle of the night, Thomas awoke and quietly opened the sliding door to the patio of their ground-level suite. He sat in the cool night air, covered with goosebumps yet again. As he rubbed at the bumps on his arms, he knew they were not caused entirely by the chilly air. His fears were coming to the surface again. His greatest concern was for Sofia. He honestly wanted her to leave for La Serena and safety, yet he knew she never would. The only thing he really knew was that if anything happened to her. he would never forgive himself and might even lose his will to go on. A few hours later, he fell asleep sitting there in the chair.

Sofia had awakened shortly after Thomas and found that he was on the patio. She also knew he needed time with his thoughts and chose not to interrupt. When she noticed that he had fallen asleep, she took a blanket from the foot of the bed and wrapped it around him, rather than disturb his sleep to make him come back inside. As tears rolled down her cheeks, she took another blanket and wrapped it around herself as she sat in the chair beside him. It was there, on the patio, that they slept until the early morning.

Thomas was the first to awaken. Sofia's head was resting on his shoulder, and he gently stroked her hair as she slept. He sat there, wide awake, refusing to disturb her sleep by getting up. He would wait until she had awakened on her own. More than an hour passed before she began to stir slightly. Slowly she opened her eyes, looked up at him, and spoke.

"You know how much I love you, my Thomas? Do you truly know?"

"Too much for your own good, or you would be on a plane to La Serena as I asked."

"No, not too much. Never too much! And do not talk about me leaving again. I refuse! You know I refuse."

"Yes, I know. What good is it to argue with a Latin woman," he said as he smiled and brushed her cheek.

"It is no good. I am happy you have learned that so quickly," Sofia teased as she pinched his nose.

"How about some breakfast, my stubborn Latin lady?"

"Mmmmm yes, I am hungry. A good breakfast! You order and I will get dressed."

Sofia went about brushing her teeth, washing her face, and getting dressed while Thomas phoned room service. When it was his turn to freshen up, Sofia replaced the blankets on the bed and then sat in silence. She heard Thomas' voice echoing from the bathroom as he spoke to her.

"Tomorrow is a big day. Pauly Sabatini and his crew will be in Rio; de Salvo will be in Fortaleza discovering a bunch of containers of junk trucks and Carlo, not sure about Carlo yet."

"I don't really want him on his way here until two days from now. I want everyone arriving on my schedule. Not all together. Nicely staggered arrivals so they don't run into each other on the plane. That would screw things up royally."

"How will you arrange that?"

"I'll have to think about that over breakfast. I'll work it out."

"I hope so. It is a little important, as you say."

There was a knock at the door and Sofia let the bellboy in with the breakfast cart. After a nice tip, he left with a smile as Thomas and Sofia sat down to a huge breakfast that they were sure they could never possibly finish. After they had eaten, they went out for a walk on the grounds of the hotel. He was finally going to see the immense beauty of this place in the daylight. He would also experience humidity so heavy that breathing was hard work. Once out in the open-air Thomas knew it would be a while before they even left the resort property. His eyes were wide and his jaw agape at the beauty surrounding him.

"Oh my God, Sofia! This is quite something."

"Yes. We are right on the banks of the Rio Negro and at least ten miles from the downtown. You like?"

"Oh, Sofia, like is not a strong enough word at all. I love it. But the heat! Good Lord it's hot!"

"Yes, I warned you. At times it is like an anvil on your chest. But you will get accustomed to it. You hope."

"Not sure that's possible," Thomas laughed, "I picked up this magazine in the room! Some interesting facts in it."

"What is it? About the hotel?"

"No. About the Amazon. Did you know it makes up five percent of the world's landmass?"

"Well, I knew it was very big. But that is a lot."

"Yes, but it is in such danger, you know. Too much deforestation! Very bad! They lose many thousands of acres every year."

"Yes, I know. It took everyone a while to realize how important this place is to the very survival of the world. At least they're making some attempts now to preserve it. The world depends upon it more than most people know."

"Shall we take a taxi to the downtown now, Thomas? See the city?"

"Sure. We can have some lunch while we're there."

They quickly hailed a cab and headed for the city center. Thomas was devouring every sight. His eyes were in a constant state of wandering from one visual experience to another. He discovered there was a great mixture of old and new in Manaus as Sofia decided to give him a bit of a history lesson.

"Europeans first settled this area in sixteen sixty-nine, with only a small fort. In eighteen-fifty a small settlement developed and became the capital of the province of the Amazonas. For about thirty years there was a rubber boom that created prosperity for the city. Actually, more so for the ruthless rubber barons that ran it! It was during that time that the Opera House, Teatro Amazonas, was built. They used Amazonian wood, Alsace tiles, Italian marble, French crystals, and gold embossing. It is very stunning. Entertainers from North America and Europe, including great opera stars, were brought in to perform for the small group of families who controlled the economy of the area. It is said that this Opera House, still used today, has some of the best acoustics in the world."

"We must see it then. You're like a walking encyclopedia about this place," he laughed.

"It is worth knowing. When synthetic rubber was invented, and as countries in Southeast Asia, using seeds collected by an Englishman in the Amazon, began producing rubber of their own, Manaus saw a rapid decline in its fortunes."

"So. what keeps it alive now?"

"It has been declared a duty-free zone and billions of dollars of goods arrive here every year for distribution to other areas of Brazil. This is possible because ocean-going ships can travel up the Amazon."

"You mean large freighters? You're kidding."

"Oh, Thomas, the average depth of the river is one hundred and fifty feet. Ships with a draft of fourteen feet can actually navigate as far upriver as Iquitos Peru."

"That's amazing. I can't get over how much you know about this place."

"I love Brazil. So, I know."

Thomas and Sofia spent a quiet afternoon touring the central area of the city. One of Thomas' favorite sites was the municipal market, Mercado Municipal. The market building itself is a cast-iron structure that was imported from England. There they found an amazing variety of tropical fruits, herbs, plants, fish, and numerous exotic jungle products.

In front of the market was Puerto Flotante, where excursions on the Amazon begin. There were boat rides to the meeting point of the Rio Solimoes and Rio Negro, fishing villages like Manacapuru and Araca, and even the archipelago of Anavilhanas

They explored such architectural pleasures as The Palacio de Justicia, Palacio Rio Negro, edificio de Correos and the church of Sao Sebastiao. By now, the humidity was getting to them both and soon enough it would, as usual, rain. He was learning that rain is an everyday occurrence in the Amazon.

"In Manaus, Thomas, when people make plans for the evening they will often simply say 'I will meet you after the rain'."

To avoid being caught in a downpour, they made their way back to the suite, both now sticky and uncomfortable from the humidity, and took a much-needed shower. What they really needed was a quiet nap in the air-conditioned comfort of their suite. Within minutes they were sound asleep. It was now almost six in the evening, and they had requested a wake-up call for nine so that they could have a leisurely supper in their room. Later, they would venture down to the bar for some drinks, music, and possibly some dancing. They planned to enjoy the evening as if it were their last.

CHAPTER 19

CARLO IS ON THE HUNT

As Thomas and Sofia had been waking up on this morning, Carlo, with head throbbing and a body that ached everywhere from a night sleeping in a chair, was regaining consciousness. As for his mood? It was foul, at best. He staggered painfully to his feet and headed to the foyer and up the stairs to his room. A good hot shower was what he needed, and he wasted no time fulfilling that desire. As he stood under the showerhead, he began to recall the previous night's conversation with Thomas. By the time he finished showering and shaving, he knew he had to find him, one way or another. It was time to call in a favor. He dressed, went back to the library, sat at the desk, picked up the phone and dialed the number for Captain Santos.

Santos was a high-ranking officer in the Sao Paulo police department. He was also the more than occasional recipient of Carlo's payments for favors performed, or investigations derailed before they had begun. Carlo needed another favor and was willing to pay well for it. Captain Santos had a serious disdain for his own first name. Carlo didn't know why, or even what it was. He had always insisted on being called, simply, Santos. It was exactly in that way that he answered the phone.

"Santos!"

"Yes, my friend, this is Carlo."

"Have not heard from you for some time, Carlo. I begin to think you forgot me. Begin to think you no longer need me."

"No, my friend. Never forget you. I'm calling now because I have a favor to ask."

"I am sure I know that. Is the only reason you ever call," he said with somewhat forced laughter.

"Well, this favor pays ten thousand American dollars. Interested?"

"Ten thousand? You sure?" the glee and the greed in his voice were obvious.

"Yes! I'm very sure. Ten thousand. Cash."

"Must be a very serious favor. That much money makes me think it is perhaps too risky."

"Not at all. It's quite simple. The money is because the favor is important, and I need it yesterday."

"Ahhh. I see. Tell me then. What is it?"

I need you to check the airlines for any flights taken by a Thomas DeAngelo. You have the authority to cut through the bullshit and get the information that I can't."

"Yes, I do. I will start with Sao Paulo."

"No! He didn't fly out of Sao Paulo. I already know that much. Try Rio. He might have been there."

"Very well. I will call you soon."

"It can't be soon enough. Thanks."

Carlo hung up the phone and went to the kitchen to find something to eat. Without Paola, he was like a fish out of water. He was almost helpless when it came to the everyday things that she had performed for so many years. Having to make his own breakfast was a disaster waiting to happen. Carlo liked his eggs over easy, and after he had ruined half a dozen of them in the simple act of trying not to break the yolks, he gave up and had a bowl of cereal. He was taking his last spoonful when the phone rang. He ran to the library and grabbed the receiver.

"Yes?"

"It is Santos. Your friend flew out of Rio to Brasilia three days ago."

"Brasilia? What the hell would he be doing in Brasilia? Who the hell could he know there?"

"You never ask me for that information, so I am sure I do not know. But he is no longer in Brasilia anyway. He flew to Manaus last night."

"Last night? Then he must still be there."

"Yes. He has taken no flight from there. I told the airline to call me if he books a flight to anywhere else."

"Perfect. Great job! Thanks, my friend."

"Yes! Your friend! And when will your, how you say, friend, get his ten thousand American dollars?"

"It'll be at your office today. You'll be there all day?"

"Yes. For that I think I can remain at my desk as long as need be. But do not forget me, friend," he said with an almost sadistic laugh.

"I wouldn't dare forget you, Santos."

"I see you understand. That is good."

"Have I ever failed you before?"

"No! But occasionally one needs to be reminded that he shouldn't. You agree?"

"Whatever you say. I have the same rule. Thanks again."

Carlo hung up on Santos and then called the airline to book four seats to Manaus. He would wait for Rico to show up at noon, and then send him to gather his two pals from the favelas. He was feeling quite chipper at this point. This irritating nemesis, this pain in the ass

Thomas would finally get his due. Yes, things were looking better every minute. Right on cue, at noon, Rico came through the front door looking his usual slovenly and brutal self.

"Rico. Get your boys. We have to catch a flight to Manaus."

"Manaus? That jungle country boss! What in Manaus?"

"Thomas is in Manaus, you dolt! What the hell else? Now get your boys and make it fast. We don't have much time."

"I go get now. We be back very quick."

Once Rico was gone, Carlo went back upstairs to pack an overnight bag. He didn't plan on spending much time in Manaus. He was like Rico when it came to jungle areas. He had no use for them. All he knew about the place was that it rained a lot and was very humid. Not his favorite kind of weather. As for the splendor of the Amazon? Leave that to the Indians and the rest of the people crazy enough to live there. He wouldn't be able to get back to Sao Paulo fast enough to suit him. Get this business done and get home. If Thomas wasn't stretching the truth, and the containers would be in Fortaleza tomorrow, there was no need for him anymore. As for Angela, he would find her soon enough and do what he should have done before. Silence her! He truly felt that the end of this nightmare was close at hand. He could feel it, and it felt good.

The flight was to depart at eight-fifteen that night. Its arrival in Manaus would be at about eleven-thirty. There were earlier flights available, but not direct. He could take an afternoon flight that went by way of Recife, or one that went through Rio and then Brasilia. In either case, the flights were interminably long and didn't arrive until after the flight he had booked. The wait gave him time to make the delivery of payment to Captain Santos. It would be very unfortunate to overlook that detail. Santos was even more ruthless than Carlo. Worse yet, he was ruthless and had the authority to go with it.

Once Carlo had made the trip to the bank, had withdrawn the required funds, and delivered them to Santos, he returned to the house to await Rico and his men. By five in the evening, they were on their way to the Sao Paulo International airport to wait for their flight. Carlo did a quick questioning of his crew to be sure they were not carrying anything that would cause a problem boarding the plane. He could never be too sure with these characters.

"Nobody has any weapons on them! Right?"

"No, boss," Rico replied.

"Not even a small knife. Not a fingernail clipper. Nothing! You understand?"

"No, boss, we have nothing."

"Good. When we get to Manaus, we'll find what we need. Then we'll do our business and get back home."

"How we find him boss?"

"We're going to have to split up. I've made a list of the hotels in Manaus. There are a lot of them. Each of us will take one area and comb the hotels. Bribe desk clerks. Money talks. With the four of us searching separately we should be able to find him more quickly."

"How we do the search?"

"For crying out loud, Rico! Do you ever think? At the airport we'll get four taxis. The drivers all carry cell phones. I want their numbers so I can contact all of you if I find Thomas. If you find him, have the driver call my cell."

"Yes, boss. Is good."

"This is important! If you find him, you do nothing. I mean nothing! You just call me, and then keep an eye to make sure he doesn't leave. You got it?"

"Yes," Rico answered as the others nodded their heads.

With the search plan in place, they boarded the airplane and prepared for takeoff. In just a few hours they would be in Manaus and on their manhunt.

Carlo sat quietly gazing out the window. He was feeling a great deal of relief, although not complete. It was good to know that Thomas was in Manaus, but the search for him could prove difficult. He could only hope they would find him before he moved on yet again. With Santos keeping an eye on flights out of the city, there were only a few other avenues of undetected escape. He could leave by car, but with limited options as to destinations, or he could take to the river and travel downstream the almost one thousand miles to the coast. In any event, it would be difficult to find him if he took either route.

When the plane touched down at Manaus airport, Carlo and his crew disembarked and hired four taxis. Carlo gave each driver one hundred dollars American for their cooperation and wrote down their cell numbers. Then each member of the search party took a list of hotels and went their separate ways. Carlo could only hope that the search would bear fruit very quickly. He wanted this over with a minimum of hassle. He wanted to get home and pick up his trucks. There were clients waiting for their arrival and the money would come just in time to save him from problems with the bank.

Meanwhile, Thomas and Sofia had gotten their nine o'clock wakeup call and had ordered and eaten a wonderful supper. By eleven they were sitting in the lounge listening to Brazilian music and enjoying a few drinks. As usual, there had been an evening rain. The temperature outside had cooled considerably and yet the humidity hung on like glue. Still, after a few drinks, they decided to stroll the grounds of the hotel. They walked hand in hand, silently, simply enjoying the beauty of the place. They had no idea that there was a choreographed search of hotels taking place in a frantic and angry effort to find them.

It was now almost two in the morning. Thomas and Sofia decided to retire to their suite at just about the same time that Carlo and his crew began to think they were wrong in searching the less expensive and more numerous of hotels. Carlo had decided that perhaps

Thomas would be hiding right where he least expected to find him. The search of the more luxurious hotels was now underway.

Thomas and Sofia made their way to their second-floor suite and he, gently kissing her lips, poked around with the key in a blind effort to find the keyhole and open the door. Suddenly, the door flew open, and Thomas and Sofia were each grabbed by the throat and dragged into the suite as the door was kicked shut behind them. To Thomas' horror, and total disbelief, he and Sofia were in the clutches of Rico. Nothing good could come of this. The end was certain now. Thomas's only hope was that Sofia would not suffer too much. He was praying that whatever the outcome was to be, that it would be mercifully swift.

Rico, now with two struggling people occupying both of his hands, realized that he would have to let go of at least one. He released his grip on Sofia and, when she appeared ready to scream for help, struck her with a backhand that sent her sprawling halfway acFedir the room. It was only a half-strength swipe from this beast, and yet powerful enough to render her unconscious. As she lay there, Rico concentrated on Thomas, who by now was turning slightly blue from a lack of oxygen. Rico pinned him against the wall, hand still around his throat, as he spoke.

"I going to have your woman. Her I keep for long time. Very long time. She be my slave always."

Thomas was sick at the thought, his mind struggling to find a way out of this. It was too painful to contemplate that there was none. Rico, realizing that he had broken Carlo's rule by not calling him when he found Thomas, reached with his free hand for the phone. Just at that moment the door practically burst from its hinges. Thomas heard the crash, but his vision was now blurry, and he could see nothing recognizable.

As Rico turned his head to see what had happened, there were three bright flashes and the accompanying muffled 'phoot phoot phoot' of three bullets making their way through the silencer at the end of the barrel of a nine-millimeter pistol. All three slugs caught Rico in the back. As he winced from the pain, he loosened his grip on Thomas' throat, letting him fall to the floor. Rico turned and, staggering, reached for the pistol he had acquired on the black market in Manaus. There was one more flash, one more 'phoot', and Rico fell to the floor with a bullet hole neatly through the head. Just to make sure, his assailant stood over him and pumped three more slugs into his body.

Thomas, by now recovering some of his breath, and his vision, looked up at this new intruder. He couldn't believe his eyes as he spoke.

"Antonio? My God, Antonio?"

"Yeah, Tommy. It's me. You ok?"

"Antonio? It's really you?"

"For cryin out loud, yes, Tommy, it's really me. I ain't no ghost."

"What are you doing here?"

"The last I looked, savin your ass," Antonio said as he laughed heartily. "That was a close call. Hey, you better check on Sofia while I get rid of this asshole."

Thomas, still struggling for breath, crawled over to Sofia. She was beginning to regain consciousness and threw her arms around him as she cried, "Thomas, you are ok?"

"Yes, baby. Look! Look who's here," he said as he pointed in the direction of Antonio, who was at that moment dragging Rico's body out to the balcony.

"Antonio? Is it you Antonio?"

"Yes, Sofia, it's me," he answered as he closed the sliding door to the balcony and drew the drapes shut, "Are you ok?"

"Oh yes! I am so fine now. It hurts a lot where he hit me, but thanks to you, we are fine."

Thomas looked at Antonio and asked, "What are you doing here? Why aren't you in Italy?"

"Ahhh! Let's just say that a hundred thousand for just opening a door and driving you to a hotel didn't seem fair. Thought you might need some more help. Now gimme a hand cleaning up some of this blood! There's not much of it. They won't find him for a while, I'm sure."

As they set about cleaning up after Rico's demise, Thomas probed deeper into Antonio's motivation.

"Please tell me the whole story, will you? There has to be more to your being here than just that."

Antonio let out a deep sigh as he spoke, "It didn't work out so good with Rosina. Or Italy."

"What happened in so little time? You seemed very happy."

"I don't know. She turned into a real bitch. Once she knew we had some money she went nuts. You know, she spent almost fifty thousand since we've been gone."

"What? How could she possibly do that in a few days?"

"You name it. She bought it. Expensive clothes, furs, jewels. She was crazy. I finally had to move the money to another account that she couldn't touch. When she found out she went wild. Next thing I know, she's gone. Good riddance. Ain't your fault, Tommy. You couldn't know."

Thomas and Sofia looked at each other and smiled. Once again, they were on the same wavelength. This time it was Paola they were thinking of. Just maybe they could get them together. Let them be a family. They were imagining what Antonio might think if he knew he had a son. They would wait for the right moment and do what they could. Right now, they needed to get out of the hotel.

"Tommy, if Rico is here, Carlo is too. We gotta get outta here, fast. No time to waste. I'm sure he ain't alone."

"I was just thinking the same thing. Our plans were to move upriver to the Ariau Towers in the morning. Guess we'll be doing it a little earlier than expected. Sofia reserved a suite there. We'll have to find someone with a boat and pay him well to get us there this early in the morning. You're coming with us, Antonio. From now on I think we all need to stick together. Tomorrow is going to be a big day."

"What's up tomorrow?"

"Some more visitors. All of whom want Carlo's head on a platter. Should be quite a clam bake."

"Sounds like fun. Lookin forward to it."

"Then let's get moving. I'm sure a taxi driver can find us someone with a boat. For enough money!"

The three of them left the suite and proceeded to the lobby. On their way down, Thomas asked Antonio,

"How did you ever find us?"

"You said you was goin to Manaus. I got lucky and picked this place to look first. A little cash and your description got me your room number. Funny thing, the guy on the desk said I was the second one lookin for ya in the past hour. That's when I knew there was trouble. When he described the guy, I knew it was Rico. I was afraid I was too late, but he said Rico hadn't come back out yet. So, you know the rest. Damn long flight to get here. Had to come through Fortaleza to Brasilia and then here."

"Well, that would explain why you wouldn't have met up with Carlo on the plane from Sao Paulo. I can never thank you enough, Antonio. Not in a million years."

"You don't gotta, Tommy. You're my friend. Aren't ya?"

"You bet. I'm your friend for life."

They managed to hail a taxi in only a few minutes. After Sofia asked some questions of the driver, they had their boat. The cabby used his cell to call and arrange their transportation to Ariau Towers. The cost was an extra fifty dollars American to the taxi driver, and one hundred for the boat. It was a bargain. When they arrived at the dock, the boat owner was waiting. After some more questions from Sofia, they headed towards the area where the craft was moored.

One look at the thing, and everyone suddenly got a sick feeling in their stomach. It was little more than a small dingy made of wood, and not looking to be in the best of condition. It was outfitted at the back with a fifteen-horsepower motor and little else. There wasn't even a single life jacket on board. Antonio was the first to pipe up with a comment.

"Holy shit, Tommy! We gotta ride in that thing? Up this river? Are we nuts?"

Thomas laughed helplessly and said, "Nope. Not nuts! Just desperate! We have no choice. I'm sure it'll be fine. Not much we can do about it anyway."

"Yeah, you're right! What the hell can we do?"

Sofia was actually the most relaxed of the three of them.

"Come on, you big boys. Don't be like little children. Let's get in the boat and get it over with," and then she climbed in and settled on the wooden seat in the bow.

"Come, Thomas," she said as she patted the seat next to her, "sit beside me."

Thomas climbed down into his position and Antonio took the middle seat. The boatman cast off the lines and settled in to start the motor. After about four pulls, it finally came to life with a great deal of sputtering.

"That don't sound so good, Tommy. Damn, why couldn't we have gotten a better boat?"

"Relax. It's going to be fine."

The boatman poked Antonio a few times in the back and mumbled something in Portuguese as he handed him a flashlight. Sofia, understanding, reached back and took the light from Antonio and shined it forward. Upriver, away from the city's lights, it would be dark beyond belief. With the load it was carrying, and the small motor, they would be fortunate to get fifteen miles an hour of speed against the river's current. That would mean a trip of two hours to the Ariau Towers. If they were lucky!

The flashlight that Sofia was holding had one primary purpose, to illuminate a small area in front of the boat in an effort to spot crocodiles that might upset the craft. There was also the possibility of running up against one of the dolphins that cruise the river. It would be, without question, fatal to end up in that river at night. The current was strong, and, in the extreme darkness, one would never find the shore before drowning or becoming food for whatever lurked beneath the murky surface of the water. The entire trip was one of total silence and intense concentration, not to mention underlying fear.

It was with great relief that they arrived at the reception dock a little over two hours later. The guards, necessary in this dangerous place at night, were somewhat surprised by their arrival. After much conversation and explanation by Sofia, they woke the manager who was kind enough, although a little perturbed, to register them and show them to their suite. There is only one suite at Ariau Towers, often frequented by the rich and famous, and Sofia had reserved it. It was ideal because of its location at the high point of the entire facility. It would provide an excellent view of all approaches. That would be critical when the other participants in this affair arrived. It was now six in the morning, and they all settled in for a little sleep. Soon enough the monkeys and birds that frequented the treetops would be creating a cacophony of noise. Best to rest for the few hours that it would be possible without disturbance.

CHAPTER 20

GATHERING THE FLOCK

It was ten in the morning in Fortaleza and Luiz de Salvo had gathered two of his men and a customs official for breakfast at the Hotel Vila Gale' Fortaleza. The ship with Carlo's containers was due to begin unloading just before noon and, by three o'clock should be on the dock. De Salvo had no idea why Carlo didn't go on this mission himself. He never involved de Salvo in the direct pickup of merchandise and was always very protective of his sources and his shipments. There was a good reason for that. Luiz de Salvo was already figuring out how to stiff Carlo for most of his money. After all, what could Carlo do about it? At the very moment of any particular whim, de Salvo could dispose of him in many ways. He never cared very much for the gringo. He liked the money he made for him, but never took any personal liking to him at all.

When breakfast had finished, de Salvo handed a wad of cash to the customs official. Five thousand dollars American was the going rate for a shipment of this size. In return for that payment, he would doctor the customs documents and reduce the import duty by more than half. That would amount to a hefty savings of over two hundred thousand dollars. It was well worth the cost. The plan was to inspect the containers and then arrange transport by truck to Sao Paulo.

If everything went smoothly, it could all be wrapped up by three-thirty and de Salvo would be on his way home. His men would remain behind to ensure the loading of the transports took place on time and then would accompany them on their trip to Sao Paulo. As they arrived at the pier, de Salvo lit up a good Cuban cigar. He couldn't help but think of what a fool Carlo had been. It wasn't hard to see the smile through the clouds of smoke curling up from his mouth.

At almost exactly three in the afternoon, the seal on the first of the five containers was broken. When it was opened, that expensive Cuban cigar fell from his mouth to the pavement. There, instead of new, Ford diesel trucks, they found nothing but rusted out hulks of old wrecks. In a panic, everyone went from container to container only to discover the same result every time. Luiz de Salvo was beside himself with anger.

"That little gringo pig. Who does he think he is messing with?" he raged, "I will kill that Yankee bastard."

As de Salvo was venting his rage, the customs official beat a hasty retreat with his cash. He wasn't about to risk having it taken away. Luiz allowed him to go on his way without interference. He knew it would be bad business to renege on a deal with a person in his position, especially over something that was not his doing.

After a hasty return to the hotel, it was time to call Carlo. Luiz picked up the phone and dialed his cell.

Still on his search, it took more than a few rings before Carlo answered in a somewhat flustered state, "Hello?"

"Carlo? What is this game you play with me?"

"Luiz? Is that you? What are you talking about?"

"Are you really in Manaus, my friend?"

"Yes. But how did you know that?"

"How did I know? You told me in your email. Do you forget so easily?"

"Email? I never emailed you. I have no idea what you're talking about, and I have a serious problem on my hands right now."

"Yes, you do! You have a very serious problem. Where are those trucks? Those bargain diesel trucks you promised me?"

"Trucks?" Carlo was now becoming a little unglued. How could Luiz know about the trucks? "What trucks?" he asked.

"What trucks? What trucks, you gringo bastard? The diesel trucks you took my money for. My quarter of a million dollars! Instead, I get containers of rusted old wrecks."

Carlo, exhausted from a night of searching for Thomas, almost collapsed to the ground when he heard those words.

"Luiz, I didn't take any money from you. I have no idea what you're talking about."

"Are you trying to make me believe that you did not email me with this plan to import twenty trucks? That you didn't ask for part of the money up front? That you did not take my money? Do you think I am stupid? Have you learned nothing about me?"

It was suddenly dawning on Carlo that Thomas was much smarter than he would have guessed. How he pulled this off, he had no idea. He knew that he must have gotten into his computer somehow, or he would have never known about Luiz. It was time to tell the whole story and hope it would spare his life. Luiz already knew all about Angela. He was the one who arranged all the forged documents to get her into Brazil in the first place. He didn't know, however, that she had regained her memory. Had he ever discovered that little detail he would have ensured that she had been killed without delay. Protecting himself would have been the priority. It always was.

"Shit, Luiz! You have to listen. I can explain!"

Carlo then told him in detail the entire situation with Angela and Thomas. He laid out the whole plan, and how everything went awry when Thomas escaped with the help of Antonio and Paola. When he finished his story, Luiz was incredulous, not to mention even more irritated.

"You stupid ass! For some money, you risk us all? Worse yet, you let that woman go back to Canada to tell her story? Why did I ever think you had any brains at all?"

"I was desperate. The bank was calling the loan on my house. I couldn't pay it. I needed the cash fast."

"I don't give a shit about your money problems. You had plenty of money. How you lost so much, I have no idea. This was a stupid plan. Where is this Thomas now?"

"I'm sure he's still here in Manaus. That's why I'm here. I'm trying to find him."

It was at that moment that one of Rico's men came running up with the news.

"Carlo, the police just take Rico from the Tropical Resort."

"What?" Carlo said as he covered the receiver of the phone, "Rico got arrested?"

"No, boss. Rico got dead. It was his body they take."

Carlo was stunned, "Dead? Rico? Holy shit!"

He put the phone back to his ear in time to hear Luiz yelling.

"Carlo? Carlo? Answer me, you shit."

"Luiz, he killed Rico. The son-of-a-bitch killed Rico."

"What? Who killed Rico?"

"Thomas! I have to find out where he is before this all turns to shit."

"It's already turned to shit, you ass," and with that Luiz de Salvo slammed the phone into its cradle and spoke to his men. "We are going to Manaus. We have some killing to do."

They were booked on the next flight through Rio but would not arrive until late in the morning. Wherever this Thomas was, they would find him, and Carlo, and dispose of them with all due passion. Luiz de Salvo was not a man to be made a fool of. Not by anyone. Ever!

Carlo, meanwhile, was now a man with two missions. First, he had to find Thomas and take care of unfinished business, and second, he had to get the hell out of Brazil as fast as possible. His life wasn't worth a red cent now, and he knew it. He turned to the two men that remained with him.

"Listen! We have to find this guy. One of you make the rounds of the rental car agencies. If they left by road we have to know when they left and what they're driving. The other one talk to taxi drivers around the hotel. See if anyone took them anywhere. I'll check the dock and see if they left by boat."

Everyone went on their way, and Carlo began talking to agents at the various cruise offices. Having no luck, he walked the boat slips questioning those aboard the larger vessels. Twice he walked right past the little wooden dinghy that had taken them upriver and was none the wiser for the experience. When the clock rolled around to almost eleven at night, they gave up the search in order to get some much-needed rest. If he was gone, he was long gone. A night's sleep couldn't make any difference.

Carlo decided to spring for two rooms at the Tropical Resort. After a meal ordered from room service, he curled up on the bed in a serious state of depression. It was doubtful he would sleep very much. How could all of this have happened? He was always so careful.

Nothing he had ever done was without careful planning. He was sure he had been the upper hand in this thing. The only wild card was that mysterious woman Thomas had been seen with at the hotel in Sao Paulo. It occurred to Carlo that she must have had a major role in all of this. The question was how?

Earlier in the day, Pauly Sabatini and his men had arrived in Rio. It was three in the afternoon when they checked in at their hotel. At about the same time that Luiz de Salvo was discovering his personal misfortune in those containers, Pauly was receiving a call from Thomas.

"Pauly! How are things in Rio?"

"Who knows? Only been here less than an hour. I never expected to be on a plane for almost eighteen hours."

"Yes! It's a very long trip if it's not a direct flight. Well, now you can catch the early flight to Manaus in the morning. It goes through Brasilia. You won't get to Manaus until midafternoon, but such is life. No rest for the wicked," he chuckled.

"Cute! Can't wait to meet you. It's gonna be a pleasure. Now where the hell is Manaus? Never heard of it."

"Well let's just say I hope you like jungle, rain, and humidity."

"I asked where. Not for a description."

"It's about a thousand miles up the Amazon River. You're going to love it. It's quite amazing."

"Yeah, I'm sure. Maybe you should write tourist brochures. What time is the flight? I have to book tickets."

"Seven in the morning. So, you had better get some sleep."

"Just one thing, Tommy! Where will I find you in Manaus?"

Thomas laughed, "If I'm lucky, you won't. You'll only find Carlo. Keep your eye on the prize, Pauly. Forget about me. It's when people get distracted that they make mistakes. You don't need any mistakes now, do you?"

"Thanks for the advice. If I need more, I'll just ask."

"By the way. There were three men with Carlo. One is dead already. Only Carlo and two others are left. Should make your work a little bit easier."

"Yeah, tough guy, thanks for the help. I'm so relieved."

"Sleep well. I'll call you when you get to Manaus."

Thomas hung up the phone and returned to his lunch. The three of them had managed to sleep until noon. Now they were enjoying a casual meal in their suite, and it was no easy task. Monkeys inhabit the treetops of the Amazon, and it was the primary reason this hotel was built at treetop level, to expose tourists to the teeming life that abounds high above the floor of the jungle. The monkeys and birds of this particular area were quite accustomed to human company and were not the least bit shy. If the opportunity arose, they would eagerly help themselves to your food. The monkeys, in fact, would often come and sit on their shoulders, chattering incessantly, in the hope of being offered a treat.

At one point, Antonio completely gave up trying to eat and turned his plate over to a persistent spider monkey that had been picking at his hair. As the monkey dug into this much-desired treat, Antonio smiled and laughed like a little kid. He was obviously enjoying this little pest.

"I think you like that monkey," Thomas said with an understanding smile.

"Yeah! He's kinda cute. Make a good pet maybe."

"Well, I'm not sure they'll let you take him home with you."

Sofia was busy feeding small portions of her meal to another little guest when Thomas asked:

"Sofia, can you check your laptop and see if, anywhere in Carlo's files, there's a cell number for Luiz de Salvo?"

"There is not. I checked before. But I can find it anyway, if you wish."

"You can? How?"

"Even here in the Amazon, they have an internet connection. I asked when we checked in. I will go into the customer base for the cell company and find what you need."

"You can do that?"

"Thomas! My poor, sweet man! Have you forgotten how good I am? You have such a short memory," she chided.

"Yes! Silly me. I forgot I have a genius on my hands."

"Not a genius. Just an expert," Sofia purred into his ear as she gave him a tender kiss that sent a chill up his spine.

"Hey, no teasing. You have work to do," he laughed.

"Yes sir. Mister boss," she joked as she kissed him yet again and then opened her laptop. As Thomas and Antonio sat and talked about nothing in particular, Sofia began her search. It hadn't been twenty minutes when she called out, "I got it."

"Already? I will never get used to how talented you are."

"I hope not. In every way," she chortled as she winked in a mischievous manner.

Thomas grabbed the phone and dialed the number Sofia had given him. It was answered by a somewhat irritated man, speaking in Portuguese. Thomas interrupted him.

"I'm afraid you're going to have to speak English if we're going to get anywhere."

"Who is this? And how did you get my number?"

"First of all, who is this? Luiz de Salvo?"

"Yes. Now, who are you?"

"Oh, I'm sure you've heard of me already. Haven't you spoken to Carlo yet? I would have thought you'd be on the phone ten seconds after those containers were opened."

"I see. So, this must be that annoying gnat named Thomas?"

"Annoying gnat? Cute! But yes, it's Thomas."

"You have created quite a situation, my gringo friend."

"I'm sure I have. To be honest, that was my intention. The question is are you joining the party?"

"Oh yes! I would not miss it for anything. I will be on my way to Manaus today. We can have a drink together. I admire such creativity. Such daring."

"Sure you do! And of course, you're being scammed out of a quarter of a million dollars would never tarnish our relationship. I'm not a fool, Luiz."

"Yes. I am sure you are not. In any event, I hope very much to meet you," de Salvo said with total sarcasm.

"Yes, well, join the club. Seems to be a lot of that going around today. I'll call you again when I know you're in Manaus. I'm guessing you'll get here sometime late in the morning. I checked the flight schedules. The earliest one you can get won't put you here until almost noon. Expect my call at twelve-thirty. Have a nice trip."

Thomas hung up and suggested that they all go for a stroll on the treetop walkways that led from room to room. It would be a nice diversion from the concerns about the next day. After a half-hour or so, Thomas took Sofia aside and asked what she thought about talking to Antonio about Paola and the baby. She wasn't so sure of the timing.

"Do you think it is good, Thomas? With what is happening?"

"Yes. I do. Imagine if something happened to us and we never told him about his son. He would go through life never knowing. Besides, I think he's a man who is suffering and is no longer concerned very much with living."

"You think so? You think he has lost his will to live?"

"It's very possible. I think he needs the motivation to keep going. To get through this in one piece."

"If you believe so, then we will talk to him."

Thomas called Antonio over and they all walked back to the suite. As they sat at the table with a cold drink, Thomas opened the conversation.

"Antonio, Sofia, and I have something very important to tell you. It's something very big, so prepare yourself."

Antonio sat there in total shock as they related the story of Paola's feelings for him and the search for her baby. When they came to the part about the baby being his, he almost fainted. It was a full minute before he spoke.

"I have a son? Paola's baby is my son? Are you sure?"

Thomas couldn't help but laugh.

"Oh, Antonio, when you see this kid, you'll realize no one could ever mistake him for anyone else's. He's the spitting image of his old man."

"I can't believe it. I always loved Paola. I just could never tell her. I had no idea she felt the same."

"I kind of assumed that. You always seemed so concerned about her. It was a bit of a giveaway."

"Are you sure she wants me? How could she, after I let all those things happen to her?"

"She knows you didn't want to let them happen. She knows that Carlo would have finished you if you had interfered. She understands! And yes, I think she wants you with her and your son. I have no doubt she loves you."

Antonio began to cry. Seeing such tears come from this big man took Thomas by surprise. He patted him on the shoulder and said:

"We're going to get out of this. All of us. You're going back to Paola and your son, and Sofia and I are going to make our life together. Everything is going to be fine. You just have to keep believing."

"It's gotta be, Tommy. I gotta see my son."

"You will. I have no doubt. Now I think we all need a diversion. We should all just relax, maybe go piranha fishing, and then get some rest for tomorrow."

"Yeah! That'd be good. Let's go catch some piranha," Antonio responded, like a man in need of something to clear his mind of this new worry.

The three of them headed down to the dock and climbed aboard the next boat heading out for a fishing trip. It was going to be a very welcome relief to have this distraction from the concerns about what might take place the next day. Thomas still had not totally devised a plan of action. This was the part he dreaded the most. He was only too aware that death would be visited upon several people. He could only hope that he, Sofia and Antonio were not among them. One thing he knew for sure was that he had to get Carlo out of Manaus, and upriver somewhere, before Pauly Sabatini and Luiz de Salvo arrived in the city. It wouldn't do at all if they were to bump into each other in Manaus or, worse yet, in the same hotel. He was wishing he had booked their rooms himself in order to avoid such a possibility, but it was too late to worry about that now.

As the boat plied its way up the river, Thomas had Sofia inquire of the helmsman about what might be found further upstream. He hadn't realized that the Ariau Towers were actually on the Ariau River, which feeds into the Rio Negro. They had traveled, in total darkness, thirty-five miles upriver to get here. It was understandable that he might not have noticed when they left the Rio Negro.

Sofia advised Thomas that, other than a native village or two, there was nothing of any significance further upstream. On their previous night's trip, Thomas had noticed what appeared to be a floating hotel barge just a few miles before they arrived at Ariau Towers. Sofia asked the helmsman about it and discovered that it was a floating hotel called the Jungle Othon Palace. Thomas immediately decided that first thing in the morning, he would send Carlo to take up residence there. As for Pauly Sabatini, he wouldn't know Thomas if he stepped on him. He and his crew would be coming to the Ariau Towers where they would be under Thomas' watchful eye. Luiz de Salvo was a different situation. He undoubtedly knew Antonio and had to be kept isolated from him at all cost. It was apparent to Thomas that he had work to do when they returned from their fishing excursion.

Meanwhile, in Manaus, the Police were not exactly involved in a heated search for Rico's killer. Antonio had paid the desk clerk very well to say that it had been Rico who had rented the room and that a few individuals, appearing to be local criminals, had checked in with him. He was quite convincing in relating the hurried exit from the lobby, just a few hours earlier, of the two men in question. Satisfied that they were looking for local individuals, the officers took down the information and then made their way, somewhat leisurely, out of the hotel as they laughed and joked with each other. After all, there was plenty of time to find the locals who committed this murder. No rush necessary tonight.

CHAPTER 21

RATTLING CARLOS CHAIN

As the boat returned to its mooring at the Ariau Towers, Antonio was grinning from ear to ear. He had caught at least half a dozen nice size piranha and was like a joyous little kid in his enthusiasm.

"Hey, Tommy? I never caught even one fish before. Never! I never even went fishin before. This was great."

"I'm glad you had fun, Antonio. You're the only one who caught anything. Sofia and I got shut out. Right, baby?"

"I don't want to catch those ugly things. Did you see the teeth on them? No thank-you! You big boys can have them all. None for me."

Thomas laughed and helped her out of the boat. He was sure that there was more to it than that. There was no doubt she was preoccupied with worries about tomorrow. Despite that, he did have to admit that these nasty little fish were just a bit disconcerting.

"Why don't we go up and grab a drink? I have to make a few calls, and I need Sofia to do one more thing before the night is over."

"Sure, Tommy. Sounds good. They gonna clean these fish so we can eat them?"

"Well, you can eat them if you want," Thomas laughed, "But I'll pass. They might bite back."

Thomas and Sofia walked hand in hand, with a grinning Antonio right behind. When they reached the suite, they ordered some snacks and drinks as Thomas asked Sofia to log on to her laptop one more time.

"What is it you need me to do now?"

"Can you open a numbered account in Grand Cayman online?"

"Yes! I can. I may have to call, too. Why?"

"See what you can find out. I think it's time we cleaned Carlo out. I don't think he'll be needing the money anymore. Later, we can donate it to the orphanage."

"Ah! My Thomas, you are so creative."

Within a matter of an hour or so, Sofia had performed her magic once again. He then had her log into Carlo's account.

"How much does he have in there?"

Sofia peered at the screen and rattled off, "Current balance, one million fifty-four thousand, three hundred and twenty-eight dollars, and twelve cents. All in American funds."

"Wonderful! Transfer one million to the account in Grand Cayman."

"Why not all?"

"A million-dollar transfer will raise enough eyebrows. Cleaning the account out completely would raise them all."

"Tommy, I thought you were going to use that to buy off Pauly and this de Salvo guy?" Antonio queried.

"I don't think my safety can be bought from those characters."

"Yeah! You probably got that right. They'd still want your hide anyway."

"Now I have to call and book a suite for Carlo on that floating barge downriver. You still have his credit card number?"

"Of course. His available balance is still over five thousand dollars."

With Carlo's credit card, Thomas called and reserved the only suite left. He was fortunate there was anything available at all. He then booked rooms for Pauly Sabatini and his men at the Ariau Towers. He was smiling at the thought of watching them check-in and them being totally unaware of who he was. He still wasn't sure what to do about de Salvo. It was likely that he would leave him in Manaus until he needed him. Timing would be everything when it came to getting him upriver. There was still the issue of deciding on a place for the final confrontation. It would have to be well up the Rio Negro, and out of the range of any prying eyes and ears.

Thomas was feeling just a little dirty about what had to happen. He wasn't someone who had ever thought he would be involved in orchestrating someone's death. He tried to smooth over the feelings of guilt by reminding himself of what they would do to him, Sofia and Antonio. It was a simple question of kill or be killed. He also considered the fact that these three men, and their crews, had undoubtedly been responsible for the deaths of many innocents over the years. Yet he didn't consider himself to be sitting in judgment. He was simply a man trying to remain alive and protect those he loved and cared for. He knew very well that the resulting carnage, should he fail to carry out this distasteful task, would spread beyond the three of them here. It would find its way to Canada and to Angela and his daughters. That was something he could never allow to happen.

With the reservation made, it was time to call Carlo and give him the instructions. It took longer than usual, at least four rings before he answered. There was not very much in the way of enthusiasm in his voice.

"Hello," he answered in a monotone and sullen manner.

"Carlo! You sound depressed."

"Tommy! I can't believe what happened to Rico. I had no idea you had it in you to do something like that."

Not wanting to let on that Antonio was in Manaus, Thomas simply replied, "Well, what can I say. Surely you didn't think I would just let him kill us without some resistance!"

"I guess not. But I still didn't expect it. The dope was supposed to call me before he did anything. If the four of us were there, you wouldn't have gotten away. That you can be sure of."

"No doubt. But, as they say, if, is a very big word."

"Was this call only to share corny analogies? Or did you have something important to talk about?"

"Actually, I've made a reservation for you. At eight in the morning, you'll be picked up at the dock and taken to the Jungle Orthon floating hotel. It's about thirty miles upriver. From there, at the appropriate time, we'll proceed to a meeting place. We do have business to settle."

"So that's where you'll be?"

"I didn't say that." Thomas laughed, "That would be too easy for you."

"This is getting a little tiring, Tommy. I hope you don't expect me to leave my men behind in Manaus. I won't do it. I'm not going anywhere without them."

"No problem. There was only one suite left available, so you'll have to share. I know how you'll hate that, but it's only one night and I'm sure they don't sWaltl all that bad."

"You have no idea! What time will you be in touch tomorrow?"

"Not sure. Not until afternoon, at least. So, get a good rest. You might need it."

"Answer me something first, Tommy."

"That depends on what is it you want to know?"

"Why the hell haven't you just left Brazil? You must know that I'm aware of what's in those containers. You played your little sting. Why stick around and keep this thing going? Why not go somewhere safe?"

"Carlo, you and I both know that nowhere is safe. You would never rest until you found me. Might as well get the whole thing over with. Whichever way it turns out."

"You have a point. I'm not a very forgiving person."

"I'm sure! By the way, you're down to your last fifty thousand dollars or so. Just thought you might like to know."

"What? What are you talking about?"

"I cleaned out most of your bank account. Just a little bargaining chip. The money is safe. You just can't get your hands on it."

"Tommy, you just keep pissing me off more and more."

"That's the point. There wouldn't be the same degree of pleasure in all of this if I didn't."

Thomas hung up the phone and began to pet a cute little howler monkey that had been staring at him throughout his conversation. As he stroked the monkey's fur, listening to him chatter away, he thought about the need to make a call to Pauly Sabatini to give him the instructions that would bring him to the Ariau Towers. He would call him in the morning, just before the plane landed, and direct him to the pier to catch the boat upriver. He even considered being on the hotel dock for their arrival. It really wasn't that daring a decision. They would have no clue that he was anyone other than a tourist. It might actually be a good idea.

Thomas's suite was in another company name that Sofia had in her little bag of tricks. It would have been ill-advised to use the one Carlo already knew about. In any case, Pauly would have no way of knowing who they were, or that they were at the same hotel. It made sense for him to think that he might as well get as close up as possible. It would make it easier to evaluate this rival and any potential threat that he hadn't anticipated.

It was early evening, and darkness was beginning to set in. Antonio had crashed on the sofa and was snoring somewhat loudly, much to the displeasure of the two monkeys perched on the armrests. After a fair bit of squealing, they seemed to decide that they preferred to go back into the trees where it was quieter and made a beeline for the nearest window.

Thomas and Sofia sat outside on the walkway just looking up at the stars that were beginning to appear in the night sky. As they sat there, side by side, and hand in hand, it seemed to Sofia that Thomas was even more lost in thought than she had ever seen him. She finally had to break the silence.

"Thomas? I can see that there is much on your mind. Would you like to talk about it?" Thomas squeezed her hand gently as he looked into her eyes.

"I was just thinking about the dramatic change in my life over the past weeks. Of course, one major change is the fact that I've found, in you, a love that is everything that I could ever hope for. That's a very good change, and one I'm grateful for."

"And the others?"

"Stop and think about it. Less than two weeks ago I was just a working guy, taking care of my kids, doing my job and going home tired every night. Since then, I've discovered that someone I thought was dead for five years had actually been kidnapped. Then I found a woman who I want to spend the rest of my life with. I've been back and forth to Brazil twice, stolen a dead man's identity, ripped a criminal off for a quarter of a million, involved Canada Customs in a scam, been held prisoner, escaped, been on the run throughout Brazil one step ahead of a man who wants me dead, and gotten myself on the hit list for two other criminal elements. Add to that the fact that you and I were in the same room when a man, in the act of strangling me, was shot about seven times. Then I ripped off Carlo's bank account for a million dollars. Oh, and let's not forget reuniting Paola with her son. And as for tomorrow? Well, tomorrow I could have the blood of a lot of people on my hands. Or I could die. I would call that just a little bit of a change in lifestyle in such a short span of time."

"I see what you mean. But you are not alone. It is the same for me. Do you feel badly about it all?"

"I hate to admit it, but the truth is I find it totally exciting. Life, except for being with you, is going to be a little boring when all of this is over."

"It's strange, I will miss the excitement and the danger too. But I will try to keep life nice and spicy for us when this is finished," Sofia said as she nibbled on his earlobe.

"I have no doubt you can, with no trouble at all. In fact, you already do. I am so happy that I found you."

"Then we are even. I am also happy that you found me. So, when this is all over, we'll go to La Serena."

The night was now pitch black. Clouds had rolled in over the forest canopy and blotted out the millions of stars that had filled the sky. No doubt it would rain soon. Thomas and Sofia retired to bed, unable to engage in any romantic activity due to Antonio sleeping on the sofa. His snoring had abated, and only the occasional jungle noises could be heard. Thomas and Sofia fell asleep in each other's arms, each feeling the heartbeat of the other against their bodies. This was the way they hoped to spend every night for the rest of their lives. Tomorrow would determine whether it would be possible.

Back in Manaus, Carlo was unable to sleep. He had informed his remaining two men that they would be leaving in the morning for upriver. His earlier phone conversation with Thomas was ringing in his ears. If Thomas had really managed to drain his bank account of a million dollars, things were going to get very uncomfortable for him. He could only hope that there was enough money left to get him out of the country and temporarily set up elsewhere. He was constantly back and forth between having second thoughts about this confrontation and then wanting it more than anything.

Carlo was sure that de Salvo was on his way to Manaus. The problem was, somehow, he just couldn't bring himself to admit defeat and turn tail. He had never run from anything in his life. With the exception, of course, of Pauly Sabatini! For that, however, he had ten million reasons. This time it was just plain revenge that kept him here. Occasionally, he somehow found himself believing that if he finished Thomas, everything would go back to normal. He was in a somewhat delusional state.

Carlo's men had managed to acquire half a dozen nine-millimeter pistols and plenty of ammunition on the black market in Manaus. The worst-case scenario, in Carlo's mind, was that de Salvo would show up and he would find it necessary to kill him as well. He had to think in those terms. He even began convincing himself that it would be the best-case scenario and not the worst. After all, with de Salvo out of the way, Carlo could just move in on his connections and go right back to business as usual.

As he paced the floor endlessly, he spoke aloud about every possible outcome. He was talking only to himself, but that didn't matter. He was a man possessed by both the torment of failure and visions of success at the same time. Thomas would have intended to rattle Carlo's cage, and yet he never would have imagined that he would be this successful. He would likely assume that he would become at least a little desperate, a little unglued, thereby diminishing his ability to function in a completely rational manner. However, how could he ever anticipate that his rival would end up a near basket case? Thomas had no idea that while he himself slept, Carlo was pacing his room and mumbling to himself, almost incoherently. He would have liked that vision.

CHAPTER 22

CHECK YOUR SCHEDULE, PLEASE!

As Thomas began to slowly awaken the next morning, he was vaguely aware of a tickling sensation on his face, accompanied by a somewhat unpleasant odor. As he opened his eyes, he was confronted with the backside of a young spider monkey that was sitting quite comfortably on his chin. He bolted upright in bed, sending the monkey scurrying hell-bent for the opposite end of the room, screeching loudly as it went.

"Awwwww, that's disgusting," he said as he began wiping his face with the sleeve of his t-shirt. He headed for the bathroom and, with serious determination, immediately washed his face.

"Damn, that's awful. I sure hope that's not a sign of how the day's going to go. Yuch!"

The previous evening, he had thought about the need to keep critters out during the night and had made sure all the windows and doors were closed before he went to bed. He guessed that this little guy had been hiding in the suite and had gotten locked in. As he spit continuously into the sink, he wished that he had been more careful.

Sofia, hearing the racket, sat up in time to see the monkey scurrying away and Thomas cursing and wiping his face.

"What happened?" she asked when Thomas had returned from the bathroom.

"If I tell you, I might never get you to kiss me again," he said with a laugh.

"Mmmmm! Nothing could prevent me from doing that."

"Yes, well, that little monkey had his butt parked on my face," he winced, as Sofia burst out in laughter.

"Well, then maybe I shouldn't kiss you until at least tonight. After you have washed your face at least five times more." Sofia winked and nibbled Thomas' ear in that manner designed to send goosebumps racing over his body.

"Listen, if you promise to kiss my ear like that instead, then I can wait with no problem," he said as he wrapped his arms around her and pulled her down on the bed, "you do know how to excite me."

In a state of total desire, they almost overlooked the fact that Antonio was asleep on the sofa. A loud yawn, echoing from the living room, brought them back to reality.

"I guess we must wait, my love," Sofia pouted.

"It appears so. Oh well, just think of how wonderful it's going to be when we're finally alone again. Oh, look at the time. I have to call Carlo and make sure he got on that shuttle boat." "Then I have to call Pauly Sabatini and get him to the docks. This is going to be a busy day of juggling murderous intent to where I want it."

"Well, I hope you are a good juggler. But you have done so well up until now, I am not very worried."

Thomas dialed Carlo's cell number, lit a cigarette and sat at the kitchen table. The very second he heard Carlo's voice he knew that the frustration level of his adversary was at a peak.

"Carlo! You sound just a little stressed."

"No shit! You think maybe?"

"How do you like your accommodations?"

"Does it matter? What's on the agenda today, smart guy?"

"Well, I just wanted to make sure you got to the Orthon alright. I'll be in touch later today. This will all be over sooner than you think."

"Glad to hear it. I'll be waiting for that call."

Thomas hung up and looked at his watch. It was just after nine and there were a few hours before he had to call Pauly. He still had to wrestle with the issue of where the final confrontation would take place. He decided to send Sofia to do some inquiring of the dock staff about what might lie upriver. She would suggest that they would want a boat they could pilot on their own to do some river touring. While Sofia went off to perform that task, Thomas made arrangements to provide boats for de Salvo, Pauly, and Carlo. He would, assuming Sofia returned with information about a good location, provide each boat with an envelope containing a map to their ultimate destination. He and Antonio would make sure they arrived first and secured a well camouflaged position from which to observe the action and, if need be, finish the job. As much as it troubled him morally, Thomas knew that none of them could be allowed to leave alive.

Sofia returned about forty-five minutes later. She had a pleased look on her face as she shared what she had discovered.

"Thomas, there is a perfect place about twenty more miles upriver."

"Really! It'll take a while to get there, but that's OK."

"Yes! There is a bend in the river at that point, and just beyond the bend is a deserted native village. There was a small group of nomadic Indians that lived there about a year ago. They have moved and the place has begun to become overgrown with vegetation again. The old man at the dock told me that there are a few huts that remain and there is a shallow area to beach a boat."

"That sounds perfect. It's unfortunate that someone has to know we're going there, but not much I can do about it. I would prefer total secrecy."

"No! It's not a problem. I listened to him as he talked about the place but then said we would not be interested in stopping there. So I had him tell me about what was farther up the river. I told him that we would just take a boat cruise and didn't want to get into any trouble in rough water or with river pirates."

"Great job, Sofia! You're pretty good at this stuff," Thomas laughed, "We might make a good pair of spies."

"Maybe so, but I will be just as happy when this is all over. I think it is enough excitement for a while."

"No question about that. Did you get the old man to make a map?"

"Yes, he marked where the village is and where there could be problems much farther upriver with unfriendly Indians. He also said that we should not even put our hands in the water. Pirahna! He said that they are very active in that area. Not like the few we found when we went fishing. Where we are going, he told me, they are quite numerous."

"Good to know. Well then, I think we have our location. Antonio? Did you hear that?"

Antonio had just finished washing up and came and sat at the table.

"Yeah, Tommy? Sounds good."

"We have the spot, now what's the situation as far as weapons go? I kind of forgot about that detail."

"No sweat! I got the gun I used on Rico, and another I brought with it. I took Rico's gun, too. Ammo, I got at least a hundred rounds. We should be fine."

"Unless the Brazilian Army shows up, Tommy. The we'd be Butch and Sundance."

"Don't even joke about that," Thomas said as he gave Antonio a slap on the back. "The police might be an issue though. I have no idea who, if anyone, patrols this area."

Sofia offered to inquire about it.

"I think they only come out if there is a problem. But I don't know. I do know that the old man told me we would be on our own that far upriver. He seemed to be saying that there would be no one to help us if we were in any trouble. I can go and ask more if you want?"

"No. It would only make him suspicious. We'll just have to assume that he's right. There will be no one around. I don't think any of the excursions they run get that far away from the hotel."

"You know how to shoot a gun, Tommy?" Antonio inquired with some concern.

"Of course. I was in the military. What have you got besides the nine-millimeter Beretta you used on Rico?"

"I got a forty-five automatic. Not those old army ones with the sloppy barrels that could miss from ten feet. This one's accurate. Then I got Rico's nine-millimeter Glock. Got about forty rounds for the forty-five and more than sixty for the nine millimeters."

"Sounds good. Might as well get everything ready. I'll take the forty-five and you keep your Beretta."

"What about the Glock?"

"Well, we can't leave our boat beached there. That would kind of ruin the surprise. Sofia, if she's willing, will have to wait a little way upriver with it. Out of sight. She can pick us up when it's all over. I want her to have a weapon just in case."

Sofia looked aghast, "But, Thomas, I never used a gun."

"It's not that hard. I'll teach you in five minutes."

"Yes, but I don't know if I could ever shoot anyone."

"If the need arises, just think about your family and your survival. Think about never seeing your family again. You'll shoot! Believe me!"

"I am not so sure, but I will take the gun anyway. How will I know when it is safe to come for you?"

"When you emptied your purse looking for lipstick the other night, I noticed that you have a whistle."

"Yes! I carry it when I have to walk at night in the cities. If I had trouble, I would blow it very loudly and pray someone would come to help."

"I'll take the whistle with me. When it's safe I'll blow it three times. One long, one short, and another long. That way you'll know it's either me or Antonio and not someone else calling you. Understand?"

"Yes! It's a very good idea. Here, you take it now."

Thomas tucked the whistle in his pocket and glanced at his watch.

"I reserved three motorboats. One for each crew! We have to make maps for everyone to find their way to that village. Sofia, I want you to get the old man to go into Manaus and deliver four envelopes to the agent that the boats were rented from. One envelope is for the agent and tells him where to deliver the boats. The other three are to be placed in the boats for de Salvo, Pauly, and Carlo. Offer the old man a hundred dollars to do it. I think he'll jump at the chance for that kind of money."

"I am sure. Are these good enough?" Sofia had traced three maps and spread them out in front of Thomas.

"Yes! Perfect. Just address the envelopes and we'll get them on their way."

"Listen, Tommy, I got two extra clips for the forty-five. We'll load them all and then you'll have about fifteen spare rounds you can carry. I got three clips for mine but only one for Rico's"

"That's fine. Fill the clip for Rico's and we'll load one in the chamber later."

Antonio went into the bathroom, out of sight of any staff that might wander into the suite to begin preparing the weapons. Thomas had Sofia request a cooler from the hotel. They would stash the weapons in it and cover them with the lunch they would have the restaurant prepare for their excursion. After all, it wasn't as if they could go marching down to the dock with pistols sticking out of their belts.

"It's time to call Pauly," Thomas said as he got up from the table. Pauly answered in his usual gruff manner.

"So, what now, Tommy? Do you have any idea how tired I am? You're wearing me out, you jackass."

"Now, Pauly. Is that any way to talk? I have a treat for you."

"And what might that be?"

"I've booked you into a place I stayed a few years back. You're going to love it. Maybe! It's called the Ariau Towers. When you get off the plane, take a cab to the dock. You'll see a water taxi from the hotel waiting to take you upriver."

"Upriver? What the hell are you talking about?"

"The hotel is built in the trees about thirty-five miles up the river from Manaus."

"You're shittin me! I gotta stay in some damn treehouse?"

Thomas was laughing heartily as he answered, "Relax! It's going to be fine. Just catch the boat. Don't be late. I'll call you there tomorrow. You have a chance to get a decent night's sleep. I think you need one"

"Yeah," Pauly growled into the phone and then abruptly hung up.

Thomas sat back down at the table. "I think he's getting a little pissed off. That's good."

Sofia was curious as to why it pleased Thomas so much to know that Pauly was so hostile.

"Thomas? Why is it so good that all of these people are so angry with you? It only makes them more interested in killing you."

"There are a number of things that can disturb the human animal to the point of recklessness and bad judgment. In this case, we can rule out lust, irrational love, and a few other emotional triggers. In this situation we have hatred. They certainly all hate me. It's a double whammy for Sabatini and de Salvo, because they hate Carlo too. Then there's anger and, in that sense, the same breakdown applies. Of course, we have greed, and each of them is guilty of that. Throw in exhaustion, which at the very least Pauly and Carlo are suffering from, and you have a group of men that are ripe to screw up. Our friend de Salvo is the only one who has not been on the chase long enough to be suffering from that problem."

"That is a very interesting theory. Let us just hope it is correct."

"Well, there's one other ace in the hole."

"What is that?"

"Confusion! While Carlo may be expecting de Salvo to come to Manaus, he certainly hopes to be gone by the time he gets here. He definitely isn't expecting Sabatini. Sabatini isn't expecting de Salvo and de Salvo isn't expecting Sabatini. Confusion! With any luck, at the point they discover this new development they will, at least for the moment, forget that I even exist. Each will be concerned with their own situation and self-interest."

"It all sounds very logical. As I said, I hope it is correct."

Suddenly Thomas pounded his fist on the table and spewed out a mouth full of obscenities. It took Sofia and Antonio each by surprise.

"Tommy! What's wrong?"

"I left out one other thing that can skew a man's common sense."

"What is that Thomas? And why does it make you swear so much?"

"Ego, Sofia. I let my ego and my desire to strut my unfamiliar face in front of Pauly Sabatini get in the way of my good judgment."

"Tommy, what the hell are you talking about?"

"I went to great lengths to keep de Salvo away from Ariau Towers because he would recognize you, Antonio. And yet out of my stupid desire to get in Sabatini's face, I'm bringing him here. He would recognize you just as quickly as de Salvo."

"That's it? No sweat! I can stay up here in the suite until we take the boat. No big deal. Don't get all up in a knot over it. You need to stay calm."

"It just wasn't smart. Now it makes me wonder what else I may have missed."

"You didn't miss nothin else. I gotta admit, I'm really impressed with how you worked this all out. It's gonna be fine."

"You may have more faith in me than I do in myself."

"Nah! You just got a case of nerves goin on. That's normal. But you gotta get over it and get your head on straight. Tomorrow all hell is gonna break loose, and you gotta be ready."

"Antonio is right. You have worked everything out so well. You cannot begin doubting yourself now."

"Well, I know one thing, without the two of you I would be a basket case right now. Anyway, you're right. I have to get back to a positive attitude. I guess I'll start by calling de Salvo. He should be checked in somewhere by now."

Thomas dialed Luiz de Salvo's cell and lit up another smoke. He was getting much too accustomed to having a cigarette in his mouth.

"Luiz? How's it going?"

"I am in the mood to meet you, my friend. Where are you?"

"Ahh, that's my little secret. Tomorrow is the day, Luiz."

"Tomorrow? And where will we meet?"

"I've arranged for a boat to be waiting at the dock tomorrow morning at seven-fifteen. You and your men will navigate the boat to a place upriver about seventy miles. There will be a map to guide you. Just follow it and you'll find Carlo. Who knows, you may even find me."

"Are you telling me that we have to go seventy miles upriver? I am not so fond of that idea."

"What? You don't like the jungle? You'd rather have a confrontation in Manaus where the police might get involved? That seems a little irrational to me."

"I guess it doesn't matter what I think. You are in control for now. Later will be a different equation."

"Glad you at least realize who holds the cards at the moment. Be at the dock at seven-fifteen. No earlier. It'll take you about two and a half hours to get where you'll be going. Just try not to fall in. Nasty things live in this river."

"Yes. Brazil is my country. I think I know about such things. I will be there tomorrow." Thomas hung up the phone and looked at Antonio.

"It's important that Carlo get to the village first. He would get spooked if he arrived and saw two boats there. Whichever of the other two arrived last would probably assume that one was mine and the other was Carlo's. I have to make sure they're spread out over a distance. Can't risk them running into each other on the river."

"Yeah, but Tommy, Carlo has to go right past this place. One of Sabatini's men might see him."

"No! I'll send Carlo out early enough. I figure he has about forty miles to cover. The man I got the boats from says they do about thirty miles an hour with a full load. That means he's there in about one hour and twenty minutes.

Luiz has about seventy or seventy-five miles to go. He'll need roughly two hours and twenty minutes. Pauly, he's the closest and will only need about an hour."

"So how you gonna get them off at the right time?"

"I have to hope they deliver the boats as I requested. Not any earlier, and not any later. I paid enough for it."

"So what time do they go off?"

"If Carlo heads out at eight, he gets there at about twenty after nine. Luiz has to head out at about seven-fifteen to get there by nine thirty-five, give or take. Pauly? We get him off at eight forty-five to have him show up at nine forty-five. Should work. I hope."

"Shit! That sounds more complicated than the bus schedules in Queens," Antonio chuckled, "But it should work out, I guess. What about us? What time do we leave?"

"We have to be on the river by no later than seven-thirty. That should give us time to set up."

"Sounds good."

"Well, now I think I'll go down to the dock and wait for Pauly," Thomas smiled at the thought. "Maybe we'll have a nice conversation over a drink or two."

"Thomas," Sofia piped up in a worried tone, "You cannot talk to him."

"I'll think about it. Anyway, I'm going down to the dock to hang out. You two stay out of sight. OK?"

"Yeah, Tommy. No problem. Just be careful. See if you can hear any names so I'll know if he brought anyone to worry about."

"I will. Be back soon." Thomas replied as he headed out onto the walkway and down the stairs to the reception dock.

CHAPTER 23

SAY HELLO, PAULY!

Thomas stood, leaning on the railing, just a matter of ten feet or so from the reception dock. He could clearly see the water taxi making its way upriver. In five minutes, it would be docking, and Thomas would get his first glimpse of Pauly Sabatini. He could feel a little boost of adrenalin causing a slight increase in his heart rate. The question running over and over in his mind was whether he would find the courage, or the foolhardiness, to talk to him. He would know the answer soon.

It wasn't difficult to determine which of the four men in the boat was Pauly. There was no mistaking the bearing and demeanor of someone who fancied himself a little Caesar, of sorts. As the water taxi tied up to the dock, Thomas was agog at the apparent size of the man. He appeared, at least in his seated position, to be more than a bit on the obese side.

The minute it was secured to the dock, three men, all dressed in Italian silk shirts, two-hundred-dollar slacks and Gucci shoes, climbed out of the boat. Then, to Thomas' amusement, it required the effort of all three of them to literally haul Pauly onto the dock. The excessive girth attached to his not overly tall frame made his movements labored and exhausting. His face was crimson and beaded heavily with sweat. Thomas couldn't help but be unimpressed with this vision. He knew he shouldn't judge a book by its cover, yet Thomas found it easy to consider

Pauly nothing more than a slovenly porker who was so out of his environment that it made him irrelevant.

As the hotel porter shuttled their bags to their rooms, Pauly and his men headed straight for the bar. The heat of the day was already getting to them, and they desperately needed a drink. Thomas saw this as his cue and followed along. He carefully looked each one of them over, taking in the measure of his rivals. Each appeared seriously weighed down by the heat and humidity. Those expensive Italian shirts were soaked with sweat and giant circles of perspiration engulfing each armpit. These were some tired individuals. As the four of them sat down at a table near the railing, Thomas thought better of taking the risk of talking to them.

Before long, Pauly finished his drink and was ready to head to his room. He spoke to one of the men he called Gino. Almost immediately, Gino and the other two followed Pauly out of the bar. Thomas waited for a while and, when he was sure they were out of sight, went back to the suite.

"Holy shit, Antonio! Pauly's a whale," Thomas whispered with an insulting laugh. "I'm sure I've seen beach balls that weren't that round."

"Yeah, Pauly always was on the chubby side."

"Chubby? I guess it has been a while since you've seen him. Chubby isn't even close. Hell, it took three men to drag his butt out of the boat. For a minute I thought they were going to drop him in the water."

"So did you talk to them?" Sofia inquired with a worried look on her face.

"I decided to follow your advice, so no, I didn't."

"I am very pleased that you listened to me."

"Did you find out who's with him, Tommy?"

"The only name I heard was one guy he called Gino. You know him?"

Antonio laughed slightly, "Yeah! He's nothin. He's Pauly's nephew, actually. If it wasn't for Pauly someone woulda put him in the landfill a long time ago. Useless!"

"So he didn't bring the cream of the crop then?"

"Doubt it. If Gino's here, he's the senior guy. What about the other ones?"

"The other two are young. Maybe mid-twenties. Never said a word. I'm sure they were just kids when you left Queens."

"That's a good thing. The young ones are all full of bullshit and carelessness. They all want to get to be made men. They want to become untouchable. So they take stupid risks. I doubt they got much experience in the rough stuff. Except maybe beatin on people who don't pay on time. Pauly has much better men to use. I'm surprised he don't have them here."

"Well, no doubt his best men have serious criminal records that would have created major problems clearing visas for them."

"Yeah! That could explain why the more dependable ones ain't here. Better for us. The older, more experienced guys are much more careful. It's better they ain't here."

"The best part is they all look like shit. It's easy to see the heat is getting to them. That's a good sign. They're dragging their asses already. Imagine what they'll be like upriver tomorrow!"

"Yeah! I been in Brazil long enough so it don't bother me too much. A lot worse here than in Sao Paulo though."

"I think we're all feeling it a little, but we're better off than they are. Sofia? You're pretty quiet."

"Just listening. I am thinking about tomorrow. I cannot help it."

"I know. You're not alone. Anyway, tomorrow comes soon enough. Let's concentrate on today. We'll just relax and save our energy for when we need it most."

With all the involved parties aware of their departure times in the morning, there was nothing for Thomas and company to do but wait. They would have supper delivered to the suite and stay out of sight, except for Thomas, until the morning. There was one item of curiosity he wanted Antonio's advice on.

"What happens back in Queens when they find out about Pauly?"

"There's gonna be somebody waitin to take his spot. They're gonna care a lot less about who killed him and a lot more about who gets his slice of the pie. Somebody'll be in line for it. Could be a small war, but doubt it. Those things get worked out one way or another. If he bit the bullet in Queens, different story. They'd be lookin' hard for who done it. But here? Who's gonna care. Foreign turf."

"That's reassuring. I don't need anybody else looking for us."

"Nah! Pretty sure there's nothin to worry about there."

At about nine o'clock, room service delivered supper to the suite. They all chose not to eat very heavily. In that kind of heat, food doesn't always digest very well and none of them wanted indigestion, or worse, the next day. Thomas had taken a short stroll along the walkway just before the food's arrival.

"It looks like Pauly and the boys have gone to bed. Can't see them around anywhere. Without air conditioning, I'm sure they're having a hell of a time sleeping. All the better for tomorrow! I hope they're good and tired when the time comes."

"We gotta get up pretty early, Tommy. Won't hurt us to get some sleep after supper."

"I'm sure that by ten o'clock we'll all be ready to pass out. One thing is for sure, I'll be combing this place for monkeys before I go to bed," Thomas joked as he winked at Sofia.

"Monkeys?" Antonio asked. He was still asleep and had missed the morning's entertainment.

"Yeah! I woke up with one sitting on my face this morning. It was a bit of a stinky situation."

Antonio gave a hearty laugh and offered, "Well, I'll help with the search. Don't want to wake up to one parked on my kisser."

With the door secured and window screens closed, they had been able to eat in peace. A few spider monkeys peered in the windows, chattering as if to be invited in, but none made it to the supper table. Eventually, no doubt in a state of frustration, they went back to roaming around the walkway in search of more hospitable hosts. They likely found someone willing to provide them with their desired treat and never found the need to return to what had been a fruitless effort at begging. Except for the occasional and far-away chatter, all was quiet. Thomas broke the silence with a comment to Sofia. "I think you should call about flights to Chile. We have to go to Brasilia first, but we should find out what the connections are. We need to have our escape plan in place."

"Yes! Maybe it is a good idea. I have no idea of the flights to Chile from Brasilia."

Sofia dialed the airline and, after a lengthy discussion with the reservations desk, shared what she learned with Thomas and Antonio.

"We can fly out of Manaus to Brasilia tomorrow night. I booked us on the nine o'clock flight. Thomas, you and I will have to take a flight from Brasilia to Sao Paulo and then on to Santiago for a connection to La Serena. We can be out of Brasilia, and on our way, at six in the evening, day after tomorrow."

"Perfect, sweetheart. We'll be in La Serena in two days."

"Yes, and I can see my family. I miss them so much."

"I know you do. I am sure they miss you just as much. Of course, it will be nice to spend at least one day with Antonio and Paola before we leave. I'm so eager to see how that all plays out. It should be very emotional."

"Oh yes! We should take a lot of Kleenex. I think we will need it."

Thomas looked over at Antonio. "What do you think, my friend? Lots of Kleenex?"

"Yeah! I think a lot for sure. I'm a little nervous, Tommy. You sure Paola will want me there?"

"I'm as sure of that as I could ever be of anything. I think I know what's in her heart."

"And my son? He really looks like me?"

"Well, he's a heck of a lot cuter, but yes, he looks like his dad for sure," Thomas teased as he patted Antonio's shoulder.

"I can't wait to see him. I don't know what I'll do when I see him for the first time."

"You'll cry, Antonio. Believe me, you'll cry. That sort of happiness can bring a torrent of tears. You're going to be a very happy daddy. And a good one."

"I hope so. That's a big responsibility. I hope I can handle it."

"You can. Besides, you'll have Paola to guide you. Listen to her. Always! She's a good woman. You know that."

"Yeah! A real good woman. Better than I deserve."

"It's the same for me. This wonderful woman here," Thomas said as he put his arm around Sofia and pulled her close to his shoulder, "is more than I could ever deserve. I'm just thankful that she's too blind to see it."

"Stop, Thomas. I am not too good for you. You will make me conceited."

"Well, we don't want that. I like you just a little humble."

Thomas placed a tender kiss on Sofia's cheek as she purred in a manner that always excited him.

"I think we should all get some sleep now, Thomas. We need to be up and getting ready by six-thirty."

Antonio curled up on the sofa as Thomas and Sofia headed for the bedroom. Since being in Manaus they had taken two showers, and not together. Tonight, they decided that they couldn't pass up the opportunity. Thomas closed the door to the bedroom and followed Sofia to the bathroom. Within minutes they were in passionate embrace under the flowing water. Their entire lovemaking session took place in the shower to avoid being heard by Antonio. Knowing that it was possible they would never have the chance again, they made sure it was tender, sensual, passionate, and long-lasting. When their emotions and passion had finally been fully spent, they were not sure they had been successful in being as quiet as they had planned. As they both giggled like naughty teenagers, they climbed into bed and, despite the worries about what might happen the next day, happily fell asleep in each other's arms.

CHAPTER 24

SLAUGHTER ON THE RIO NEGRO

Thomas was up, and raring to go, at six in the morning. He poured himself some fresh mango juice and lit a smoke. He would let Sofia and Antonio sleep a while longer as he pondered the complexity of the boat schedule he had worked out. Thomas had paid for the boats with Carlo's credit card number and wasn't worried about any chance they could be traced back to him. What did concern him were the few details that could throw the entire schedule out of sync.

For one thing, all it would take was a late delivery of one of the boats. That possibility was not at all unlikely given the laid-back attitude of many Brazilians of this area regarding punctuality. Thomas had offered a one-hundred-dollar bonus for tiWalty delivery and hoped that it was sufficient to ensure at least some devotion to fulfilling that obligation.

The other item of concern had to do with the speed at which they proceeded upriver. If they made the estimated thirty miles per hour, everything would run like clockwork. A mile or two here or there would not create any serious difficulty, but a significantly slower boat, or slower driver, could make a mess of everything. All Thomas could do was keep his fingers cFedired, pray, and hope everything ran smoothly.

As he was butting out his cigarette and pouring another glass of juice, Sofia came and sat next to him.

"This is the big day, Thomas. I am a little nervous."

"That makes two of us. No point in pretending that it's nothing to be worried about. All we can do is follow the plan and hope everything comes out the way we want."

"And pray. Don't forget the prayer, Thomas."

"I've already said a dozen, I think," Thomas replied as he smiled and kissed Sofia softly. "I can't accept the possibility that you were brought into my life just so that it could all end up badly. That's not acceptable. I have to believe that we came to be with each other for a better purpose than that."

"I am sure of it."

The bear-like yawn coming from the sofa served to announce that Antonio was awake. As he rubbed the sleep from his eyes, he plodded, rather heavily, over to the table and took a seat.

"It's showtime, Tommy. You ready for it?"

"Do I have a choice, my friend?" Thomas patted Antonio on the shoulder and smiled. "I have you on my side. That makes all the difference. I know I could never pull this off without you."

"Not so sure about that. Then again," Antonio gave a hearty laugh, "ya never know."

There was a knock at the door and Thomas got up to answer it. It was a bellhop delivering the lunch the kitchen had prepared for their excursion. Once they were alone again, Antonio set about wrapping the guns in a plastic bag, covering them with ice, and then with the food that had been provided. Once the cooler was securely packed, they all set about dressing appropriately for the day. To Thomas, that meant long, cotton, khaki pants, a long sleeve cotton shirt, and good hiking boots. Despite the heat, he preferred to have as much of his skin covered as possible. If something planned to go crawling around on him, it would have to get through his clothing first.

Sofia would be remaining with the boat and didn't need to be so concerned about the spiders and other such things that inhabit the jungle floor. She chose a pair of shorts and a t-shirt. Antonio, taking a cue from Thomas, made sure he was well covered. By seven o'clock they were in the boat and heading upriver.

The trip was a quiet one. There was no conversation as everyone simply sat, thought, and took in the sights along the Rio Negro. They spotted the occasional alligator sunning itself on the shore, a reminder that they would not care to be in the water. Almost exactly one hour after they departed Ariau Towers, they arrived at the bend in the river, just downstream from where they would put ashore. Thomas, at the helm, slowed the boat to a crawl as they searched the bank for signs of the abandoned village.

"There, Thomas!" Sofia called out. "I see it there. Maybe fifty feet further up the river."

"Good eyes, Sofia. Now let's see how close we can get this thing to the shore."

Thomas steered the seventeen-foot-long craft toward an area that appeared to offer an opportunity to actually beach the bow of the boat. He was bang on, and the bow slid nicely about two feet onto the somewhat muddy ground, while still leaving the motor in deep enough water.

On their journey from the hotel, Thomas had taken the time to show Sofia how to operate the craft. She was a quick learner, and he could see no difficulty for her in navigating a short way upriver, anchoring, and then returning to pick up him and Antonio. As he gave Sofia her final instructions, Antonio unpacked the guns and handed Sofia the Glock. Thomas reminded her how to use it, insured the safety was set and that she knew how to disengage it if the situation required her to do so. She seemed prepared, and Thomas and Antonio gave the boat a push back into the water and sent her on her way upstream.

Before they set out to explore the area and select a good hiding place, Thomas drew Antonio's attention to a spot on the muddy shore. "See that?"

"What? That big smudge?"

"That's a slide mark. See the footprints? There was an alligator here. At least I hope it's a case of 'was here' and not 'is here'. Keep your eyes open."

"Damn! I'll keep em wide open."

"Let's smooth this mud out with some branches. We have to erase our footprints and then we'll find a place to set up. We need good cover with a good view of this area. I can see some huts over there. We'll check them out first."

After a fair job of wiping away the evidence of their arrival, they inspected the three ramshackle huts that were still standing. Made of branches, twigs, and leaves, they weren't the sturdiest of structures. Finally, after a good walk around, they settled on a spot in among a large area of broadleaf flora, slightly behind the huts and with a clear view of the whole area. It took a little convincing to get Antonio to lay down in that mess of undergrowth, but eventually, they were both nicely settled and well camouflaged. Now they had only to wait what might be as little as five minutes for their first visitors. That would be Carlo and his boys, if things went as planned. If the schedule held, there would be no more than fifteen-minute intervals between arrivals. Thomas was just slightly on edge. What he heard next didn't help the matter.

"Hey, Tommy. I think I'm halucinatin."

"What? What do you mean?"

"I'm sure I just saw that big log move."

"Big log?" Thomas' eyes were so wide open that they were like saucers. "What log?"

"Just beside you there. Maybe five feet to your right."

Thomas slowly turned his head as he felt his heart begin to pound. If there is such a thing as being prepared for what you will see, and yet not prepared, this was it. Thomas fully expected that he knew what would be there, and yet hoped that Antonio was indeed hallucinating. He wasn't.

Not more than six feet to his right, Thomas saw the form of the dreaded Anaconda. He was sure it rivaled the longest one ever recorded, in the range of thirty-seven feet. The snake was partly coiled, and its huge head was pointing directly at Thomas, its eyes upon him, its tongue flicking rapidly as it took Thomas' measure.

"Antonio," he softly whispered while looking directly into the snake's eyes, "do you have your silencer on?"

"Yeah. What's up?"

"That's no log. It's an Anaconda. If it moves for me, shoot it. And please, don't miss. Right in the head! Anywhere else is a waste of a bullet."

"No problem. I got a bead on him. Why not just finish him now?"

"I'm not interested in killing him unless it's to save my butt. This is his territory. We're the trespassers. Anacondas will only feed every few weeks. I'm certainly hoping that this big boy has recently eaten."

As Thomas and the anaconda continued their staring match, he could hear the sound of an approaching boat. It was time to make a decision about this unexpected threat. It wouldn't do to have this thing lurking nearby, waiting for an opportunity to strike. Just as Thomas was preparing to tell Antonio to shoot it, the snake found its attention drawn towards the water's edge where Carlo's boat was being beached. Slowly it began to move away in the direction of the nearest hut. Thomas watched, as its huge body slithered into the hut through a hole in the branches and leaves that made up the outer wall. It seemed the snake was more interested in avoiding these new intruders.

"Damn, that was close, Tommy."

"Yeah! Hope there aren't any more around. We'll have our hands full enough. I'm glad we didn't have to kill it."

Carlo's men had dragged their boat up on the bank of the river. Slowly, they were making their way towards the clearing in the center of the huts. They were still too far away for Thomas to hear what was being said, but there was a great deal of conversation going on. Most of it was coming from Carlo.

"Damn, Tommy! Carlo looks like shit."

"He does look pretty rough. He's going to look a lot worse in a little bit, I think."

Carlo was now near enough that Thomas could make out some of his ranting.

"Son-of-a-bitch! Where is that bastard? If this is another one of his little jokes, I'm going to spend a week killing him."

"Maybe he just late boss," one of Carlo's favela hoods chimed in.

"Yeah. Late. Maybe. Let's look around a little. Find a good place for you two to hide. Let him think I'm alone."

Carlo and his men began checking out the hut that was farthest away from Thomas and Antonio. They looked behind it, around it, inside it and then, satisfied in some manner, moved on to the second one. Having finished that examination, they were approaching the third hut when all three of them heard the sound of another boat. Carlo was more than slightly animated as he directed his men,

"That has to be him. We'll hide in here until he gets ashore."

The three of them quickly entered the hut to wait.

"Holy shit, Tommy! Did they just go in there with that friggin big snake?"

"I think they did. This should be interesting."

"How come they ain't come runnin out yet? Maybe the snake got em. You think it did?"

"He could only get one at a time. The others would be running like crazy. Or shooting! That anaconda might have snuck out the other side of the hut or could be hiding in that pile of leaves we saw inside. Can't be sure! We'll know soon enough if he's in there."

"Hey, Tommy! Here comes de Salvo and his men!"

Thomas looked towards the river's edge to see three men approaching the clearing. Once again, it wasn't difficult to tell which of the three was at the top of the food chain. While Pauly had looked like some overweight Roman Emperor, Luiz de Salvo was tall, dapper, and looking fairly fit. The two men with him looked as mean as anyone could ever be. Each one was at least the size of Antonio. Maybe even bigger!

"The show should start soon. Carlo must be pissing his pants about now."

Thomas wasn't far wrong. Over in the hut, Carlo was beside himself with anxiety. "Shit! What the hell is de Salvo doing here? That bastard Thomas set me up. That dirty son-of-a-bitch."

In the back of his mind Carlo knew he had taken on the wrong man. He knew he should have just disposed of Angela and been done with it. Too late now! His life was on a major downward spiral and there was no way out without finishing off de Salvo and his men.

"We have to take them out. I'll take de Salvo, you take the one on his right and you the one on his left," Carlo hastily tossed out his instructions.

Before anyone could even take aim, the sound of the final boat could be heard making its approach. Carlo instantly changed his command. "Wait! That must be that pain in the ass, Thomas. We'll get all of them at once. No sense scaring him off with gunfire."

Back in the underbrush, Thomas and Antonio were biding their time. With any luck they would never have to fire a shot. Not likely, but a hope, anyway.

"That's got to be Pauly. Shouldn't take them more than half an hour to get his lard ass out of the boat," Thomas quipped.

"You're a cruel man, Tommy," Antonio chuckled admiringly.

"Nah. Just truthful."

Luiz de Salvo and his men had been wandering around the clearing talking in Portuguese when they heard the boat arrive. Thomas had no clue as to what they were saying, but he suspected that they assumed the boat would be bringing Carlo to the gathering. When Pauly, Gino, and the other two Queens hoods entered the clearing, there were more than a few moments of awkward silence. Inside the hut, Carlo was having a serious fit.

"Jesus! Sabatini's here? Holy shit. Damn! Thomas, you bastard! You smart, sadistic bastard. If I get out of this, there is no place you will ever be able to hide."

Carlo and his men decided to keep out of sight and see what developed between de Salvo and Sabatini. With any luck, he thought, they would kill each other.

After a period of silence, Pauly was the first to speak.

"Who the hell are you guys?" he demanded.

Luiz de Salvo was having none of it.

"This is Brazil, my country, so I am the one to ask the questions. Who the hell are you?"

"I'm Pauly Sabatini. Supposed to meet a guy here."

Luiz glared with a fearsome look in his eyes.

"I am supposed to meet someone here too. What is the name of the man you are to meet?"

"Who the hell is asking?" Pauly demanded, as if he thought he was still in Queens and all powerful.

Luiz saw no harm in answering, "I am de Salvo. Now who do you meet here?"

"A crumb by the name of Carlo."

"Carlo? You are meeting Carlo?"

"Yeah! You know him?"

Luiz laughed derisively, "Don't tell me! You are the fool who allowed Carlo to steal your money? Your ten million dollars?" Luiz was by now laughing hysterically.

Pauly was losing his cool. Hot and sweaty, and on the verge of collapse, he was in no mood for this.

"You find that funny? It's a big joke to you?"

"What I find funny is that this Thomas, whoever he is, has pulled off one hell of a trick. He's brought us all together. He knows we both want Carlo's head. So, might as well work together."

Pauly was mulling over this proposition as Thomas and Antonio were discussing their perception of what was taking place.

"I don't know, Antonio. They seem to be getting pretty chummy over there. Not a good sign. Something had better happen soon."

"Then why don't we make something happen?"

"What do you have in mind?"

"Somebody has to start the shootout," Antonio answered as he took aim with his Beretta.

There was a slight muzzle flash, the almost inaudible 'phooot' of the silencer and a nine-millimeter slug penetrated the skull of one of de Salvo's men. Antonio had started the action for them.

By the time de Salvo's man hit the ground, everyone remaining standing had their guns drawn. Unsure whether to point them at each other or start spraying the surrounding area with a hail of bullets, they stood quiet and almost motionless. Their eyes surveyed first each other and then their surroundings, looking for any sign of movement.

Over in the hut that served as Carlo's hiding place, the anaconda had been lying in wait beneath a large pile of foliage. Thomas had been wrong about this snake. He definitely hadn't eaten for a while and was more than hungry. In one quick strike, it had one of Carlo's men by the head, its body already beginning to coil itself around this new victim. Carlo and his remaining gunman had only one choice. They bolted from the hut with guns blazing in the hope that they would surprise de Salvo and Pauly and finish everyone off in short order.

Until the gunfire had begun, Sofia had been preoccupied with an alligator that had been cruising near the boat. Its eyes were like little balls floating on the surface of the water while its body lurked below. It was eyeing this potential meal and biding its time. The hail of gunfire sent shivers down Sofia's spine and caused the alligator to become a memory. No more than a quarter of a mile upriver, she could hear every shot. She was praying none of those bullets had found Thomas or Antonio. Her ears strained, waiting for the sound of the whistle that would let her know that at least one of them was fine.

The first to go down in the shootout was Gino. Shortly after he bought it, Pauly and his other two henchmen were felled. Luiz de Salvo and his last man were firing in all directions as Carlo was making his way to the river. From their hiding place, Antonio and Thomas opened up on Carlo's only remaining hood, and he dropped to the ground in a heap.

Luiz, now realizing they were being fired at from another direction, turned his attention to the area where Thomas and Antonio were hiding. He and his still standing partner forgot about Carlo and opened fire on the underbrush. In the hail of bullets that traveled in both directions, de Salvo and his man finally went down. Thomas had taken a bullet in the shoulder and was wincing in pain.

"Tommy! You ok?"

"Yeah. Just grazed me, I think. No entry. Go get Carlo. I'll be fine. He can't be allowed to get away."

"He won't," Antonio assured him as he began a run towards the river.

He could hear Carlo trying to start the boat. He was having trouble because he had flooded the engine.

When Antonio reached the bank of the river, Carlo had his back to him as he struggled with the motor.

"You ain't goin nowhere, Carlo," Antonio hurled the words like daggers.

Carlo slowly turned around to face him.

"Antonio? Thank God! Listen! We have to get out of here. Let's try the other boat."

"I ain't goin nowhere with you."

"Hey, Antonio! Come on. Listen, if it's about you helping Thomas escape, forget about it. It's ok. We all make mistakes. I forgive you. I need you. We're blood! Remember?"

"We ain't blood, Carlo."

"What are you talking about? Were cousins for crying out loud! That's blood family." While he spoke such reassuring words to Antonio, Carlo was slowly retrieving his pistol from his back pocket.

"We ain't cousins."

"What are you talking about? Of course we are."

"Nope! I was adopted. So you see, no blood. No blood between us at all."

Carlo pulled the pistol from his pocket and swung it towards Antonio. Before he could pull the trigger, Antonio put a bullet in his chest, sending him falling backwards out of the boat and into the water. Carlo struggled to keep his head above water as the current swept him up and pulled him downstream. Antonio fired four more rounds as the body approached the bend in the river. Carlo was gone.

Back in the clearing, Thomas was checking the bodies to see who, if anyone, was still alive. No one was. It was Antonio who told him they were one body short.

"One of Carlo's guys ain't here. Better look for him before we go."

"Yeah! I suppose we should. I don't remember seeing him come out of the hut."

"Me either. Guess we outta take a look."

They approached the entrance very cautiously, Antonio taking one side and Thomas the other. They both peered around the corner at the same time.

"Oh, man, that's disgusting."

There, partly stretched out on the floor, still trying to swallow its prey, was the anaconda. Nothing could be seen of Carlo's man except from the knees down. The rest was well on its way to the digestive tract.

Together, they returned to the beach, laughing and crying at the same time. Thomas pulled out the whistle and gave the signal for Sofia to pick them up. Those three sounds were the sweetest Sofia's ears had ever heard. She started the motor and began to proceed downstream to retrieve her man.

CHAPTER 25

LEAVING MIGHT BE WISE

With three other boats crowded together at the shore, Sofia had no choice except to pull parallel to their sterns so that Antonio and Thomas could climb aboard from one of them.

Once they were settled, Thomas took the helm and opened it up full throttle. Immediately, Sofia noticed the blood on his shirt.

"Oh my God! Thomas, you have been shot?"

"It's alright, honey. Just a graze! It'll be fine."

"Yeah, Sofia! You shoulda seen your man. He was somethin else. And that snake!"

"Snake? I don't want to hear. You are both alive. That is all I care about."

"Hey, Tommy, we gotta keep an eye out for Carlo's body."

"Well, right now you had better get rid of the guns. Toss them in the river. They'll never be seen again."

"I'll toss yours and Sofia's," and with a quick throw the Colt forty-five and the Glock were on their way to the bottom of the Rio Negro.

"I'll toss mine in a bit. Just gotta make sure about Carlo."

"Antonio, we haven't seen him yet. Good chance an alligator got him. Or Pirahna! He could never survive in this water. Certainly not with a bullet in his chest."

"Yeah! You're right," Antonio replied, tossing his Beretta into the water while Thomas expressed another concern.

"I have to believe that someone downriver might have heard all that shooting. Sound carries pretty well over water."

"Guess we outta come up with a story. Just in case."

"How about this? We're enjoying our little boat trip when we hear gunshots just as we're approaching the river bend. We see some boats and guess that they may be poachers or, worse yet, river pirates. Just as we're passing, a stray bullet hits me in the shoulder. We're scared to death and make a run for it down river. Sound good?"

"Yeah, Tommy! Sounds perfect. Just in time, too. Look!"

Speeding upriver, directly at them, was what appeared to be a police or army patrol boat. On the bow were two uniformed and heavily armed men. Sofia immediately decided to put the terrified tourist act into play. She stood up and waved her arms frantically as Thomas slowed the boat to a crawl, and then stopped dead in the water. By the time the patrol boat had come along side, with its full complement of five soldiers carrying automatic rifles, Sofia had managed to muster up a torrent of tears to go along with the frantic Portuguese. The soldiers listened intently as Sofia told them the story. She explained that Thomas and Antonio did not speak Portuguese and were on their first trip to the Amazon.

One of the soldiers, an officer, began speaking to Thomas in English. "You tell me what has happened here?"

Thomas repeated the story they had agreed upon, the one Sofia had undoubtedly already told in Portuguese. It was just the officer's way of checking for the truth and being sure the stories matched. Once satisfied, he asked if Thomas needed medical attention. Thomas said he was fine and would get bandaged up at the hotel. In a matter of five minutes, the patrol boat with its well-armed occupants was on its way upriver to check out the situation.

As Thomas restarted the motor and gave it full throttle, Sofia used some water from the cooler to clean his wound.

"I do not like this. You could get a bad infection."

"Don't worry. Check the storage compartment. There may be something helpful in there." Sofia popped open the compartment and pulled out a large first aid kit.

"Wonderful! There is peroxide and iodine here. I can clean it very well now." With cotton swabs she soaked the wound in peroxide, letting it bubble completely before dabbing it dry and applying more. When she was satisfied that the peroxide had done its job of killing any germs in the wound, she applied a liberal coating of iodine and then covered it with a gauze bandage.

"There! Now it will be fine. I am so happy it was only what you called a graze. English is such an odd language. I always thought that graze was something cows did."

Thomas couldn't help but laugh.

"You're right. Both ways. It is something cows do, and goats and horses, but also has a different meaning. And yes, English can be a very odd language."

The trip back downriver was much quicker. Going with the current, they were able to make the return trip in less than forty-five minutes. When they pulled up to the dock, there was a crowd of curious people gathered. A fisherman had come down river and regaled them with a tale about some shooting he had heard. Sofia related their story in Portuguese as Thomas laid out the English version for the guests. After fifteen minutes of fielding questions, they excused themselves and went to their suite to pack.

Thomas called the check-in desk and advised the clerk that, after their harrowing experience, they felt the need to return to Manaus and would he please arrange transportation in one hour. With serious apologies for their situation, the clerk offered another night's stay at no cost. Thomas thanked him, politely declined, and set about packing. They would be on their way to Brasilia and Antonio's first encounter with his son.

Antonio was in the bathroom washing up when he called out to Sofia. "Hey, Sofia! You got any nail polish remover?"

"Yes. Why?"

"Thomas and I should wash our hands with it. Gunshot residue. Just in case. Don't need to be in any Brazilian jail. Wouldn't be my idea of fun."

"Good idea, Antonio! See, Sofia? He is indispensable."

"Yes, he is! We owe him everything. Absolutely everything."

"Yes, we do! We can never forget that. If he is ever in trouble, or in need, we have to do whatever we can for him."

"I agree. We must take care of him as he has done for us."

Overhearing the conversation, Antonio shouted out from the bathroom, "Will you two cut that out? You don't owe me nothin! If it wasn't for you, Carlo woulda finished me off sooner or later. So, we're even."

"OK, big guy. We're even," Thomas shouted back. Then he leaned towards Sofia and whispered, "No way we're even! Right, babe?"

"Not even close. We owe him forever."

"That's my girl," Thomas whispered as he took Sofia in his arms and pressed his lips softly against hers. He loved her lips, so full, so soft and warm. He could kiss her for hours. Unless Antonio had other ideas!

"Hey! You guys wanna quit makin out and get ready to go? I gotta see my son you know," he growled in the manner of good-natured ribbing. "Besides, it's makin me think of Paola and I don't wanna get all mushy like."

"I'm afraid he's right, Sofia. We have to get ready to go. Besides, watching him get all mushy wouldn't be a pretty sight."

Within the allotted hour, they had finished packing, said their fond farewells to a few of the monkeys that frequented their suite, and headed for the dock. Once they were aboard, the boat taxi left its berth and started wending its way down river. As it reached the Rio Negro, they noticed the patrol boat making its return trip. Two of the three boats left at the landing were following close behind with soldiers at the helms. Stacked in the belly of the lead boat was a pile of bodies on their way back to Manaus, probably for final identification. The soldiers waved as they passed by. It was clear now that there would be no trouble with the police. If they had wanted to question them for further information, they would have stopped them right then and there.

Upon arrival at the dock in Manaus, Thomas hailed a taxi, and they were on their way to the airport. They would have a wait of a few hours, but no problem. It was an opportunity for them to reflect on the day's events. Thomas had no way of knowing if he had actually killed anyone this day. He only knew that he had emptied a clip of ammunition in the direction of three men. They could have fallen victim to his bullets, or Antonio's. Either way, there was still the need to deal with the knowledge that he had blood on his hands. It would not be an easy thing to live with, no matter the circumstances. He could only hope that it would all eventually fade into the darkest recesses of his memory.

Once onboard the plane, there was very little conversation. It was after nine and they were all quite tired. Before long, each was asleep. They only awoke from their slumber when the stewardess tapped each of them on the shoulder and advised them to fasten their seat belts for landing. They were coming into Brasilia already.

When the plane finally parked at the arrival gate, Antonio was so eager to disembark that he was the first one to the door. It was all that Thomas and Sofia could do to keep up with him. Outside the terminal, they hailed a taxi and Sofia gave the driver Paola's address. They would make a hotel reservation when they arrived at her apartment. At that moment, the only thought on anyone's mind was getting Antonio to his son.

When the taxi pulled up in front of the apartment building, Antonio actually began to shake. Thomas couldn't help but notice.

"Hey, buddy. You nervous?"

"Yeah, Tommy. I ain't never been so nervous. Look at me, for God's sake. I'm shakin like a scared little kid."

"Well, I'd be shaking too if I were in your shoes. But it's all going to be fine. You'll see."

As they were entering the building, Thomas dialed Paola's number. Fortunately, it was her who answered and not someone else in the family. In that event he would have had to give the phone over to Sofia so she could handle the Portuguese part of the conversation.

"Hello?"

"Paola? It's Thomas."

"Oh, Thomas! Everyone is good? You are still in Brazil?"

"Yes, we are still in Brazil."

"Thomas, did you talk to Antonio? Did you tell what I say?"

By now the three of them were standing in front of the door to the apartment.

"Yes. I talked to him."

"Yes? Really yes? What he say?"

"He said that you should open your front door."

"What? What about my door?"

"Paola, open the front door. Please! There's a surprise for you. I think you're going to be very happy."

Thomas could hear a lot of chatter in Portuguese as the sound of Paola's footsteps made their way to the door. When she opened it and saw Antonio standing there, she dropped the phone and just looked up into his eyes as she started to cry. Within seconds, Antonio had taken her in his arms. Paola was half Antonio's size and she almost disappeared in his grasp.

"We have a son, Paola? Is it true he's mine?"

"Yes, Antonio! I could never tell you. I am so sorry I didn't tell you. Will you forgive me?"

"There's nothin to forgive. Can I see him?"

"Oh yes, my Antonio! Of course, you can see your son."

Everyone in the family was peering out the door at this tender scene and whispering to each other. There were giggles, smiles, and tears from everyone. Antonio was realizing that he was home. He was just beginning to understand that this was his family. As they made their way to the living room, everyone wanted a hug and kiss from this sentimental mountain of a man. There was a steady stream of tears running down his face.

"Antonio, Victor is sleeping. That is his name. Victor! Do you like?"

"Yes. It's very nice."

"Good. Now we must wake him so he can see his daddy."

Victor was sprawled on Paola's bed. She softly cooed in his ear and stroked his hair until he awoke. He sat up, sleepy eyed, and listened as Paola spoke. Then he looked at Antonio. It was as if there was an instant recognition. Victor stood on the bed, on wobbly legs, and reached out his arms to his father. Antonio reached down and gingerly lifted him up. They both smiled. Victor gave him a kiss on the cheek and then gently rested his head on Antonio's shoulder. "You were right, Tommy. He does look like me, but better lookin."

"Yes, well, maybe he got the 'better looking' part from Paola," Thomas teased.

"Yeah. Probably. She is beautiful. Isn't she beautiful Tommy? Isn't my Paola beautiful?"

"Yes, she is, Antonio. You are a lucky man. You have a beautiful woman who loves you, a handsome son who will adore you, and a family of relatives who will treat you like a king. You're all set, my friend."

"Yeah! Sometimes life gets good."

Paola's mother had brewed some good Brazilian coffee and was boiling some milk. Thomas liked the way some Brazilians add milk to their coffee, boiling it first so that everything remains hot. He always found that it did make a wonderful difference in the taste.

Now, everyone crowded around the kitchen table to hear all about the events in Manaus. There were almost constant exclamations of surprise and horror at what they were hearing. Everyone wanted to know about Thomas' wound and to comfort him. The highlight of the conversation was when Antonio told the story about the anaconda and its meal. When he got to the part about legs sticking out of the snakes mouth, Paola's younger sister bolted for the bathroom, gagging all the way. Everyone had a good laugh at her expense before she returned with a sour look on her face.

After another brief period of conversation, Thomas and Sofia said their goodbyes to everyone. They promised that upon their arrival in Chile, they would call Paola and Antonio. All four of them knew that there was a bond between them that could never be broken. It was a connection as strong as family. It would live for as long as they did. After a flurry of hugs and kisses all around, Thomas and Sofia were on their way.

Thomas had called and reserved a room at the same hotel he had used on his last trip to Brasilia. There could be no more using Carlo's credit card, though. It wouldn't be well advised. The authorities would look pretty hard for someone using a dead man's credit cards.

Once in their suite, Thomas and Sofia raced each other for the shower. It was distinctly possible that this could turn into an all-night affair. There had only been the one opportunity to enjoy each other's passion at the Ariau Towers, and they were determined to make up for lost time. If the previous opportunity had been burdened with the realization that it could have been their last, this one was filled with the joy of knowing there were many more nights of passion to come.

After a highly sensual and romantic session, they sat on the sofa and recounted the day's events and how fortunate they were to have survived. There was some, not much, but some regret for the loss of life on the part of those who had designs on killing not only Thomas, but surely Angela and Sofia as well. He had to admit that his conscience would have suffered much less had those criminals been spirited off to prison for the rest of their lives instead of being gunned down in the middle of the Amazon. He comforted himself with the knowledge that, with de Salvo's and Carlo's connections, it would have been a very unlikely scenario. Finally, after three in the morning, they fell asleep.

After a short night of rest, they had room service deliver what turned out to be a marvelous breakfast. Sitting on the balcony as they ate, Thomas expressed his concerns about the visit to Chile.

"How do you think your family will react to me?"

"I think they will like you very much. Well, actually my mother will be another matter altogether."

Sofia laughed at the thought of poor Thomas undergoing her mother's inspection.

"She's a tough one, is she?"

"You will see. She is a wonderful mother, and I love her, but she can be very difficult at times. I am sure she will not be pleased that I took such a risk with my life in order to be with you."

"Well, then maybe we shouldn't tell her that part," Thomas said as he leaned over to kiss Sofia's ear.

"You think you are joking, but you are not. I think it is better that we tell her nothing about it. At least not yet."

"Believe me, I have no desire to tell her anything about any of it. It's going to be tough enough to win her approval without divulging that information."

When their breakfast had been eaten and their bags were finally packed, they headed for the airport and a flight to La Serena by way of Sao Paulo and Santiago. Tomorrow, they planned to be on the beach in La Serena, enjoying the sun and the surf.

CHAPTER 26

THE CITY OF THE BELLTOWERS

The trip from Santiago to La Serena, on a LATAM flight, was less than an hour. Thomas spent much of the time looking out the window at the spectacle of the Andes. It seemed to him that the aircraft never reached an altitude higher than the mountains themselves. The steep, rocky crags of the mountainside were such a dark shade of gray that they were almost black. He couldn't help but think of what it would be like to be stranded there. The movie 'Alive', and its true story of soccer players stranded in these mountains after a plane crash, replayed in his mind.

"Thomas, I must tell you something. It worries me because I should have told you before now. But I was worried about what your reaction would be."

"Sofia, I cannot imagine anything that would be a problem for me or change my feelings. So, it's best that you trust in me and tell me."

As Thomas took her hand in his she looked into his eyes and said:

"I have a daughter."

Thomas leaned back a little, a serious look on his face and said:

"Are you telling me that not only do I now have, in my life, the love of the most beautiful and wonderful woman I have ever known, but I also get another daughter to hold in my heart? Best surprise ever, Sofia. I can't wait to meet her."

By now, tears were rolling down Sofia's face as she asked; "It makes you happy?"

"It sure does, Sofia. I couldn't possibly be happier. What's her name?"

"Her name is Maria. Do you like it?"

"I do. It was my maternal grandmothers name, so it's special."

Sofia, relieved and very happy, nestled in his arms for the brief remainder of the flight.

Shortly, the plane began its descent to La Serena. Its flight path now approached the Pacific Ocean and a coastal view much more to his liking. Soon, he could see the city, spreading out from the shore towards the mountains that were now a short distance in the background. What he could see from the air was pleasing to the eye.

"La Serena is often called the City Of The Bell Towers, Thomas. It was founded by the Spaniard, Pedro de Valivia, in fifteen forty-three. It is Chile's second oldest city, after Santiago."

"It looks to be a beautiful place. Not very green though."

"The northern area of Chile is quite arid and receives very little rainfall. Unlike the southern areas of the country, La Serena has a coastal desert climate. There are typical desert characteristics, including cactus and scrub brush. We can take a short drive to where there are more fertile areas. The world-famous Chilean grapes are grown there. The vineyards stretch for miles. They are so symmetrical. Such neat rows of carefully planted vines. It is something to see."

As the plane settled on the runway, Sofia leaned over and kissed Thomas on the cheek.

"I am home now, and I am so happy you are here with me."

"So am I. I'm looking forward a more peaceful time together."

"We must get you settled somewhere and then I will go to see my Maria."

"Someplace simple this time. I think I'm out of luxury mode," Thomas quipped as they made their way down the stairs to the runway.

"There is a simple place with some cabanas. It is near the beach. I think it will be fine for you."

"Sounds good. We should go out for supper after I get settled in. You, Maria and I! I'd love that."

"I guess we will see what Maria thinks of you," Sofia said as she gave him a pinch.

The taxi ride to the Cabanas Hostel del Mar took no more than fifteen minutes. Sofia was right, it was a simple place, yet nice, and the cost was a quite meager thirty-two dollars American per night. That was more like Thomas' normal budget. Sofia accompanied him to his apartment and helped him to get settled. It was a decent little place with a living room, small kitchenette, bedroom and bathroom. There was a balcony that gave a view of a small yard between the building and the fence separating it from the street. This would suit him just fine.

"OK! Thomas, I must go home now. I will call you when Maria and I are leaving to come and get you. There is a nice little restaurant on the beach. It is called La Table. I think you will like it."

"Anywhere that we're together is fine. I'll go for a walk along the beach, but I'll be back in time."

"OK. I must shower, change my clothes and get Maria ready. So, it will be more than two hours, I am sure."

"No problem. After my walk, I'll take a nap until you call. I'm still a little tired from all of this traveling."

After numerous kisses and tender displays of affection, Sofia left for home. Thomas took a quick shower, dressed, and headed down the block to the beach. The waves from the Pacific Ocean were quite lively this afternoon. There was something very relaxing about the sound they made as they crashed over the shore. Thomas went into a small store that was right on the beach, bought a pack of smokes, and then sat in one of the many benches that dot the sidewalk all along the beachfront. What Thomas found amazing was the fact that no hotels or residences were allowed to be constructed anywhere on the beach area. There were a few stores and restaurants, but nothing else. The beach belonged to the people and was not to be gobbled up by a handful of wealthy individuals who would deprive the masses of their use.

A small island sat a few miles offshore. Sofia had told him that boat trips could be taken there to observe dolphins as well as the penguins that inhabit the place. He was looking forward to that.

An hour had passed since Thomas left his cabana and he began to make his way back to the Hostel del Mar. The staff there proved to be more than kind, and quite friendly. Although almost no one there spoke any English, they communicated just fine. The women that performed the housekeeping chores were all smiles and courtesy. Thomas was enjoying the idea of this simpler, less grandiose, way of life. This was more his style.

Shortly, Sofia called to say that she was on her way to pick him up. Maria, she said, was quite enthusiastic about the whole thing.

"I am so surprised, Thomas. Maria seems excited about meeting you. It is not like her at all."

"Well, that's a good sign. I'm just as excited about meeting her. It should be interesting. Especially since she doesn't speak English."

Thomas laughed a little at the thought of trying to communicate with a ten-year-old whose language he didn't speak.

"Do not worry. I will translate for you. It will be fun, I am sure."

Thomas set about getting ready. Once he had cleaned up and dressed, he sat at the table and poured himself a glass of Pepsi. Within minutes there was a knock at the door. As it opened, Sofia entered, followed by a somewhat shy little girl. For a few moments, Maria almost hid behind her mother. Thomas was struck by how pretty this child was. She had long hair that went well below her shoulders. Her eyes were big and beautiful, and like her mother's, were the deepest brown. Maria began to smile as she overcame some of her shyness. Once they had been introduced to each other, she rushed over, gave Thomas a hug and kiss, and then returned to her mother's side.

"I don't believe! I have never seen her do that. I think she likes you already."

"She's wonderful. Such a beautiful child! It's not hard to see in her eyes that she's a sensitive and caring person."

"Yes! She is. Sometimes a little selfish, but still, she has a very good heart."

"I have no doubt she's a wonderful kid."

As they departed Thomas' cabana, the evening was beginning to move towards darkness. The walk to La Table was only about five minutes and soon they were seated at their table and placing their order. Maria sat acFedir from Thomas. It didn't take long for them to be in conversation, with Sofia translating. Thomas asked about her cats, school, and anything else he could think of. Maria wanted to know about Canada and his daughters. It was a very sweet and touching occasion. This wonderful child, who didn't know what it was like to have a father, and a man who knew everything about having daughters, came together despite a language barrier.

The entire evening went so well that Thomas and Sofia were both surprised. They had not expected Maria to be so receptive. Whatever Maria saw in Thomas, she seemed very comfortable with the situation. She appeared to take to him instantly and displayed honest affection. It was a relief to Thomas and Sofia.

All too soon, it was time for Sofia to take her home. They said their goodbyes, and Maria once again gave Thomas a hug and kiss. He knew without hesitation that he would love this child as if she were his own. He already felt an intense fatherly attachment to her. It never cFedired his mind to think of her as anyone else's daughter. If anything, he found himself regretting having missed the first ten years of her life. He was thinking in terms of being a good father to her for many years to come. Of course, that was assuming that Sofia would consent to marrying him. He had yet to ask that critical question. Now, here in La Serena, he would discover the answer.

Once she had returned home and prepared Maria for bed, Sofia called Thomas to tell him how well she felt the evening had gone. She assured him that Maria had liked him and was looking forward to seeing him again. She considered it quite a big step for her daughter to find any attachment to a man in her mother's life. Thomas was unable to hold back the tears of happiness. He knew that Maria was her mother's heart. If she had taken a dislike to him, the relationship might have found it difficult to survive. He totally expected, and supported, Sofia's desire to place Maria's well-being above all else.

Once the conversation with Sofia had finished, Thomas decided that it would be a good idea if he called Angela to let her know that everything had gone well. She was more than happy to hear from him.

"Thomas! I have been so worried. Are you still in Brazil?"

"No. We left Brazil yesterday."

"We?"

"Yes! Sofia and I."

"Ahhh, so that's her name. How are things going with you two?"

"Wonderful! Couldn't be better. I met her daughter tonight. She is the sweetest child. Everything is perfect."

"I'm happy for you, Thomas. I remember everything now, and I know that what you told me in Sao Paulo was right. We must each go on with our lives."

"We will. Each in our own way."

"What about Carlo?"

"He's dead!"

"Dead? Is he really? I hate to sound so thrilled, but he certainly deserved it."

"He did for sure. There was quite a bit of carnage in fact."

"What do you mean?"

"A lot of men died on the Rio Negro. I don't feel that good about it, but it was necessary if we were going to survive without any future threats."

"How many, Thomas?"

"There was de Salvo and two of his men, Carlo and two animals from the favelas, Pauly Sabatini and three more from Queens. Oh, and Rico was killed the day before them."

"My God! How could you possibly have survived all of them?"

"I wouldn't have survived even Rico if it hadn't been for Antonio."

"Antonio? He helped you?"

"Yes! The big guy had gone to Italy with a Brazilian woman, but it didn't work out. He knew I was going to Manaus and tracked me down. Just in time, too! Rico literally had me by the throat, Sofia was unconscious on the floor, and the end was certainly near."

"Oh my God! But you know, I always thought Antonio was a decent guy in many ways. He never fit as a bad guy."

"He's a great guy. We'll be friends for life now."

"Well, I am so happy that you're fine. Tell Antonio I said thanks for keeping the father of my children alive for them."

"I will. Speaking of children, did you know Paola had a baby three years ago?"

"Yes! Carlo made her give it up."

"Well, did you know whose it was?"

"I had no idea. It was never talked about."

"It was Antonio's."

"Get out! You're kidding! Really? Wow! Does he know?"

"He didn't, but he does now. He's in Brasilia with Paola, starting a new life with her and his handsome little son. You have to see this kid. Spitting image of his old man and sweet as can be."

"That's great! I'm happy for him. He deserves it for keeping you alive. Now when will you be home?"

"I'd say about a week. Have to spend some time with Sofia and Maria, enjoy some recovery time, then I'll return home. Tell the girls I love them and miss them. I think you can tell them the whole story now but leave out the part about people dying. Would not be good to have that information being talked about around town."

"Yes, I think it's time they knew just the basics. I'll give them your love. Take care of yourself!"

Thomas crawled into bed, exhausted from the events of the past week, and immediately fell asleep. He didn't awaken until one of the room attendants knocked at the front door with his breakfast. As he sat enjoying his coffee, juice, and cornmeal bread, a very polite and friendly woman set about cleaning his apartment. He knew he was going to enjoy his stay here.

Over the next week, he got to spend time with Sofia every day. On at least four occasions, she brought Maria along. When they were together, they would go to the beach, or shopping. When they stayed around the Hostel del Mar, Thomas would push Maria on the swing next to his cabana, go swimming in the pool, or play ping-pong with her.

They were definitely developing an attachment to each other. Perhaps Maria was finally prepared to accept a father in her life. Over the course of the week, Thomas had brought up the possibility of marriage with Sofia. She had indicated that it was something she was considering, but that it was not a decision that she had ever thought she would have to make. So she was still thinking. Then, one afternoon, as they sat on the sofa in Thomas' cabana eating pizza, Sofia, in a very shy way, simply said, "I want to marry you!" as she took a bite of her pizza. It just came out, just like that! Her mind was made up, and Thomas was taken by surprise.

"Sofia? Did I hear you correctly? Are you agreeing to marry me?"

"Yes! I have made my decision. I want to marry you. I am sure it was meant to be."

"Oh, Sofia! You just made me the happiest man in the world. I'm going to have a beautiful and wonderful wife, and a wonderful new daughter. I am so happy."

It was decided that Thomas would return to Canada, and they would plan to marry near the end of the year.

On Thomas' final night in La Serena, the three of them went out for a late supper. When Sofia and Maria showed up at his cabana, Maria presented him with one of her favorite little Teddy bears to take home with him. She wanted him to have something special to remember her by. At La Table, as they ate supper, Thomas told Maria how much he would miss her. As soon as Sofia translated the words, Maria slumped down in her chair and began to cry softly. Her big brown eyes, filled with tears, could break any heart. Thomas went and knelt beside her chair, holding her in his arms as he tried to reassure her and ease her pain. When he told her that he would be back, she looked at him with those sad eyes and simply asked, "Promisito?" He reassured her that it was a promise.

As they walked to the corner so that Sofia and Maria could hire a taxi, Maria positioned herself between them and held their hands. Sofia was surprised, once again. "Thomas, I have never seen her do this. Never! She has given you her heart for sure."

"I think she's smart enough to know that I'm not here to take her mother away from her. I'm here to make us a family and to love her as my own daughter."

"I think you are right. She understands you are real."

When they reached the corner, before they entered the taxi, Maria threw herself into Thomas' arms, hugging him tightly and sobbing heavily into his chest. It was breaking his heart. After a few moments, Maria stepped away, grabbed Thomas in one hand, Sofia in the other, and pushed them together. She then stepped back and watched them have their own tender moment. This was another huge step for her. In the past, she was far more likely to get between her mother and anyone who tried to get near her. Thomas had always respected Maria's presence and did not get even slightly physical with her mother when she was around. Now, Maria was saying it was alright.

The next morning, Thomas prepared for his flight home. Sofia would come to have lunch with him, but not go to the airport. She was sure she would not be able to handle it. It would be too painful. Thomas agreed, because he knew it would be difficult for both of them. After lunch, Thomas spent the afternoon walking near the beach. At half past three, he took a taxi to the airport, and by five o'clock he was on a fourteen-hour journey home. His adventure in Brazil was over. He would return to La Serena towards the end of the year, marry Sofia and they would all live a very happy life in Canada.

CHAPTER 26

CARE FOR A TWIST?

It was early evening on the Rio Negro, thirty miles upstream from the Ariau Towers. The Brazilian authorities had, earlier that day, recovered the bodies from the clearing on the south bank of the river. They had also recovered two of the three boats that had been beached there. Antonio had told Thomas about Carlo's difficulty in trying to start one of the boats and, Thomas assumed, that was the reason they didn't see three boats return with the authorities. The truth was when the authorities arrived, a third boat was nowhere to be found. As far as they knew, there were only two to be returned to Manaus.

At the very moment that Thomas, Antonio, and Sofia were boarding a plane to Brasilia, a small band of four Amazon Indians was cautiously approaching a boat that had drifted into some fallen trees along the shore, upriver from Ariau Towers.

With spears at the ready, ever silent, and more than curious, the four natives peered cautiously into the entangled craft. What they saw was a smallish man, not much larger than they were, and presumably dead. One of the natives gently prodded the body with the tip of his spear. To his surprise, it moved. The four of them jumped back from the boat and conversed amongst themselves as if trying to decide what to do about this discovery.

It seemed that the only decision they had reached was to prod the body once more. Again, there was the same result, followed by yet more conversation. Finally, someone made a decision. The man was hauled unceremoniously to the shore. The Indians removed a few large leeches that were attached to the body. These little bloodsuckers, three at a time, could drain a man of a pint of blood in just an hour. A dozen or so could drain the entire blood supply of a man's body in an almost equal period of time.

The Indians hastily threw together a few tree branches, connected with leaves and vines, to make a litter. This served as a means to drag whomever this strange intruder was back to their village. The tribal leader would decide what to do. The village was a few miles inland from the water and the trek was through thick jungle that required frequent use of a machete. Almost an hour later, the Indians and their trophy entered a clearing containing six or seven crude huts like those downriver.

There was an immediate gathering of native men and women, all of whom were, for the most part, naked. The men all had fiercely painted faces, sported nose rings, and carried spears. The women were unadorned and wore only simple loincloths. A few of them held small infants to their naked breasts. Young children, as curious as children anywhere, ran back and forth, to and from the litter that had just been dropped to the ground with a loud thud.

Within minutes, there were at least two-dozen men and women standing, or squatting, all around this unconscious stranger. There was a cacophony of noise, arguing, and the smoking of rolled up leaves. This was an unexpected dilemma for them, and they had no idea what to do. A few hours of this indecision had passed before the tribal leader gave the direction to treat this individual, at least for the time being, as a guest. As soon as that decision had been expressed, the women moved the litter into one of the huts and placed it on a bed of leaves.

There, in the simple structure of branches and twigs, they set about cleaning the body of the muck accumulated from its time spent in the river. It wasn't long before they discovered a hole clear through the man's chest and out his back. Using traditional plants and herbs, they provided what treatment they could and then departed.

How the bullet that Antonio had put into Carlo's chest managed to miss his lung, and any other vital area was a mystery. It seemed that, at least up until this point, Carlo had survived. The fact that he was in the hands of an untamed Amazon tribe, in a serious and feverish medical condition, and more than one hundred miles from the nearest hospital, certainly made his future seem more than bleak. If Thomas had been aware of this circumstance, he surely would have been praying that his future was non-existent. But that, as they say, is a whole other story.

Manufactured by Amazon.ca
Bolton, ON